DON'T FENCE ME IN

The first few months I was on the road, I bluffed my way through everything. For instance, in Chicago I went to an Army-and-Navy surplus store and spent $82.50 of my hard-earned Pizza Place $200 on a sleeping bag, a backpack, and a hunting knife. If a man was giving me a ride, and his arm started to crawl along the back of the seat toward me and he said, in a certain weasely kind of way that I must've heard at least fifty times, "Doesn't a girl like you get a little *scared* hitchhiking alone?" then I'd whip out my knife. I'd open it, and very slowly begin cleaning my nails.

"Oh, no," I'd say, perfectly deadpan as I peeled the dirt out from under one fingernail after another. "You see, I know self-defense."

Bantam Books by Paul Zindel
Ask your bookseller for the books you have missed

CONFESSIONS OF A TEENAGE BABOON
THE EFFECTS OF GAMMA RAYS ON MAN IN THE
    MOON MARIGOLDS
THE GIRL WHO WANTED A BOY
HARRY AND HORTENSE AT HORMONE HIGH
I NEVER LOVED YOUR MIND
MY DARLING, MY HAMBURGER
PARDON ME, YOU'RE STEPPING ON MY EYEBALL!
THE PIGMAN
THE PIGMAN'S LEGACY
A STAR FOR THE LATECOMER (with Bonnie Zindel)
TO TAKE A DARE (with Crescent Dragonwagon)
THE UNDERTAKER'S GONE BANANAS

TO TAKE A DARE

Paul Zindel and Crescent Dragonwagon

BANTAM BOOKS
TORONTO • NEW YORK • LONDON • SYDNEY • AUCKLAND

RL 6, IL age 12 and up

TO TAKE A DARE
A Bantam Book / published by arrangement with
Harper & Row, Publishers, Inc.

PRINTING HISTORY
Harper & Row edition published March 1982
Bantam edition / April 1984
2 printings through December 1985

Grateful acknowledgment is made to the following for permission
to reprint material copyrighted by them.
*The excerpt on page 41 from "Born to Run" © 1975 by Bruce
Springsteen and Laurel Canyon Music Ltd. Used by permission.*
*The lines on page 47 from "Nothing Like a Hundred Miles" by
James Taylor © 1976 COUNTRY ROAD MUSIC, INC. (BMI).*
*The lines on pages 47–48 from "For the Roses" © 1972 Crazy
Crow Music. Used by permission. All rights reserved.*
*The lines on page 59 from "Amelia" © 1976 Crazy Crow Music.
Used by permission. All rights reserved.*
*The excerpts on pages 110, 111, 115, 140, 142; Bill Haymes:
words of songs "Hear the Music," copyright © 1981 by Bill
Haymes; "Frozen Somewhere Blues," copyright © 1981 by Bill
Haymes; "Taking Leave of the Nest," copyright © 1976 by Bill
Haymes. Used by permission only. All rights reserved.*
*The lines on pages 139–140 from "Guilty" copyright © 1973 WB
MUSIC CORP. & RANDY NEWMAN. All rights reserved. Used by
permission.*
*The excerpt on page 142 from "Rainbows All over Your Blues"
(John Sebastian) copyright © 1970—THE HUDSON BAY MUSIC
COMPANY. Used by permission. All rights reserved.*

ISBN 0-553-25898-2

Published simultaneously in the United States and Canada

PRINTED IN CANADA

COVER PRINTED IN U.S.A.

11 10 9 8 7 6 5 4 3 2

This book is for Bill Haymes,
friend and partner,
who is one for the duration.

C.D.

AUTHOR'S NOTE:
Because I make my home in a small Ozark Mountain tourist town, some readers may assume that the town depicted in much of *To Take a Dare* is an only slightly fictionalized version of this town. They are correct, though I have tried to picture the town not as I see it, but as seen through the eyes of a sixteen-year-old runaway, Chrysta.

Because the book's setting is "autogeographical," some readers may assume that the characters, too, are drawn straight from real life. In this, however, they would be mistaken. Chrysta, Luke, Dare, Nettie, etc., have their only real life in this book.

C.D.

Luke has been saying that I should write all this down, this whole crazy period from when I was twelve or so until now, which is sixteen. He says I've been feeling guilty about it long enough and the best way for me to stop is to get it out of my head and down on paper. Luke is big on writing things down.

But I've been putting off writing about this time, especially the part of it with Dare. Luke says I put it off because I don't really want to face it, but I do.

It's so complicated. Where do I begin? Do I start in Benton? Or in Excelsior Springs? Who started all those things that snowballed into that sad mixed-up time and the mixed-up kid that Dare was and that I was?

I don't know, though I do know where it ends—with my starting to be happy for the first time in my life, and in love, and straighter (at sixteen) than I ever, ever dreamed I'd turn out to be. It also ends with Dare, who went the other way. And there was nothing I could do for Dare, nothing but let him go.

I will always feel sad, though, just sad sad sad when

*I think about crazy Dare with his stringy blond hair
and his one wild earring. He had half the girls in
Excelsior saving earrings for him. If they lost one of a
pair of pierced earrings, they knew what to do with the
other—save it for Dare.*

*And when I remember Dare's thirteenth birthday,
which was the last time I saw him, I want to cry, still.
His thirteenth birthday was even worse than mine, and
mine was pretty bad.*

That seems as good a place as any to start.

1

On my thirteenth birthday my father called me a slut once too often, my dog was hit by a car, and I lost my virginity—what was left of it.

When I was twelve and a half, I was the one who would go in to buy the beer for the kids in my crowd, because I looked—easily—over eighteen. I never got asked for I.D. In three or four months between twelve and thirteen, my hips rounded, and my waist went in, and I got these great big breasts, and suddenly I had this body that nobody knew how to deal with, me least of all, though I quickly learned. When my mother, who is very, very fat, tried to give me the requisite talk about my being due to get my first period soon, she just couldn't pull it off. "Sweetheart," she began, "you're almost a woman now—" which, except for the "sweetheart," is a line she got, word for word, from a U. S. Government pamphlet called *Telling Your Teenager the Facts of Life* (I know, because I saw the pamphlet lying on the hall table, took it up to my room, read it, and put it back).

But after Mom's lead-in, she stopped and in this thoroughly bewildered, tearful way said, "But you're *not* almost a woman *yet*, Chrissie, you're still my little *girl*." If there was anybody in that family who was a little girl it was her, though she was always—especially when she put dinner on the table—telling me what a great mother she was. That "little girl" remark made me feel really terrific at her great empathy over what it was like to be the only girl wearing a C-cup bra at Benton Middle School. Little!

At any rate, I did my usual reassuring number. "It's okay, Mom, don't worry. I understand."

"You do?" she said, sniffling back her tears.

"Yeah, Mom," I said, "I do."

Neither of us clarified things further, so I have no idea whether she thought that what I understood was that pretty soon I'd be menstruating and could get pregnant, or the fact that *she* still thought I was her little girl. But she seemed comforted, and never brought it up again. When I did get my period, about a month and a half later, I didn't bother telling her.

I have a pretty weird family. I mean, not just hard to get along with, but out-and-out *weird*.

For as long as I can remember, I knew that my mother was different from other mothers. Even when I was a very little girl, I felt that she needed looking after or protecting, that she was weak and helpless, like a giant, slightly retarded baby. She lived in her own little world, probably because she was so fat she didn't much want to go out into the real world (where people stared at her—I mean, she was a size 62). She was blobbily cheerful as long as she was left undisturbed. She used to go out of the house to shop for food, but for the last few years I lived at home she even stopped doing that, because a new market opened that did deliveries, so she could just phone in. By the time I left home, the only thing she'd go out for was Mass, once in a very long time.

But no mention was ever made of her spaciness and bizarre behavior at our house when I was growing up, because if you referred to her weight or her eating, or if you didn't do something she wanted you to do right away, she'd start crying. "Humor her, Chrissie," my father must've told me privately a million times as I was growing up, and both of us did. For instance, my mother had told me, when I went into first grade, that I shouldn't visit other girls because if I went over to their houses, I would have to invite them back over to our house and "other people's children make me nervous." What's strange to me now is how I never, not once, rebelled, though I was lonely most of the time and wished things could be different.

Humoring Mom was pretending not to notice her craziness—like ignoring the fact that four gallons of mint-chocolate-chip ice cream that I knew were in the freezer one morning when I went off to school were lying empty in the garbage can when I got home.

My father and I also ignored her bit with the U. S. Government pamphlets. You see, once there was some little blurb in the paper, on the same page as Ann Landers (which was the only part of the paper she read) about how you could send off for a list of free U. S. Government pamphlets. She got the list, and she ordered every single one, every topic from reproducing African violets by root division to installing home sprinklers and fire-alarm systems. She used to quote from them often, whether or not it had anything to do with the occasion. She'd begin by saying something like "You know, I was just reading somewhere that—" My father and I knew where "somewhere" was: either the pamphlets or Ann Landers, who she used to refer to simply as "Ann." Twice a year the good old U. S. Government would send her a list of new pamphlets available, and twice a year she'd send off for them.

You get the picture—Mom was bonkers. Period. But, I always thought, mildly bonkers. Now, Luke and Lissa tell me you can't change the past and what's done is done, but still, if I had just had any idea... But I'll get to that part soon enough. You can judge for yourself whether good old Mom was only mildly demented or a first-class A-number-one twisted-up sicko.

Now Dad, Dad was not crazy. But he was very negative about everything, and he was into this weird martyred religious trip. He was always saying that his life was a continual disappointment to him but he'd accept it because what the hell else could he do, that's the breaks and they're rotten, but it's God's will and his cross to bear. His cross to bear: that's how he put the fact that his wife was grossly obese and out of her gourd, that he didn't have a son, that he'd never be rich even though he "damn near works himself to death, and I don't have to tell *you*, Chrissie, how much of it goes on food bills for you-know-who." He laid tiles for a living and considered it his cross that people were buying cheap polyurethane bath and shower stalls instead of having real tile installed—which is what he apprenticed to a master tile layer for seven years to learn how to do and now he was becoming obsolete. I heard him repeat this number over and over again during the first thirteen years of my life, and it left me feeling shaky and anxious and guilty inside, as if I was responsible because my father was so unhappy: I loved him, but I couldn't do anything to make him happier.

For all my father's crosses, he did seem to care about me until those last few years before I left home. When I was a little kid, Dad and I used to talk a lot, and do things. I used to help him work on the car on weekends, handing him wrenches or whatever he needed, and he'd show me all the parts of the car: This was the fan belt, this was the radiator, and so on. He was a lot nicer on weekends, though he complained about his crosses and warned me about how tough life is and how "you gotta watch yourself every minute." But he tried—he really tried—to be a good father. That he was such a total bastard later can't take that away. I used to come into the bathroom and keep him company when he shaved in the late afternoon. He had a heavy beard, and on weekends he'd shave twice a day, once in the morning and once in the afternoon, because if he didn't he'd have a five-o'clock shadow. I'd sit on the clothes hamper and just watch him and talk to him.

One of the things we talked about was what books I was reading. He used to compliment me on my reading— he would ask me which book I was reading and what it was about. I remember telling him all about Helen Keller, and *The Diary of a Young Girl* by Anne Frank. He was interested, and proud, too—I guess because he wasn't very well educated and he never read anything outside of the paper and *Popular Mechanics* (and a couple of times I found *Penthouse* in the garage—but who buys *Penthouse* to read? And with Mom like she was, who could blame him?).

Now, about my reading: That's important. I used to—and still do—read all the time. My third-grade teacher read *The Secret Garden* out loud to my class, and when she finished I got it out of the library and read it to myself twice, and that got me started. Since that time I've always had a book I was in the middle of,

usually a novel or a biography (Luke says that's why I'm
the world's most educated high-school dropout).

I loved reading so much because, really, what else
did I have (other than Marshall, my dog, who I'll tell
you about in a minute)? Mom was in another galaxy; I
loved Dad but he was on a constant downer. I didn't
have any friends at school, either: I'd gotten into the
habit of keeping to myself, first because of Mom's
warning, and then, later, when I got old enough to see
how bizarre my parents were, because I didn't want to
attract attention to myself. I was afraid that maybe I
was as weird as they were, and if so, it was better to
keep it under wraps than to be actively unpopular,
which I was *sure* I would be if I was ever really found
out by the kids or teachers at school. So I stayed very,
very low-key: I had my nice little B+ average, I spoke,
but only when called on, I never got into trouble. And I
read.

On Saturday mornings, Dad would drop me at the
Benton Public Library—my favorite place in that whole,
boring, straight little burg—while he did errands. When
he picked me up at noon, he'd comment on how many
books I had checked out. "*Seven?* And you're gonna
read all them books in one *week*? A real intellectual!
Another Einstein!" He must've said that every single
Saturday from when I was eight up to when I was
twelve, which was when we stopped doing anything at
all together except fighting.

My father also used to be very sympathetic about my
animals, which were the only important part of my life
besides reading. I used to bring home stray animals
pretty often. They seemed to find me, cats with infected
paws and no tags, puppies that were just wandering
around that people must've left out to fend for themselves,
and birds with broken wings. My mother used to fuss

about the dirt and disease and expense whenever I brought an animal home, but my father stood up for me (for once) instead of "humoring" her. "Be *glad* she has a tender heart, Annette," I remember he once told Mom. My father would drive me over to the vet, Dr. Avner, if an animal was really sick and needed attention, and he'd help me write and phone in classified ads for the *Benton County Courier* about the animals once they were well again, either to locate the owners if it seemed like the animals had just been lost or, more often, to find new homes for them.

Of course, what I wanted more than anything was to be allowed to keep one of them—a dog, a cat, I wasn't particular. I wanted a pet of my own desperately. But my mother was adamant; that was out of the question. Dad went along with her, but he kept my hopes alive by saying, "Well, maybe someday."

Someday came, finally, one Saturday when Dr. Avner called us about a year-old Airedale he had, named Marshall. Marshall chased cars, Dr. Avner said, a serious habit which his owners—who lived on a very busy street, in a house that had no backyard—had been unable to break him of. Marshall had just been hit by a car for the second time, and he, Dr. Avner, had just finished "patching him up." No, he was just banged up a little this time, nothing serious, but the first time he'd had a leg injury that had left him with a slight limp. Dr. Avner said the family that owned him had decided to find him a new home somewhere, either out in the country or somewhere where he could be penned in. Dr. Avner was calling us, he said, because we might know of someone; we had found homes for so many animals.

So Dad and I drove over there, me begging, "Please, Dad, if he's a nice dog—do you think I could keep him?

Maybe? Please? We could fence in the backyard; no one ever goes in there anyway. Please?"

"You *know* how your mother feels," Dad kept saying, strict, but in a nice way. "And do you know what fencing costs? Do you? It's an arm and a leg, I'm telling you. No, we keep him just till we find him a home, and we keep him tied up. But maybe if no one calls ... Nah, well, someone will, and your mother don't want a dog around the house, no use you getting your hopes up. You can't always get what you want, Chrissie, and the sooner you learn that, the better. Life is tough, and it don't hurt to learn it young. Save you a lot of heartbreak."

But before Dad completed his lecture (which I knew by heart backward and forward anyway), we were at Dr. Avner's, and he came right out as soon as we stopped the car, with sweet old Marshall-dog on a leash. Marsh was brown and black, like all Airedales, with curly short hair and a little upright stubby tail just wagging away. He had a boxy sort of head, which he tilted up toward me, and his little cute folded-over ears perked up, listening. Dr. Avner handed the leash to me, and we walked to the car, and the minute I opened the door Marshall jumped in, completely trusting. On the ride home, he settled himself next to me on the seat, half on my lap, sitting up attentively with his nose pressed against the glass.

I wanted Marshall so much, more than any of my other animals, even more than this darling little half-starved kitten I'd found once, all black with one white paw. I'd cried when I'd had to give her away, but that was nothing compared with how much I wanted Marshall. Every so often he would turn from the window to look at me earnestly and give me a few friendly licks on the cheek, then he'd go back to checking out the view.

"Oh, please, Dad? Please?"

"Chrissie, I told you *no*," he said sharply, then he sighed and glanced over at us. He shook his head. "He is a nice-looking dog, I'll say that much." He sighed again, and was quiet for a moment. I held my breath—I thought he was considering it, and I didn't want to nag. Finally, he said, "Well, I'll speak to Annette about it."

And so I got to keep Marshall. I'm still not sure how Dad talked Mom into it. She kind of sulked for a couple of days, but she didn't throw one of her crying fits. Marshall stayed politely out of her way. I took care of feeding him, walking him, everything. Dad fenced in the backyard with chain link the weekend after we got Marshall, and I'd pen him up back there after breakfast on school days, so Mom wouldn't have to deal with him at all. Gradually—I thought—she accepted his being there.

Once, during the first month, Marsh got out. I think because I didn't drop the latch all the way shut. I hadn't left for school yet, and when I heard him barking at the front of the house I went racing out, just in time to see him charging after a brown station wagon. Even with his gimpy leg, that dog could *move* when he wanted to! I tore after him, yelling, "Stop, Marshall, stop, stop!" The lady who was driving the car saw me in her rearview mirror, figured out what was going on, and was nice enough to pull over, which allowed me to catch up with him. I thanked her (she was wearing sunglasses and had her hair in a bandana—she was the kind of lady who probably jogged every morning and was a Girl Scout leader—the kind of lady I used to wish was my mother), and I grabbed Marshall by the collar and marched home with him. Once her car was out of sight, he followed me willingly. Marshall was very obedient, except when there was a moving vehicle. Then he just couldn't help himself.

After that, whenever I put Marshall in his pen, I double-checked to make sure the gate to the yard was latched securely. Always.

Every day when I came home from school, Marshall and I would take a long walk together (Marsh on a leash, of course, in case he saw cars). When we came back, we'd go up to my room, and I'd lie on my bed reading until the late afternoon, one hand on sweet old-Marshall-doggy, who lay snoozing beside me. Those afternoons were the most peaceful times in my life then. I know Marshall was only a dog, but he was the only one I loved who I really, 100 percent, *knew* loved me back. Who knows what Mom felt underneath all her spaciness and fat? Maybe affection . . . sometimes. Dad, I think, cared for me, at least when I was little (although what happened later makes it hard for me to believe), but even during the years we got along he was never what you would call demonstrative. The Perrettis did not hug and express their feelings like they say Italians do. I remember once during one of those endless heavy dinners, when the TV was on, that commercial for long distance phone calls, the one that says, "Reach out, reach out and touch someone," came on. And suddenly this thought flashed across my mind—here we were, the three of us, such a *short* distance from each other, just a few feet of table separating us—but we couldn't *begin* to "reach out and touch."

But I did have Marshall. There was more love and joy in *one* of his tail-wagging, jump-up-and-down, lick-your-face, body-quivering greetings than in a year of my father's nightly "Phew, what a day," as he slammed the door in the early evening, announcing his arrival. Or my mother's hazy, distracted voice floating down

from upstairs after I came home from school, "Oh . . . hello.
Is that you, dear?"

"Yeah, Mom," I'd call up to her, as I put down my
books and headed for the backyard to let Marshall out.
Marshall never had to ask if it was me, I'll tell you that.

2

I accepted that weird life when I was a kid, never
thought about rebelling. But Luke says (Luke's majoring
in psychology) I just kept it pushed down, and that's
why it exploded out of me all at once, when I got my
breasts. My very noticeable breasts.

Boys—or at least a certain kind of boy—began paying
attention to me then, and at first it embarrassed me.
After a lifetime of trying to keep a low profile so the
kids at school wouldn't find out what fungi I and my
family were, after a lifetime of feeling like my only
friends were animals and my only escape was into a
book—suddenly my own body had *forced* me to be
noticeable. There was a lot of snapping of my bra strap
and that kind of thing, which I *hated*, from boys my
own age. But older boys started talking to me too, and
that was different. At first I was scared, but I found out
I could talk back to them, and they'd listen, and talk
back to me, and that was flirting, and I could do it
pretty well.

One of those boys was Donny Figeroa, a phoney

punk dropout. He was tall, seventeen years old, and with his dark wavy hair, blue eyes, and dimpled chin, he would have been very good-looking if he hadn't had so many pimples. A lot of the kids looked up to him because he had this threatening, experienced air and everyone knew he had two cousins in Chicago who were in a street gang called the Destroyers. Donny was very turned on to me, and that gave me a lot of status among the kids right there. I mean I was just a *few months over twelve*—and here's Big D, all of *seventeen*, coming on to me. That I acted so-so with Donny only increased his desire, which gave me even more status. It seems stupid and shallow now, but then—then you have to understand that I was hungry for status. And it happened so fast.

But once I understood that being "built" meant I could say anything and boys would act like it was the most fascinating thing in the world, I couldn't help but use it. Part of me felt like it was cheating, but what else did I have to offer? I didn't know if I was nice, or intelligent, or interesting, or talented; if I "had personality." All I knew was I had big attention-getting breasts. I decided I would keep my body in good shape and never, never get fat like my mother. So what if it was not really *me* that boys liked? Even the girls who had previously only tolerated me were suddenly hanging out with me. Of course they were just jealous of me—or of my breasts—but so what? I was popular. Suddenly.

I remember once looking at the back of a *Cosmopolitan* magazine where there was this ad for a bust developer that showed a diagram of a breast: the fat cells, the mammary glands, the pectoral muscles above the breast. And I remember thinking how strange it was that a few fat cells on my chest could make such a big difference.

*   *   *

Everything changed at home, too. But at home I was very *un*popular all of a sudden. Especially with Dad. He started acting like everything I did was a crime.

The first time I remember it happening was one Sunday afternoon when I was sitting on the clothes hamper in the bathroom, talking to him as he shaved, just like I always had. I had just finished reading a book about two teenagers, sisters, and one of them dies of cancer, and I was looking forward to telling him about it. I knew he'd enjoy hearing about it because it was so depressing. Dad was standing in front of the mirror, his face all covered with white shaving foam and his razor in one hand, poised and ready to begin. Then suddenly he looked over at me. His eyebrows pulled together. He frowned. Then he glared at me. Then he looked down at himself—he was wearing, as he always did when he shaved, a white cotton undershirt and these baggy blue boxer shorts. Then he looked at me again, and glared even more furiously.

"Get out, now. You're too old for this, Chrissie. You shouldn't be in here," he said, in a low, angry voice.

I didn't ask him why he was angry. I didn't argue. I just got out.

And from then on, everything I did was wrong.

It was, "Your mother's right, enough's enough with the animals. I've had it with those mutts. Don't argue with me, Chrissie. I said *don't argue*. One more word out of you and I'll take Marshall to the pound." I didn't say a word, because it was urgent that I keep Marshall, who was now my only friend at home. But also, protesting and making a fuss wasn't my way—yet.

Of course, as for my father and me talking or doing any of the other things we used to do together, all that went too. It was, "I don't want you out here under the car anymore, Chrissie, it doesn't look right, grease all over you, a girl your age." It was, "Get your nose out of that damn book, I'm talking to you!"

Now Luke says that maybe when I developed I looked like my mother when *she* was young, before she got fat and crazy, and he—my father—was afraid he'd be attracted to me, and that's why he started acting so mean. It sounds logical. But I shouldn't have been punished for something that wasn't my fault, that wasn't even wrong or bad anyway but just a natural thing. And I couldn't even begin to understand at the time what was bothering him. All I knew was that, for no reason at all, my father was being mean to me.

At the same time for reasons I *could* understand, I was suddenly very popular at school. Well, you can guess what the combined effect of those two things was. I underwent a complete transformation.

3

By the time I was twelve and a half, there was no more nice, mousey, unnoticeable Chrissie. That person was gone. No more shirtwaist dresses in little flowery prints, no more kilts and cardigans and loafers. At school I was Chris, not Chrissie, and I lived in tight jeans and T-shirts in the summer or tight turtleneck sweaters in the winter. I used to wear strings of beads if they were the right length—just long enough to hang off the shelf of my breasts, dangling, from there, out into space. I started wearing high-heeled shoes, Candie's, with those crisscrossed straps in bright green or red or purple, and wooden heels. They were uncomfortable, but I thought they made my figure look even better, and they made a loud, dramatic clicking sound when I crossed a room. I started chewing bubblegum and wearing green eye shadow and that lip gloss that you put on with a brush and that looks wet and sticky, and so much black mascara that my eyelashes stuck together in clumps. Even my spaced-out mother noticed something.

"Sweetheart," she said to me one day when she passed me on the stairs.

"What?" I said. I snapped my bubblegum aggressively.

"Don't you think you're wearing a little too much makeup?"

"No," I said, snapping again.

"Well . . ." She paused. "Well, I just wanted to be sure." Then she went down and I went up.

That night at dinner she said brightly, "You know, I was just reading somewhere that you can catch eye infections from using mascara for too long. You should buy a new tube every few months, not keep using the old one."

"I go through about a tube a month," I said, which wasn't true but was the kind of belligerent remark I had taken to making. "So I guess I'm safe."

"All that mascara certainly adds a lot to your cheap look," said my father. "What's gotten into you, Chrissie?"

My mother stared at the wall.

"It's not cheap," I said. "It's three ninety-five a tube."

"For this I spend hours on a scaffold, tiling a slanted ceiling for some rich dingaling's hot-tub room?" asked my father rhetorically. "So *she* can spend three dollars and ninety-five cents a month on her eyelashes? That does it. I'm cutting off your allowance."

"Fine with me," I said, shrugging. I had been thinking about trying to get a job after school at the Pizza Palace (called the PP) anyway. But even if losing my allowance had bothered me, I never would have admitted it.

You see, I had discovered the incredible rush you get from just being deliberately obnoxious, pushing as hard as you can. That was why I pretended to be tough and threatening, even when I knew underneath, all along, that I wasn't really a punk. Later on, Dare couldn't believe I understood why he sometimes just *had* to act up and be bad, even when he didn't want to and knew better. But I did understand. Being bad—fighting and being deliberately irritating—made me feel *alive* in a way I had never felt when I was nice and unnoticeable, and once I got started sometimes I couldn't stop.

"You know, I never had an allowance," my dad went on. "I had to *work* for everything I got. My father gave me five dollars once for my birthday, and this was a big thing to me, Chrissie. I never forgot it. I *appreciated* it." He snorted and shook his head in disgust. "Three ninety-five a month for mascara so she can look like—"

"Like *what*?" I said, daring him.

My father stared at me. His eyes narrowed. "You know what you're asking for now, don't you, Chrissie? Now *my* father used to take a strap to me if I ever so much as—"

"So?" I said, narrowing my eyes right back at him. "So? So what if your father did it to you? I'd like to see you try it with *me*."

He stared back at me for a minute with such anger I really thought he *would* go after me, and I felt myself tensing, filled with adrenaline. But suddenly his expression changed. He dropped his gaze, and he just looked sad.

"Oh, Chrissie," he said softly, shaking his head. "Chrissie, what happened? I don't know what happened to you. What'd I do to deserve this? You used to be a good kid, Chrissie. I just pray you're not out there doing what you look like you're doing. You look like a . . . a degenerate. You look like a slut."

"Would anyone like dessert?" said my mother.

I was and I wasn't doing what my father was afraid of. I *was* drinking beer—some, but not a whole lot, because I'd seen kids get sloppy drunk, and I wanted to stay in control in order to pull off my aloof leader-of-the-pack bit. Now that I had status I wasn't going to blow it by barfing all over my shoes; no way. For the same reason, I smoked dope, but never a whole lot, and I never messed with anything other than weed. I'd smoke when it was offered to me, but never enough to get silly, never more than a couple of tokes, just enough to relax me a little. I never bought it myself, either—and I could've, too, for after the mascara fight with Dad I had gotten the after-school job at the PP, busing tables and doing the setup for the salad bar late in the afternoon, so I had a little cash.

As for sex, well, I had started making out pretty heavily with a number of boys, particularly Donny Figeroa. But the strange thing was, although I was acting sexy, I didn't really enjoy making out, and deep inside I wondered what the big deal was about (actually I never did find out, not until I met Luke). I just wasn't turned on, though sometimes, thinking about it later, I'd get a little turned on. At the actual time, though, I was usually bored. Or, if it was with a boy who was grabby or rough, I'd just be grossed out, though I'd keep on doing it, pretending it was wonderful.

I put on a great act. Inside me, of course, a lot of things were still the same. I still loved Marshall better than anyone else on earth, and at home, whenever I wasn't fighting with my father, I'd go upstairs to my room, close the door, and read, sweet Marshall all spread out next to me.

But if you had seen me in my punk disguise you never would have realized that I was really an animal lover and a bookworm. And you never would have guessed that I was still a virgin. But I was—until my thirteenth birthday.

4

Around the time I got big breasts, I decided I'd never get fat like my mom, and I started taking out all these books on diet and nutrition from the library. I remember one called *You're Being Poisoned!* which had a lot of gross facts in it, like that the chemical used in fake vanilla extract was the same thing they use in dog collars to kill fleas. The next time I bought Marsh a flea collar, I checked the label against the label on a bottle of imitation vanilla in the kitchen, and sure enough, it was the same chemical, one of those long, unpronounceable ones. I couldn't believe it! Anyway, that made me decide that not only would I never get fat, I would also try to stop eating things with artificial flavors and colors and preservatives and junk in them. Another book I read, *Moods and Foods*, said that people could go crazy from eating too much sugar, and I wondered if that was what had happened to my fat mother.

Now when I say my mother was fat, I mean that though she usually wore those loose-fitting knee-length housedresses, you could still see her hips and stomach and fat ass melting and quivering into each other—her legs like two massive tree trunks of pinkish white, wobbling, dimpled, unhealthy-looking flesh. She wasn't plump, or solid, she was really *fat*, like something out of a freak show, like someone who if you see them walking down the street or in a store or something, you're embarrassed—you don't know whether to look at them or turn away. Mom had really pretty, small, delicate feet, too, which made me sad because I couldn't help comparing them to the rest of her. I felt sorry for her, but her overweight revolted me. I couldn't help thinking, *God, what if I turn out like that?*

I began fixing my own breakfasts and lunches to take to school, because I knew Mom would not be able to deal with fixing anything different from what she usually fixed. My meals were the kind of healthy stuff you'd expect a *mother* to be pushing on a teenager, whereas what Mom ate you'd expect some real abnormal teenager to eat.

One morning, about a month before my thirteenth birthday, my mother was watching me suspiciously as I prepared my standard breakfast: a poached egg, 100 percent whole wheat bread, and half a grapefruit. She sat at the kitchen table, eating *her* breakfast. She had a package of eight cinnamon rolls in front of her, as well as a dish of powdered sugar, a tub of diet margarine, and a huge mug of black coffee. She'd break off a piece of cinnamon roll, slather it with diet margarine, and then dip it in powdered sugar and scarf it down with a gulp of coffee. I knew she'd be through with that package of rolls and maybe started on her second package by the time I left for school.

"How can you *eat* that food?" she asked me.

"What do you mean, how can I eat this food? This is normal, ordinary food, Mom. *You're* the one who eats weird stuff." Since I'd undergone my transformation, I'd stopped handling her with kid gloves, and she'd taken it surprisingly well: no crying fits. I thought she had, by this time, retreated so far into her safe, insulated world that nothing touched her or bothered her anymore.

"But it's so—" she paused and gestured dreamily with her puffy, sugar-dusted hand. "It's so . . . I mean, grapefruit without *sugar*? That's too *sour*. I can't imagine . . ."

"It's *good*, Mom," I told her. "You've just polluted your tastebuds by eating so much sugar that—"

"No, it's *not* good," said my mother firmly, and I knew from her tone of voice that whatever I said would make no difference. Still, I figured that this was as good a time as any to approach the birthday food problem.

You see, on my last birthday, which fell on a Saturday, my mom ordered *three* cakes—one served at each meal—besides making an astounding amount of so-called birthday food supposedly for me.

"Annette, don't you think three cakes are a little much?" my father asked.

She said, self-righteously, "How *could* you *think* of depriving your daughter of *cake* on her birthday?"

And I covered for her, like I always used to do since I was still being nice, sweet Chrissie. "Gee, I bet I'm the only kid at Benton Middle School that got *three* cakes on her birthday!" Believe me, I was practically choking on the crumbs when I said it. I didn't even *like* sweets.

Well, my mother beamed and she looked triumphantly at my father as if to say, "You see?" and he sighed and left the room. But I felt sick inside. Mom was supposed to be doing something for *me*, for my birthday, but as usual she had managed to twist it so she could get what *she* wanted—extra food—and I had to act as though it was so wonderful.

But I wasn't doing that anymore, I was saying what I felt, and with my birthday coming up I knew I'd better warn her about the food. So on the day of the grapefruit discussion, I said, "Hey, Mom, listen, all this reminds me—please don't do a big fuss on my birthday, okay? I don't want a cake or a whole lot of food, okay? Do you understand, Mom? I'm eating differently now, you know? More natural foods?"

She nodded, but she had that glazed, dreamy look and I could tell she was somewhere else. "Remember when I used to make those little apple fritters when you came home from school?" she said thoughtfully. "You used to *love* those. They were fried. You know, recently I was reading somewhere that although there are over two hundred known varieties of apples, only eight are grown commercially."

"I don't care, Mom." But I don't think she heard me, any more than she'd heard me all the years when I'd said, "That's interesting, Mom."

I also knew she had been reading the U. S. Government pamphlet *Apple Varieties for the Home Garden*.

5

Marshall woke me up on my birthday like he always did: by standing on his hind legs at the head of the bed with his front paws braced against the side of the bed, staring me awake with his big brown eyes and his dog ESP. The minute I woke up, his stubby little tail started thumping back and forth, and he leaned his head over to nudge my face and neck with his cold, wet nose. I petted Marshall and told him how wonderful he was and fussed over him for a few minutes before I got out of bed. Marshall didn't care whether or not I wore mascara or how big my breasts were. He just loved me, and I loved him. Most days, waking up with him was the best part of the whole day.

It certainly was *that* day.

When I went downstairs to feed him and saw my mother bustling around the kitchen, the table set, my birthday present, wrapped in pink-and-white paper, beside the plate, my worst fears were realized. She had made scrambled eggs with salami and jalapeño peppers, enough for a dozen people; a platter of sausage patties; another platter of those little frozen miniature cocktail-size tacos; a fruit salad made of canned fruit, Cool Whip, and miniature marshmallows; hot cocoa; and—you guessed it—a cake. This cake said

Happy 13th Birthday, Chrissie

in a swirly blue-icing script, and it was a sheet cake. It had little plastic figures of a rock band on a little plastic stage: a drummer, two guitarists, and a singer who all had early Beatles haircuts. I guess the lady at the bakery had told Mom that the rock-singer motif was the perfect choice for teenagers.

I felt sad, sad and sick. "Mom, you didn't remember."

"Of course I did, dear!" she said. She sounded very cheerful. "See, I made you a *special* birthday breakfast!"

I looked at her, standing there in this enormous red housedress with white and yellow and pink flowers, and these ridiculous white fluffy slippers on her feet, and suddenly I went from sad to absolutely furious.

At that moment I saw something so shocking, but so obvious, that I stood there stunned, astonished that I had never seen it before. *Mom wasn't spaced out because she couldn't help it. It was something she did so she didn't have to do or hear anything she didn't want to! So other people would do things her way! And it had worked!*

What I'd always thought of as her weakness was really Mom's way of being *strong*, stronger than Dad or me. All my life she'd floated around, this fat vague messy blob who Dad and I pitied—but she *always* got what *she* wanted. We had been duped! I saw it with an intense and devastating clarity: Mom's complete selfishness. It was so much meaner—no, sicker—than Dad with his temper storms. Because even if Dad was calling me a slut, I knew what was going on. With Mom I never *understood* what was happening—I just ended up doing things her way and feeling guilty but untrue to myself at the same time.

And I got absolutely enraged. My hands trembled. My heart started beating hard. And I hated Mom. I hated her fatness. I hated the pretending I had done for her: pretending I was happy, pretending I thought she was the world's greatest mother, pretending I loved the greasy, heavy, unhealthy food she was trying to shovel down me. I hated that I had never had friends, never made them because they were "other people's children." And good old Mother had to be spared the agony of being "nervous," and if her daughter was lonely and needed companionship, well, that was just too bad. I hated her because I couldn't begin to tell her how much growing breasts had changed my life and how confused I was. I hated her because she never went out of the house, because she would never jog, or wear sunglasses and a bandana and drive a car, because she would never be anything close to normal, and because she had forced Dad and me to live our lives tiptoeing around her.

I *hated* her.

And the gross-out, sicko, unhealthy birthday breakfast spread out on the table—that capped it for me.

I said, "You don't really expect me to eat all this garbage, do you, Mom?"

"Well, I can save anything you don't eat now for later."

"Right, Mom," I said. "Save it where, in your stomach? With all the other garbage and leftovers you eat? You're just one big fat leftover yourself, you know that?"

She stared at me. Her face lost color and her mouth hung open.

"Go ahead, Mom, *eat* all that crap! *I'm* not going to! You did it for yourself, why don't you just admit it?"

She looked like a wounded animal. I wanted to hurt

her, and I felt victorious. But at the same time part of me was appalled. Still, I couldn't have stopped if I wanted to.

She looked at me, gave me a look so terrified that my heart turned over. She bolted from the kitchen.

I felt sick. Two voices in my head screamed at each other. One said, "You rotten, wretched, cruel little bitch! How could you? Go apologize!" The other said, "She deserved it! She deserved it! She *is* hateful! Don't fall for it this time!"

I left my birthday package, still wrapped, by my plate.

I went back to my bedroom to get Marsh (since Mom didn't like him, he wasn't allowed in the kitchen). "Here, Marsh, old boy, good old dog!" I called, and he came bounding out enthusiastically, leaping up cheerfully, nuzzling me with his round nose. I ruffled his curly fur and he followed me downstairs. I opened the back door. We went out to the yard and I sat on the ground a moment. Marshall caught my mood then, and quieted down, draping himself over my lap and turning his friendly, intelligent face up to gaze at me, asking, "What's wrong?" with those soulful brown dog eyes.

"Oh, Marsh, Marsh," I said, and I folded myself over his lean curly-furred warm body. I hugged him and laid my cheek against his back, and I stayed there for a long, long time.

Marshall licked my face and wriggled around a few times as if to remind me, "Look, whatever it is, we can talk about it later. I'll be here—you'd better go to school now." He followed me ruefully to the gate, sad to see me go but doing his duty, staying like a good dog when I stepped through and pulled the latch securely down into its holder. I checked the latch, like always. I turned once as I walked away, and saw him watching me through the chain link, following me with his eyes.

When I came home from school at three thirty my father was sitting on the front porch waiting for me. This was so unusual that I knew something was wrong (usually Dad didn't get home till six thirty or seven). Why was he here? Maybe my mother had had a heart attack from everything I had said to her. I felt sick.

"Chrissie, I have something to tell you," he said. "Let's go inside."

He held open the door and gestured me toward the living room, a dark ugly room with a stale smell. The couch and armchair had plastic covers over the upholstery so they wouldn't get dirty. There was one little window and a brownish braided rug from Sears on the floor.

I sat in the armchair. "What's up, Dad?" I asked guiltily.

"I hate to tell you this, Chrissie," he said, "especially on your birthday. But Marshall's been hit by a car."

"No!" I said. I stared at him. Fear.

"Yes," he said. "I'm sorry."

"No," I said. I began trembling. "Dad, where is he now? Is he at the vet? Is he okay?"

My father didn't say anything.

I got out of the chair. "Dad, he's not dead? Dad, is he dead?"

"Chrissie, I'm so sorry—"

"IS HE DEAD? IS HE OR ISN'T HE? WOULD YOU TELL ME?"

"We can go to the animal shelter right now if you want and get a new one—"

"You're saying he's *dead*?" I sank back down into that

armchair and put my face in my hands and started sobbing. And then suddenly I stopped. It was impossible. "Marshall is dead" were words that didn't mean anything. "What happened?" I said.

My father, in his plaster-dotted work overalls, sighed deeply and rubbed his chin. "Well, you know how he loved to chase cars," he said. "He was chasing one down Maple Street, and another came across Bridge Street and didn't see him, and—"

"But how did he get *out*?" I said, puzzled. "How could he have gotten *out*? I left him locked in the backyard before I went to school this morning. Maybe it wasn't Marshall. Maybe it was some other dog, maybe—" I stood up to run to the backyard.

"Sweetheart," said my father more gently than he had spoken to me in months. "There's no doubt. It *was* Marshall. You must not have latched the gate this morning."

"But I DID!" Suddenly I was screaming. "I DID!" I saw the flat aluminum piece slide into the catch. I saw myself checking it. I saw Marshall watching me through the gate. Marshall—dead? Gone forever? My friend? My sweet doggy Marshall?

"Well, he must have gotten out somehow, then."

"How? How? *How*?" I was crying, now, again.

"Well, I don't know. What does it matter, Chrissie? He got out somehow—now he's dead. I'm sorry, but that's how it is."

"That's how it is? *How* he got out doesn't matter? You know what happened? I'll tell you what happened! My *mother* let him out! My own *mother*!" Rage boiled in me, racing through my veins. "How could she do that? How *could* she? How could Mom let Marshall get killed?"

"Chrissie, don't you *dare* speak that way about your

mother! You know your mother would *never*—I won't have it! I won't. I'm telling you. I know you're upset, but—"

"You're goddamn right I'm upset! Mom killed him! I *know* she did! She killed my best friend! Because *I* left Marshall locked in the backyard! I know it, and there's no way, *no way*, he could have gotten out, and it had to be Mom! It had to be! I hate her! I *hate* her!"

Dad walked across the room, pulled me up out of the chair, took me by the shoulders, and shook me hard. When that didn't make me stop crying, he slapped me across the face, hard. In the silence that followed, he said, in a low, hissing voice, "I don't care *what* happened, Chrissie, do you hear me? You are not going to talk this way no matter what—"

"No, you *don't* care what happened, do you?" I said, dry eyed now, and hard and cold. "You've never cared about me, why should you start now? And Mom? That's a laugh, she never cared about anyone but herself, not for one minute. Well, you know what? I've stopped caring about *you*, too. I give up. I just don't care at all. I'm through trying to please you 'cause it's impossible. I—hate—you. Do you understand? And I—hate—Mom. And from now on I'm going to do whatever the hell I want because I—don't—care!"

"I thought," said my father in a low voice, "that you were already doing that. Dear God, I swear I don't know how you turned out this way. It makes me sick. You're no daughter of mine, you miserable, filthy, foulmouthed slut." He shook his head and left the room.

That night I went out with a bunch of the kids. We went over to Paulette Steves's house, because her parents were away, and we smoked some weed and drank beer. But being stoned only made me feel sadder. It was as if I was looking down on the sadness from somewhere else, instead of being right in the middle of it. I was numb. And I wanted to be numb, even sadly numb. I just didn't want to think or feel anymore. Happy birthday, Chris!

Being stoned made it possible for me to appear calm and collected, my usual public self. It was important to me that I not break down and start crying. I didn't want anyone to know. Not Donny, not Paulette Steves, not anyone. Now, of course, it seems stupid to me that I spent all that time hanging around those kids but never talking to them about anything important, just constantly putting on this big act of Chris, the stacked teenage rebel queen, the toughie. I remember wondering sometimes if all of them were putting on acts too—if each of the kids had their thing that they were doing to disguise what was really inside *them*, too.

That night I was with Donny Figeroa. After we got stoned at Paulette's and listened to her new Pink Floyd album, I remember we went to the PP and had pizza. I hadn't eaten all day. I was pretty hungry, and the dope made every bite of the pizza delicious.

Donny was sitting next to me, his arm draped around my shoulders. "Mmmmm-mmmm! You sure look good tonight! Gooo-oood!"

Even in public, Donny didn't stop pestering me about going to bed with him. I was sick of it. But it did seem pointless not to. I mean, why not? Very few of the girls I knew were virgins. My virginity was just a technicality, anyway, since I'd already done "everything but" with Donny and almost that much with a couple of other boys. I was secretly hoping that if I went all the way I *would* feel something, and then I'd understand what sex was about and I'd know I was normal.

But why did I say *yes* that particular night? Maybe I

was tired of fighting. Maybe my father had accused me so often that I thought I might as well live up to his accusations. But there was something else, too. I had this idea that losing my virginity would change me, would make some big difference.

And I was so lonely that night.

It wasn't the most romantic place in the world: a damp vacant room that used to be a laundry room in the basement of an apartment building Donny knew. We used to go there a lot, to make out. He brought along a sleeping bag he kept stashed in the trunk of his car.

"Come on, Chrissie, *please*?"

I was so sick of arguing.

"God, you come on hot, but you're so *cold* when it comes right down to it!"

Cold? Donny couldn't imagine how cold I was. Stoned, I let my mind drift onto cold things. Icebergs, white icebergs bobbing along slowly in bubbling red rivers of blood, floating in my veins.

"Stop teasing me, Chrissie!"

And then Donny actually grabbed and shook me. That made twice that day I'd been shaken. *Who is this urgent, pimply kid shaking me? Who am I, the rag doll with the big tits, being shook? Or shaken? Or shooked— no, that's not right. Shaked. Shocked.*

"Come *on*, Chris, *please*! You know, I just don't understand how you can act like you do and look like you do and still be such a goddamn prude."

Finally I said, as if from a great distance, "Sure thing, Donny. You convinced me."

But as he started making love to me, he said, "You know, Chris, you *could* be a little more enthusiastic."

I remember I laughed—a quick, unfunny snort.

It was cold in the laundry room, and I remember the zipper of the sleeping bag was cutting into my back. But I didn't move the sleeping bag or say anything to Donny because it seemed too much trouble. I just wanted to get it over with; heaving, grunting Donny, with his beery breath, and his pathetic enthusiasm, my hands resting lightly on his back, mountainous with pimples. A warm body close to me, on me, in me... but a zillion miles away.

And so I lost my virginity. And it was a new physical sensation, that's all. Not a turn-on, not painful, not anything. Zip. The same numbness I'd felt all evening, only more so.

It wasn't until I met Luke that I finally understood, and experienced, what the big deal over sex was all about. But of course, that night with Donny I had no idea that I ever would find out, or be with someone like Luke, or be happy.

And losing my virginity hadn't changed anything. Everything was exactly the same.

When I got home it was after midnight and my parents were already in bed. I finally opened the birthday present. It was a perfect clincher to that whole day.

They had gotten me a white dress, all lacy and frilly and girlish, with a pink ribbon threaded through those little tiny narrow shoulder straps.

Now you've got to understand that it wasn't just that I didn't wear dresses anymore; it was that I couldn't have worn that dress even if I had wanted to, even if I had liked it.

Being a 36C, I had to wear those heavy-duty three-hook bras with the great big thick shoulder straps. And wearing a bra like that, there was no way I could wear

anything strapless or with thin little straps or with a
halter top that tied around the neck or with a skimpy
neckline. I couldn't. This dress that my parents were
giving me was made for someone else.

I remember shaking my head, somewhere near crying
or laughing but not doing either. They don't see me, I
thought. At all! Period! I'm invisible! They think they
love me, but it's not *me*. It's some make-believe charac-
ter called Daughter, not *me*.

And they got Daughter a pure, innocent, white dress,
like a nine-year-old might wear to first communion.
What a choice, I thought, remembering the gray laundry room in the basement, the sleeping bag on the
concrete floor. What perfect timing!

There was a half bottle of catsup in the fridge. I got it
out. I took that frilly little dress with its pretty pink
shoulder straps and I spread it out over the kitchen
table with its skirt neatly flounced out. Then I took that
bottle of red, red catsup and shook it out all over that
frilly white dress.

6

The first time I told Luke about everything that I've
written down here so far, he said, "I'm surprised you
didn't take off the next *day*, Chrysta."

But I didn't. I didn't run away until nearly ten
months and about ten boys later.

After my Happy 13th, home—if you want to call it

that—had become a war zone. Mom just avoided me; I *never* saw her. When I was around the house she'd just stay barricaded in her bedroom, the TV blaring through the closed door.

But my father and I did not avoid each other. I think we each felt that if we stayed out of the territory we had formerly occupied, it would have been a victory for the other. So we kept our regular routines, tossing a few verbal bombs at each other whenever our paths crossed. These brief battles all boiled down to his calling me a degenerate slut and my saying that he was the world's shittiest father. But this was all just friendly chitchat compared to what happened when he found the pills.

You see, I got the clap. Gonorrhea. VD.

I'm not sure who I got it from, not that it matters.

After I went to bed with Donny Figeroa, I slept with about ten other boys in Benton, all in that same crowd. I just felt, "Why not?" Nothing seemed to make any difference to me, not in any part of my life. Sex was just something to do, something it was easier to say yes to than say no to. I never enjoyed it particularly—it was just as zip with the other boys as with Donny, but I did it anyway. Since my father was calling me a slut every five minutes, I felt I might as well live up to it.

I knew I had the clap before I went to the doctor because I had symptoms (I found out later a lot of girls don't). It burned whenever I peed—really hurt—and I knew, I just knew, I had it. I told Tom Wallach, the boy I was going with at that point. I had to tell someone, and I didn't know who else to tell. Tom was pretty nice about it. He drove me to Bloomberg, where there was a doctor his sister had gone to. I told Dr. Lundbeck that I was Liz Schmidt, 24, a divorced secretary, and I gave an address in Garden Hills, and I got diagnosed. When the nurse asked me who I'd had "sexual contact" with, she had this disgusted expression on her face. I hate to think how she'd have looked had she known I was only thirteen. The nurse told me that a letter had to be sent to my "contacts" telling them they'd been "exposed," and you can bet I thought fast and lied through that too. But when I got back to Benton I told all the boys I had gone to bed with, which completely trashed whatever was left of my reputation. Not that I cared.

Finally Dr. Lundbeck gave me a prescription to have filled. I had it filled in Bloomberg (with money I'd earned at the Pizza Palace) and I started taking the capsules. But my father found the pills and he just flipped out.

Of course, Dad had no right poking around in the bottom drawer of my dresser in the first place. At first he thought the yellow-and-orange capsules were dope. "You just sit your cheap ass down and start talking, young lady. . . . For starters, who is Liz Schmidt? I asked you a question! And what are these? 'Uppers'? 'Downers'? Start talking. I suspected this. You've changed too much for it to be a natural, normal thing! I knew there had to be drugs involved! Now you answer me, or I swear I'll turn you in to the police!"

He probably thought that he sounded real hip and aware, but to me he sounded like he'd watched one too many *Rockford Files*.

I kept quiet, not sure whether it was worse for him to think that the pills were dope or for him to know what they *really* were. Eventually, of course, he called Lundbeck and got it all figured out. And then, Dad just—exploded. Lost it. He Frankensteined from his usual self into a certifiable, raving, vicious monster. He never let up from that point on. I was a slut, a whore, a prostitute, cheap, filthy, foul, diseased, perverted, a hopeless case, ungrateful, unfit, conniving, disgusting, incorrigible, better off dead, belonged in a detention home, and on and on and on and on. His face would get twisted up with hatred as he made his accusations—he didn't even look like himself.

And he *kept* the tetracycline. I was supposed to take two four times a day, but instead of letting me hang on to them and take them as I needed to, he would dole them out to me.

Before I could open my mouth in the morning, the second I'd walk into the kitchen for breakfast, he'd say something like "Haven't you forgotten something?"

"No, Dad, I haven't forgotten."

"Well, what do you say, you little slut?"

"May I please have my pills, Dad?"

"What kind of pills?"

"Tetracycline."

"For what?"

"For gonorrhea, Dad."

"Very good! A-plus! Here you are, Chris. One, two little pills for you now, three, four for later. There you go. Now isn't that nice? You can cure yourself of this slimy disease you picked up by screwing your brainless head off, and once you're healthy—why, you can go right back to screwing to your heart's content! If you *have* a heart! You're lucky I even let you stay under the same roof with us, you slut! You're lucky I let you have these at all! I wonder if you wouldn't be better off with your kind of people, dying of your own filthy diseases in some gutter somewhere—"

My throat would tighten so hard I could hardly swallow the pills. I knew that however bad I was, I didn't deserve this. I managed to keep from crying the first two times he did it, but on the third, I couldn't help it. Tears began to roll down my face. Where was the old Chris, the one who could always come out fighting? She was gone then, gone as much as sweet, innocent, prissy Chrissie had gone.

"That's right, cry!" my father screamed. "That's a nice mature reaction. A nice *adult* response! If you want to act like an adult when you're a child, you have to take the consequences! But no, you don't want to do that! You expect to do whatever dirty, filthy thing crosses your mind and get off scot-free! Why weren't you crying the first time you spread your legs, huh?"

I was supposed to take the tetracycline for ten days, and then return for a check-up. But my father found them on the third day I was taking them. I got through three more days of medication—with Dad doling them out and carrying on. By that time the symptoms were gone. By that time I also think I would have shriveled up and died if I had had to listen to any more of my father's abuse. It seemed like anything would've been better than staying. I thought about killing myself. But I was too angry. If I had thought killing myself would've made my father feel guilty, then I might've done it. But I knew Dad would see my death as another cross for *him* to bear, part of his weird ego trip on how much he suffered. He might secretly be relieved that I was out of the picture and not causing trouble. Well, I wasn't going to give him that satisfaction.

I was going to live. So I ran away.

7

I left home with nearly $200 saved from the P.P., and enough rage and hurt at my parents to keep me running, I thought, forever. I also left with something else, something dangerous harbored inside me—but that I didn't know about. I didn't find out until much later.

Luke says it's not important for me to tell everything that happened to me in my two and a half years on the road, because—he says—the real story didn't start until I came to Excelsior. Well, I couldn't tell everything even if I wanted to, because I don't remember it all: I met so many people, and stayed so many places, and worked so many jobs, one after the other.

But some of it I do remember, and some of it I do need to tell. Because if I hadn't done some changing and growing up before I hit Excelsior, if I'd blown into town the same tough, bratty, mixed-up kid who left Benton, there wouldn't *be* any story. I never would have seen what Excelsior had to offer, and even if I had, I wouldn't have been able to take it. And give to it.

For a few months after I split, I mostly acted like my old Benton punk-queen self. I still wore a lot of makeup, wore my good old wooden-heeled Candie's, and had fights with my parents—but now only in my mind. I never called them, though I thought about it a lot. But I always ended up with "Why should I?"

Mostly I hitched, though now and then I traveled by bus or train. When money ran out, I learned how to get a phoney Social Security number and a job. Looking old for my age helped a lot—I put down "24" on the job applications, and never, not once, did I get so much as a skeptical look.

Right after I split, I worked for a few weeks in Chicago in another Pizza Palace, where I not only did the salad bar but made the pizza in the afternoons. But Chicago was only a couple of hours from Benton, and I kept worrying my parents would catch up with me, so pretty soon I hit the road. When I was out of money, in those first few months, I'd stop in a town and meet a boy and let him buy me a meal and sometimes give me money. Sometimes I'd pay for it by spending the night with him—but a lot of times, much more often than not, I didn't have to. Which was good, because I didn't *want* to. I still didn't feel anything much, outside of wishing I was somewhere else. I'd lie there, supposedly making love, but really thinking about the book I was reading, or what time I'd leave in the morning, waiting for it to be over. Sometimes my father's ugly words would come into my mind. I'd chase them out, but of course when you try to not think of something, you're still thinking of it, so it didn't do much good.

I traveled a lot. So many towns and cities were ugly, scarred by factories and fast-foot places and discount stores and used-car lots. I learned how to work each of them the same way. The action usually spread out from the bus station or the train station, and every Pizza Palace or McDonald's was stamped out of the same mold. I could get a job in a fast-food place anywhere, and I did, though I rarely ate in them. Chicago was the same as Milwaukee was the same as Des Moines.

But the people I met were different. I met truck

drivers, other runaways, college kids, Jehovah's Witnesses, hippies, preppies, Hare Krishnas, and even a few Indians. Once I got picked up by chicken thieves in a beat-up truck, once by marathon runners on their way to a race in Cincinnati. Another time there was an old couple in a Buick who had a parrot, Chico, in a cage with them in the car. They kept talking to him, but the only thing Chico said, at least while I was in the car, was "Play it again, Sam."

I stayed with some students in Boulder, Colorado. I lived in Topeka, Kansas, for a few weeks with a boy named Tom who sold weed. I spent nearly two months in Taos with Daniel, a housepainter who wanted to be a poet and always listened very intently to song lyrics. Daniel was pretty quirky. You couldn't call him "Dan" instead of Daniel or he'd get upset. And if a record by Joni Mitchell, Bruce Springsteen, Bob Dylan, Paul Simon, Jackson Browne, Randy Newman, or Michael Franks came on, you had to shut up so he could hear the words, or he'd get upset. Before, the music I'd heard had mostly been top-40 stuff, background at the PP or other places I worked at, or over car radios when I was hitching—and I was surprised at how much I liked listening to the words too. But eventually I got sick of Daniel going "SSSSSHHHHHHHHHH!" all the time, or "DANIEL, *NOT* DAN!" I wasn't about to put up with that for long, since I'd been *ssshhhhh*ed all my life. So pretty soon I moved on again, though with song lyrics and music running through my head: like Bruce Springsteen's line "Tramps like us, baby we were born to run."

Daniel was really nice-looking—6 foot 3, blue eyed, with curly blond hair. I was pretty attracted to him. We shared a few interests: natural foods, reading. He was patient enough to teach me how to drive, too. And I liked Daniel—though not enough to tell him who I really was. I thought, at first, that he might turn me on sexually: but nothing. I decided there really was something wrong with me after all, if Daniel couldn't do it for me. I decided, after I left Daniel, to avoid sex as much as possible for a while. I did, too, and felt good about it.

I remember after I'd been on the road oh, maybe three months, this well-meaning high-school teacher named Harold Jenkins picked me up hitchhiking outside of Des Moines, Iowa. I'd waited about five hours for a ride and it was drizzling outside and I was tired and cold and fell asleep almost the second I got in the car. After I woke up, we got to talking a little, and he told me about "his kids"—in his classes, that is—and said he was worried about my safety, being female and hitchhiking alone. He said about ten times, "Look, the world is not as nice a place as you or I might want it to be. There are good people, but there are a lot of loonies. A lot of loonies on the road."

"I've told you," I repeated to him, each time getting more annoyed, "I can take care of myself."

"But *part* of taking care of yourself is that you've got to consider what *could* happen to you. You've got to take responsibility for yourself in the world *as it is.*"

Well, this really pissed me off. I mean, I didn't want to spend my time thinking about all the bad things that could happen to me. If I had, I couldn't have done it, and I *had* to do it. What other choice did I have? Go back home? I remember thinking, man, no matter *what* the loonies on the road might be like, they couldn't be half as bad as the two I left behind in Benton, Illinois. Where did this guy get off? "Look, this is my life, and

I'm going to live it the way I want to. I asked you for a ride, not a lecture, and believe me, if I can't have one without the other I'll get out right here and now."

"No, no, I'm sorry," he said quickly and dropped it, but after that the atmosphere in the car was tense. The next time we stopped at a gas station, I split to the highway while he was in the bathroom, and caught another ride almost immediately. Later, going through my backpack, I found a ten-dollar bill tucked in that Harold Jenkins must've stashed there when I was sleeping, and I felt badly that I'd been so rude to him. Long after that ten bucks had been spent, his words came back to me. And I wished I could apologize to him, but of course, I couldn't.

Except here, I guess: Mr. Jenkins, wherever you are, I'm sorry.

The first few months I was on the road, I bluffed my way through everything. For instance, in Chicago I went to an Army-and-Navy surplus store and spent $82.50 of my hard-earned PP $200 on a sleeping bag, a backpack, and a hunting knife. If a man was giving me a ride, and his arm started to crawl along the back of the seat toward me and he said, in a certain weasely kind of way that I must've heard at least fifty times, "Doesn't a girl like you get a little *scared* hitchhiking alone?" then I'd whip out my knife. I'd open it, and very slowly begin cleaning my nails.

"Oh, no," I'd say, perfectly deadpan as I peeled the dirt out from under one fingernail after another. "You see, I know self-defense."

I never got bothered. But one day a college-age guy with shag-cut blond hair responded, with great interest, "Oh, really? Karate?"

"Uh-hunnh," I said, acting bored.

"Where'd you do your trials? I just got my black belt."

"Did I say karate?" I said quickly, racking my brains. "Actually, it's a, uh, combination of karate, kung fu, and tae kwon do. The best points of each. They don't give belts."

"Oh," he said puzzled. "I've never heard of it. What'd you say it was called?"

"Uh, ka-chung fundo. It's kinda new. But *real* effective."

After that I retired the nail-cleaning bit from my repertoire.

Yet underneath the Chris who was bluffing every second, there was another Chris. I mean, whoever heard of a teenage hippie-punk kid, a high-school dropout, who was a compulsive reader? But there was always a paperback in my backpack, from the bookstore in the last city I'd been in (*bought* from the bookstore; I never ripped anything off because I was afraid I'd get caught and found out as a runaway). I read *Rebecca* and *The Scapegoat* by Daphne du Maurier, all of Tolkien, all of Paul Gallico, lots of Ray Bradbury, and even that weird story by Franz Kafka about the guy who wakes up one morning and discovers he's a cockroach (I felt that way, only in reverse—I had woken up and discovered my *parents* were cockroaches). I read if it was light out and not too windy by the side of the road as I waited for rides. I read in little diners as I slurped down hot bowls of chili (usually the cheapest thing on the menu) and pretended not to notice the rednecks and waitresses and truck drivers staring at me as if I was from Mars. During off hours at the fast-food places where I worked, I read between customers. Wherever I bedded down for the night, I read a few chapters. In New Mexico crash pads. In student apartments. In motels.

Wherever I was, if I was there for more than a couple of days, I scouted out the public library. Even if I couldn't take anything out because I wasn't a resident, I could sit there in that quiet atmosphere and read all day. I read all of *Catcher in the Rye* in one sitting in this great old library in Chicago one winter day, fairly soon after I left home. I remember the chair I was sitting in was blue, and there were those great big oak library tables, and it was clean and light and warm and safe and quiet, except for the hiss of the radiators. There was a faint musty smell, and it was snowing out.

So I was still two girls, just as I'd always been. One was Punk-Queen-Chris-Who-Gets-What-She-Wants-and-Doesn't-Take-Any-Shit. That Chris was tough, a survivor. She could think fast, lie her way into a job, or talk her way out of being raped by some drunk guy who'd picked her up hitchhiking. My inner Chris, though, was the complete opposite: so beaten down by her previous life that she was always frightened, sure that sooner or later she'd be caught, busted as a runaway, and hustled straight back to Benton or off to juvenile detention. This Chris was afraid to make friends or tell anybody the truth about herself, though she wanted to desperately. She was scared to death at the very moments the other Chris was recklessly barging in and out of risky situations.

But the scared, quiet Chris was also the one who was looking for answers, who was reading and wondering "Why?" and thinking about her life all the time.

And one of the things I thought about was "Will I ever be the same all the way through—one girl instead of two?"

*   *   *

But gradually, my life on the road began to change me. The Punk Queen started to get edged out. First, of course, my appearance changed—you can't wear Candie's if you're running down the shoulder of an interstate waving your hands excitedly because after two hours a car pulled over for you a few hundred yards down the road. You can't wear eye makeup if your only mirror is a jagged half mirror above a dirty sink in a Mobil station at three A.M. in North Dakota and the guy driving the Hev-In-Lee Yogurt delivery truck is waiting for you outside, his radio tuned to an all-night country-and-western station for truck drivers.

And slowly I began to feel like there was more to me than just a good body, though I wasn't sure what. And sometimes I began to feel like somehow, I wasn't sure how, things might just work out for me.

By the time I lived with Daniel in Taos, I was on a different circuit from the one I'd been on when I first left Benton. I wasn't wearing makeup anymore, and my Candie's had been replaced by sneakers and a pair of comfortable sandals. I found myself working in natural food stores and restaurants instead of Colonel Sanderses and Pizza Palaces. I found myself starting to relax, just a little, though never so much that I told my whole story to anyone.

I think reading may have been one thing that helped me keep it together as well as I did—that and feeling like I *had* to keep it together because I had no real alternative. Books gave me something to escape into, and they also offered me a way to see how other people had problems in their lives, as bad as mine or worse, and how they worked them out. Of course, I was also seeing that "live and in person" through all the different people I met, people who gave me rides, people who I worked with. And the music helped too. I remember once getting let out in the middle of nowhere in Texas, and I couldn't get a ride for the longest time. A sandy wind was blowing up little eddies of dust, and tumbleweed, this light, bushy plant which sort of rolls itself up in a ball, was bouncing along in the wind. It got darker and darker, and it was cold, and the wind was sighing more and more loudly, and it was pretty spooky. No cars at all were coming by, and I felt scared—really scared—and as lonely as I'd ever felt in my whole life.

But, still, it wasn't lonely in the way I'd felt when I'd lost my virginity to Donny Figeroa on the laundry-room floor. It was a different kind of loneliness. And better. Like *knowing*, for sure, that I had only myself to count on, only myself in the whole world, and so I'd better be strong and not freak out.

So I started singing, just all of a sudden, singing out loud in the Texas dusk that was turning to night, singing out loud as the wind rose and sighed and the tumbleweed blew down the highway in its eerie, ghostly way. As the moon came up, I sang that James Taylor song, the one that goes

> *There's nothing like a hundred miles between me and*
> *   trouble on my mind*
> *there's nothing like a hundred miles*
> *show me the yellow line.*

And I sang some Joni Mitchell songs, like the one that goes

> *Sometimes I get that strong longing I want to settle*
> *down and raise a child up with somebody—but it*

passes me as the wind blows I'm a wild seed, let the
wind carry me.

Now, I have a voice like a crow, and I would never
sing in front of anybody, even now. But that night, in a
Texas wasteland, the sun down and the moon rising,
cold and lonely and scared, grit blowing into my eyes, I
sang my lungs out, and it was great. And in the middle
of that loneliness I felt an emotion that was so foreign to
me that it took me a while to put a name to it. Finally I
did, though—it was triumph. I felt triumphant.

Not long after that, a van came by filled with five
longhairs headed for Austin, Texas. I went with them
and I wound up getting a job waiting tables at the Beer
Garden at Armadillo World Headquarters for two months.
Which makes me realize, as I write this, that to be
honest I have to add another item to my list of things
that helped me come out okay: luck. Because I *was*
lucky. Things like the van ride to Austin and the job at
Armadillo World Headquarters just happened to me.
And I never got ripped off, I never got raped, I never
got busted as a runaway, I never got down to my very
last dollar (though I got down to five dollars several
times), and I was never hungry for more than a day or
two. Always, something would turn up: a ride, a job,
somebody to buy me a meal or slip me a few bucks or
let me spend the night on their couch. Sure, I met
quite a few jerks, but I met a lot more good people. I
used to think that it must just seem that way, because
after my parents anybody halfway sane would be peaches
and cream. But when I met Lissa, and later Dare, and
heard about *their* lives on the road, I decided I really
had been lucky after all.
It was certainly luck that led me to my job at

Henley's Big Sur Inn. And to Lissa. And, later on, to
Excelsior Springs.

8

I knew I was heading for California; every runaway is.
It's all the songs about California, and books and movies,
I think, which make it out as something more than just
another state. Which is all it is.

It wasn't like I had a particular job or destination in
mind for when I got there—it was the idea of California.
Looking back on it, I think I felt about going to
California a little like I'd felt about having sex—that
doing it would change my life and make a difference.
You'd think after sex turning out like it had, I would
have known better.

I wound up working at a place called Henley's Big
Sur Inn. I stayed there for almost four months, longer
than I had worked any other job since I'd left Benton.

I was a maid and dishwasher at Henley's. I had a
tiny, bare cabin all my own, off in the woods, a little
behind the Inn's main building. It had white walls and
an uneven floor and a single bed with a holey white
chenille bedspread and a table and chair. I got three
meals a day, and a hundred dollars a week. I had a
regular schedule, which began with my washing the
breakfast dishes and ended with my washing the dinner
dishes. In between, I cleaned cabins 1 through 8. I had

two afternoons off a week, and on one of them I'd usually catch a ride with Jean-Paul, the gloomy French chef, to the nearest city, Carmel, where I'd pick up a paperback at the bookstore. Jean-Paul, if I caught him in a good mood, would occasionally show me some culinary trick, like once he taught me three different ways to thicken a sauce, but most of the time he—like everybody else—left me alone. It wasn't me especially, everybody left everybody alone. Everyone kept to themselves. I wonder now, after coming to Excelsior and finding it so much the opposite, if maybe it had to do with the place itself.

It never actually rained there, but the sun never shone brightly either. Nothing final or definite, the weather and the people both gray and chilly: not like movie-and-song California. And yet, in its way, Big Sur was beautiful.

Just to the left of the driveway at Henley's there was this one spot where, whenever the fog lifted, you could get a good view of the ocean, gray-blue with white frills of waves, crashing into huge gray boulders far below. It seemed right to me that instead of the California I'd always pictured—golden sand beaches, girls in bikinis, and boys carrying surf boards—I'd found this wild, violently beautiful California, steep and rocky and isolated and hostile, with the angry surf bashing into the stones.

Most days, I used to walk out to that point where you could see the waves and just stare out for a while. And I'd always pass this phone booth, one of those clear plastic outdoor ones, which stood just outside the main lodge. And I'd find myself imagining calling somebody up from that phone booth. My parents. Daniel, the housepainter. Or good old Harold Jenkins, that high-school teacher who picked me up that time, who probably would've been the only one happy to hear from me, and I bet he would've remembered me, too. But of course I had no idea where he lived or even what school he taught at. "Hi! This is Chris, remember me? Well, you'll never guess where I am! Listen, I can see the Pacific Ocean right from where I'm standing. . . ."

No, I'd think every day, looking out at those endless waves. There's nobody I can call. Nobody in the whole world.

And at those moments my longing to love and be loved and to have a real home and real friends would pulse so hard and deep in me I could hardly keep it down.

But something was beginning to build in me: an urgency I couldn't describe. Maybe I was scared to—it was that strong.

I remember the moment I decided to quit Henley's.

I was knocking at the door of 5, the Inn's biggest cabin. It had three bedrooms, a fireplace, the works.

That week a family was staying there. Even though I heard voices inside, no one answered my knocking. I knocked harder.

Finally the mother's voice came floating down from upstairs. "Sarah? Find out who it is."

I could picture the mother, leaning over the sink in one of the upstairs bathrooms, putting on mascara. She was one of those tasteful, sleek women. She probably paid fifty dollars for a haircut and spent all her time at a health club doing sit-ups. The kids were bratty, always whining. Her husband smoked a pipe.

Right behind the closed door I heard the little girl's shrill voice. "Who is it?"

"The maid," I said, shifting my weight, a heavy armload of sheets and towels pressed against my chest. *The maid.* Well I was, wasn't I?

"Mommy!" I heard the girl shriek up to her mother. "Mommy! It's the maid!"

I'm not "the maid." I know it. Then what, what?

From upstairs the mother's voice floated down again. "Tell her we'll be out in a few minutes and she can come then."

The little girl opened the door then, and looked up at me. "Come back later," she commanded. Then she shut the door in my face. It was time to move on.

But California was as far as I could go. I'd come all the way here, crisscrossing the country from Benton, Illinois, north and south and up and down, but always vaguely heading west, to golden California. So now what?

I decided to head to L.A. It got sunnier the farther south I got. An easy hitch, until I hit Oxnard, a city just north of L.A. There, a car let me out to one of the most unwelcome sights a hitchhiker can see: a line of six or eight other hitchhikers already waiting on the on ramp. I glanced at them and then looked away, sighing as I climbed out of the car. I walked to the end of the line to wait my turn, and as I eased my backpack off, I heard a male voice say in astonishment, "It's *another* chick!" I looked up and discovered, for the first time in about two years on the road, another girl who didn't appear to be with anyone.

She had this wild sand-colored hair, shoulder length, that stuck straight out around her tiny heart-shaped face. It was as if she'd stuck her tongue in an electric socket and the voltage had gone straight to her scalp. What made the hair seem even more dramatic was that the girl was so small—only five feet or so. But she wasn't delicate. She was tight, muscular, tough: After I knew her better I came to think of her as pure, compressed energy.

She was wearing jeans, big clunky running shoes with white socks, a green T-shirt, and a faded blue jean jacket, cut Hell's Angels style. But it was all clean—she didn't look grungy or beaten down. Over one shoulder she had this giant floppy suede purse, purple, with long strings of fringe hanging down.

She walked over to me—after shooting a disgusted look at the guy who had made the "chick" comment—and asked me, "Hey, do you have a Tampax?"

I said, "Uh, sure, I think," and began digging around in my pack. "You going over there?" I asked her, gesturing with my head toward a Denny's across the street.

"Yeah, I guess." She squinted at it. Her hazel eyes were large, and her lips were full. Exaggerated features. Like a pretty monkey.

"I'll come too," I said. "I want a glass of orange juice." I did, but I was also interested in her. Something about that monkey face was immediately likeable.

"Okay." She shrugged, then nodded and suddenly grinned. I saw her left front tooth was slightly crooked, giving her a raffish, crazy look. I found the Tampax and handed it to her. "Hey, thanks," she said, still sizing me up. I slung my pack back on, and we headed across the street. "Bye-bye, gurrr-rrrruls!" called the same boy who had spoken earlier, in a sleazy falsetto.

"Jerk," the girl said to me. "He thinks that's witty. Height of wit. He's been putting the make on me for *one* hour, and I'm reeeal bored with it, know what I mean?"

I nodded.

"Yeah," said the girl, amused, glancing at me

appraisingly and taking in my figure. "I bet you do. Oh lucky lucky you. I'm Lissa, by the way, short for *Me*lissa, which my white trash mama used to pronounce M'lissa—two syllables. You?"

"Chris," I said. We reached the restaurant and she pushed open the door. The interior was dark after the glare outside, and I blinked. Lissa immediately headed for the bathroom, but a bleach-blond waitress, who looked like her hair had been glued on and her makeup applied with spray paint, stepped in front of her. "JUST a minute, young lady! *If* you are one, it's hard to tell! Rest rooms are for customers only!"

I started to say, "Well, I—" but Lissa, swiveling around with her hands on her hips, interrupted me. Narrowing her eyes at the waitress, she hissed, "Well, it's a goddamn good thing my friend and I are customers then, isn't it? Otherwise I'd have to do it on the floor, wouldn't I? Now are you going to take her order, Bleach Brain, so we can *become* customers, or am I going to have to squat down here under one of the tables?"

And with that she marched into the bathroom.

The waitress's mouth hung open, then she snapped it shut. Although I was as shocked as the waitress, I moved to a booth—we were the only ones in the place—and sat down. The waitress hurled the menus onto the table. Then she rolled off, to return with two plastic glasses of water, which she slammed down. Then she announced, "Your friend has quite a mouth on her."

I thought of all the times waitresses had told me rudely that rest rooms were for customers only, and how I had always meekly explained that I *was* a customer, feeling self-conscious. And I thought, *Hey—runaway or not, grungy or not, backpack on or not, hitchhiker or not, I have a right to be treated politely.* After all, in my many stints as a counter girl or waitress, *I* always tried to be nice to everyone who came along.

And just like that, I looked up at that waitress, absolutely deadpan, and said quietly, "I guess she must've figured that *mouths* were the local fashion. Two orange juices, please."

"That's *all* you're having?" The waitress glared at me.

"I'm going to wait to order the rest until my friend comes back from the bathroom."

"You know"—the waitress put down her pad on the table and raised a forefinger warningly—"you know, if I was your friend's mother, I'd—"

"But," I said, "you're not. You're her waitress, and mine, and I'd like my orange juice, please."

Fifteen minutes later, when Lissa still hadn't come out and the waitress was all but having convulsions, I went in to make sure she was okay.

And there was Lissa, running shoes on her feet, T-shirt and jacket on top, but in between—zip. Bare-ass. She was holding her jeans up to a hot-air-blower hand-drier thing. She looked ridiculous—those little tiny bare buns poking out—but I freaked. I hardly knew this girl! What if she was certifiably cuckoo? What if the waitress came in? What if we got shipped to the police station and—

"Lissa! Are you crazy?"

"No, just, um, imaginative. I got blood all over the crotch of my jeans and underpants, see, and I rinsed it out, but I have to dry it out a little before I can put it back on. It's a reeeal drag. Why, is Neon Face giving you a hard time?"

"A little. You think you could wear a pair of mine?"

We looked at each other.

"Well—" Lissa hesitated. "Well, I don't want to, you

know, bleed all over *your* jeans or something—I mean, these'll be dry in a few minutes and—and, listen, there's no way they'd fit anyway—"

Like me, I thought, listening to her, she's like me! It's hard for her to accept favors. "I'll get a pair, let's try," I said, and went back out. Bleach Brain rolled up again. "Now listen, miss—" she began, waving her forefinger again, as I stood by the booth, digging around in my pack. "Two orders of dry whole wheat toast!" I said, and marched into the bathroom, carrying a pair of jeans and a piece of rope I kept for tying things to my pack. A few minutes later, Lissa and I emerged, she wearing my jeans. They were hugely baggy on her, rolled up at the ankle and tied at the waist with the rope. We nearly collided with the waitress, who was bringing the toast. Speechless, she blinked at Lissa's new attire, and Lissa quickly pirouetted on her toes, posing like a fashion model. "And *this* year," she said in this la-di-da voice, "we have this *smashing* new look for spring, all the rage in Ox-Turd." She spun again, and strutted to the table.

And that's how I met Lissa, my first friend—and still my best, other than Luke. And over orange juice, dry whole wheat toast, and finally salad for me and a turkey sandwich for her, Lissa told me about herself and I told her about myself, and she talked me into going to New Orleans with her to the Mardi Gras. We would stay with Jake, a friend of hers, and then, maybe, the two of us would get jobs and a place of our own.

By the time Lissa and I split from California three weeks later (we stayed at this apartment of some friends of friends of hers in L.A.), I knew all about her and she knew almost everything about me. I knew she was eighteen and had run away from home in Mississippi when she was fourteen. I knew if she pulled back her

hair there was a scar right along her hairline, where her
mother had thrown her into a radiator when she was
four; I knew she'd been beaten by her mom all her life.
I knew her father was an alcoholic tire salesman who'd
drifted from job to job to finally no job. Lissa dismissed
him with one contemptuous word: "pitiful." Her older
brother, Jimmy, had tried to molest her when she was
thirteen, and when Lissa tried to tell her mother, "That
bitch beat me within an inch of my life, and you better
believe that as soon as I *could* run after that, I did. You
know, Chris, I could *seriously* hate her if it wasn't such
a damn waste of time." I knew that after a series of
hair-raising adventures on the road and a lot of sex for
survival's sake ("Let's face it, Chris, I was a regular
Pop-Tart") she'd finally drifted to New Orleans, where
she had had the good fortune to become friends with a
thirty-nine-year-old gay guy, Michael, who more or less
adopted her, and "just, you know, helped me talk it out
and see my way clear of that shit. Or start to. Saved my
damn life is what he did." I also knew that Michael
had—and she could say this cheerfully, with her crazy
crooked smile lighting her face, "pushed me out of the
nest, so I could learn to live without him, you know,
like a mother bird pushes a baby bird out, otherwise
the stupid lazy little sucker'll just sit there and open its
mouth for food and never flap its own damn wings."
Michael was now in Toronto, helping to found a gay
counseling center; Lissa sent him a postcard every few
weeks. "Since I don't have a regular address, most of
the time I can't hear back from him, though every once
in a while, if I'm in a place for a couple of weeks, I do,
and that's always a reeeal up for me, you know? But
even when I don't hear from him, just knowing he's
there and that he cared, he fucking *cared* enough to
take me in—*and* let me go, that gets me by."

As for me, I told Lissa everything about myself except my age. I was almost sixteen when we met, and I'd been on the road about two years, but I thought she might drop me if she knew I was underage, or not treat me as an equal. Of course, now I know that Lissa would've accepted me whether I was six, sixteen, or sixty-five—that's just how she is. But then, even though I wanted to trust Lissa, and did 99 percent of the way, I told her I, too, was eighteen, and that I'd split when I was sixteen.

I had plenty of money—nearly $600 from my stint at Henley's, and Lissa had a little over $300, from cocktail waitressing in L.A. Lissa had a fit when she saw I was carrying my money in cash, especially when hitchhiking. "Girl, are you clean out yo' head? Haven't you ever heard of traveler's checks?" Of course I hadn't, but Lissa taught me: You get 'em at a bank, you can cash 'em anywhere, if they get ripped off the traveler's check company pays you back. And so we traipsed off to a bank, and I got traveler's checks. Lissa was always teaching me stuff like that.

"You know, Lissa, if we wanted to we could just take the bus from here to New Orleans." Some of Lissa's on-the-road stories had scared the hell out of me, like the time she told about when "some drunk crackers in Alabama" had played Russian roulette with a gun held to her head.

But Lissa said, "Nah, we should hitch, it'll be safe, with two of us, and besides, we need to save our money to put down on a place once we get to New Orleans. Anyway, I just have the feeling that we're going to get good rides."

She was right. Our first ride took us to Flagstaff, Arizona, a clean, piney city in the mountains. And our second ride was with a University of Arizona student who was going—get this—straight to New Orleans, for Mardi Gras! "Did I tell you we'd be lucky, babycakes, or did I tell you we'd be lucky?" Lissa gloated, her big eyes opened extra wide with pleasure, as we slung our stuff, my backpack and her duffle, into the car trunk.

Tim was the student's name. He said he'd "enjoy the company" on the road, but then hardly said a word to us after that. Maybe listening to me and Lissa jabber away was company enough for him.

Tim's car was a dirty-white sixty-seven Mustang. He planned to drive it straight through, but by the time we reached Tucumcari, New Mexico, he was weaving all over the road, and Lissa and I talked him into stopping at a motel for the night. I think he had visions of some wild orgy, because he quickly agreed, and then kept insisting—right at the front desk, in front of the motel clerk—that we all three share one room. He looked really disappointed when it sank in that Lissa and I were going to get our own room and that was that.

Anyway, the three of us had Mexican food at the motel restaurant, and Lissa and I went to our room. I showered, and then Lissa did—I remember hearing her singing from the bathroom,

> *"I pulled into the Cactus Tree Motel*
> *to shower off the dust*
> *and I slept on the strange pillow of my wanderlust."*

I smiled because that was a Joni Mitchell song, one of the ones I always found myself singing when I traveled, and it felt good to have a friend at last. "Good night, babycakes," said Lissa from the other double bed. "Good night," I said from mine, and my last thought, before I fell asleep between the clean motel sheets, was that I was glad the two of us had money (we were even chipping in to pay for gas), so Tim couldn't pressure us into going to bed with him because he was paying our way, as so many boys had done, both to Lissa and me, in the past.

The next day, when the three of us climbed into the car after breakfast, Tim had to turn the ignition key several times to get the car started. He looked worried, and Lissa and I exchanged glances—would we make it to New Orleans in this car after all? But it finally started, and when we got on the road, the Mustang seemed to run fine. But after we stopped for lunch, the same thing happened—trouble getting the car started, but okay once we got going.

We stopped for dinner in a greasy little diner in Arkansas—we were going to try to make it to Little Rock, and spend the night there. But when we got back in the car, it wouldn't start at all. Zip. Tim tried it over and over again, saying "Shit" each time, and in the neon light from the diner I could see Lissa biting her lip.

Finally we went back into the diner, and Tim used the phone to call Larry Evans, the nearest mechanic, who the cashier recommended. Larry came out—he was driving a Jeep, custom painted a turquoise blue—and looked at the Mustang's engine with a flashlight. "Probably your alternator," he said. "Maybe I can get to it tomorrow. Maybe." Then he offered the three of us a ride into the nearest town, where, he said, there were plenty of hotels. As we drove in, I tried to make polite conversation with Larry because I thought it was pretty damn nice of him to come out and look at our car when it was already after dark and he didn't even know us, but Lissa and Tim were both so bummed out about the delay that they weren't saying much. I asked Larry a little about the town we were coming to. He said it was small, "twelve hundred people or so," and a tourist town, and "the weirdest place you ever saw." He said that the town motto, since the 1880's, had been, "Where the misfit fits."

"What did you say the name of this town was, again?" I asked him, intrigued.

He said, "Excelsior Springs, Arkansas."

9

Lissa and I were sitting on the bench on Main Street in Excelsior, Tim was still in his hotel room apparently sleeping. I was in a great mood. Even though it was early March, it was a warm, sunny springlike day, and the sky was a bright blue without a single cloud. We had just had a great breakfast in a little cafe, and I had for once broken my poached egg habit to have whole wheat pancakes floating in butter and honey. They tasted just right to me, right for the day, right for Excelsior Springs. I felt full and happy and safe, like I could sit on that bench forever, watching people go by, and that would be enough to keep me happy for the rest of my life.

Lissa, on the other hand, was in a foul mood. She had just called the mechanic and learned that the car wouldn't be ready until late in the afternoon. She sat on the bench, swinging her legs and scuffing her feet back and forth on the sidewalk, her lips pressed together.

The bench where we were sitting that day was right

in the middle of town. Now you have to understand that Excelsior Springs is not your nice, neat, average straight town with the streets laid out like lines on graph paper. Main Street wound its way up a hill, making a sharp curve in the middle. The hills weren't flattened out for the roads and houses, and I think it somehow gave Excelsior this feeling of everything getting along. The buildings looked like they just grew where they were, nobody tried to force them into place, and the hills and rocks and trees seemed to say to the houses and the people, "All right, fine, sure. You're welcome to stay." And that's how I felt—welcome, and good, and safe. Excelsior was like someplace I had always imagined, but was never sure where it was or what I was looking for. Now I had found it and I *knew* this was where I wanted to live. I felt like I had come home. I told Lissa that.

"Home!" she snorted, flipping her hair back over her shoulders. "How would you know anything about homes, you *or* me? Huh, Chris?"

"You don't get a special feeling here?" I asked.

"Well, it *is* pretty hip for a little town out in the sticks, but still. I know *I'd* get bored here in a flash. And I bet there's not much money around; I bet you could make ten *times* as much in New Orleans."

"Well, maybe it would be worth it to earn less money if you could live in a place you really liked."

"Oh, Chris." Lissa looked at me, shaking her head. "You're hopeless. You have this silly romantic idea that . . . Shit. I mean, you've never had a home and neither have I, except temporarily with Michael, but at least I'm—I'm realistic. I don't ask for much, so I don't expect anything, so I don't have to be disappointed all the time. See, when I left home, if that's what you want to call it, I decided that home is where I plant these two feet *now,* today, and home'll probably be a different place tomorrow. And family is gonna be any good people I'm lucky enough to meet along the way, and if I don't meet any, fine, I can take care of myself, I always have, anyway. Don't you see, Chris? Home is a fairy tale, something somebody made up to sell Mother's Day cards with. Maybe I've been around on my own a little longer than you, Chris, or maybe . . ."

Her voice trailed off. I said, "Or maybe we're just different."

I sat on the bench in silence. The day was still sunny, but there was something cold, suddenly, between us. "Look," I said, more gently, "maybe you're right, Lissa, but maybe I just know this place is home the same way I knew we'd be friends. Right? Remember?"

Lissa squinted at me through one eye. "Oh, all right, all right. Forget it, it's not important."

"No, I mean, I never had a close friend before you, I didn't know that there was such a thing, I mean for me, but when I met you, I just knew. I *knew* we'd be friends. I know you hate the word 'vibes,' but—"

"Oh, puke," said Lissa, dabbing at her eyes with her fingers. She took a deep breath. "Oh, God. Lay it on thick, why don't you? Now see what you've made me do? All this sentimental crap." Then she suddenly gave me her big uneven, snaggle-tooth smile, and said, "Okay, you get good vibes from Excelsior. You expect me to cheer, Chris? It means I'll have to go on to New Orleans without you, turkey." She sniffed. "You any good at writing letters?"

"You could stay," I suggested. "You could stay here in Excelsior with me. We could get a place together here instead of New Orleans."

"Nope," said Lissa, now in good form. "Are you kidding? *I'm* going to New Orleans, and I don't hold the fact that you are a *fool* if you don't come with me against you. You're the one who's so vibed out by Excelsior, *you* stay here with all the hippies. Where are they all from, anyway? I thought they died in the sixties."

A woman carrying a braided rag rug had come out of a store called 100 Calico Cats. The store—one of many craft stores in Excelsior—had patchwork quilts and patchwork pillows piled in the window, and the woman was wearing jeans and a shirt with a patchwork yoke. She looked maybe 35 or 40, and she had long black braids. She started shaking the rug out into the street. With every shake, her braids bounced. She smiled at us, nodded, and went back in the shop with her rug.

"You don't think she looks nice?" I asked Lissa.

Lissa sniffed. "She's not bad if you like middle-aged hippies. Which I don't."

"You're such a snot."

"Look." Lissa nudged me. "Here comes a *non-*middle-aged hippie. And a cute leetle *baby* hippie."

Two people were walking toward us. There was a guy in his twenties with a long reddish ponytail and a scraggly beard; he was wearing a small backpack.

And then there was this kid.

The kid looked like he was maybe ten. He also had long hair, blond, loose, and stringy and looking like it hadn't been washed in a while. He had these long bangs that kept falling in his face, and he would toss his head back every few steps to get the hair out of his eyes, which were green. He was wearing jeans, and an undershirt. You could see his scrawny little ribs. He was barefoot and he was wearing a large earring made of feathers in his left ear. He had this trying-to-be-tough posture—hunched over a little, eyes slightly squinted, no smile. A don't-mess-with-me look.

But he had this perfect angel kid's face. Big green

eyes with long lashes, a cute little turned-up nose—he looked like he could be advertising back-to-school clothes for JC Penney.

The two of them stopped. The older guy slipped off his backpack and sat down on the bench next to Lissa; the kid remained standing, one hand on his hip, thumb of the other hooked through his belt loop.

"Mornin', ladies," said the older guy. He had a southern drawl. "How you two doin' this fiiiine mornin'?"

Lissa, completely unpredictable where men were concerned, snapped, "None of your business, you brainless buzzard!"

I thought Lissa's outburst uncalled for. The guy looked totally shocked. But the kid giggled. The kid looked at me to see if I thought it was funny. Our eyes met and we clicked, and he smiled. It was a bright, quick flash of a smile and it completely lit up his face. I smiled back.

"Lissa!" I said to her. "He was just trying to be nice; you don't have to bite his head off." And then, to Ponytail, I added, "You have to excuse my friend, she has terminal cancer—of the tongue."

"I reckon you two aren't from around here," said Ponytail, and added to Lissa, "Don't take offense, darlin': I was just bein' friendly."

"My name's not darlin'," she said, "It's Lissa."

"I'm Rick," he said.

"I'm Dare," said the kid.

"Dare?" I said. The kid nodded. "Like, I dare you?" The kid nodded again.

"It's short for Darrell," said Rick, "but he don't like to tell people that." Dare glared at him, then said to me, "What's *your* name?"

"I'm Chrysta," I said. The name Chrysta just came to me that second, but it felt right, it felt more like me than Chris or Chrissie or Christine ever had. Chrysta. I liked it. I *really* liked it. Lissa stared at me. She knew making up names off the top of my head was not my usual style. But I didn't miss a beat. I continued, "Lissa and I just got in from L.A. She's on her way to New Orleans, but I might stay here."

"Well, Excelsior's 'bout as fine as they come," said Rick. "Good people. Lotta music."

"Lotta home-grown," said Dare, smirking. "Wish I had some right now. Hey, man, you got a cigarette?"

"Lotta work durin' the tourist season, that's from April through October," Rick said, getting out a cigarette from a box in his pack and handing it to Dare. Dare examined the cigarette and said, "Aw, not this low-tar shit."

"Take it or leave it," said Rick offhandedly, continuing to us, "In season, all the hotels are lookin' for people. Especially in October, 'cause a all the tourists comin' to see the foliage."

"Foliage?" asked Lissa.

"Yeah," I told her. "Like leaves, right? They grow on trees? They turn colors in the fall? Ever heard of them? Well, a lot of leaves together are called 'foliage.' Some people find it pretty."

"Pretty," she agreed. "But borrrring." She yawned a pretend yawn, as Dare, who had been digging around in his pockets, finally found a weather-beaten package of matches. I idly watched him trying to light his cigarette.

"*Borin'?*" Rick was looking at Lissa in astonishment. "Honey, did I hear you say *borin'*? Darlin', watchin' the leaves change, watchin' Nature do her eternal dance— not only is that the only trip there is, it's the only one we're *all* takin', I mean *all* of us, whether we know it or not. Now, the Indians, see, they knew how to go with the *flow* of Nature, they saw the earth as their mother and they couldn't rip off their mother."

"Maybe that's why leaves bore me," said Lissa acidly. "I could rip off my mother in a minute if she had anything worth taking." I watched Dare trying to act nonchalant as he tried to strike one match after another. None of them caught.

"Well," Rick said, "I didn't mean mother like *that*, I meant mother on a *higher* level: Mother Nature, who is one heavy lady. You see, uh, what'd you say your name was, darlin'?"

"Lissa."

"You see, Lissa, that lady, Mother Nature, she can teach you a lot. Now, in this town, we're especially tuned to *learn* what she's teachin' us, because Excelsior's, like, built between two mountains, and the energy gets trapped between 'em and it kinda *vibrates* back and forth. That's why it's such a *high* place."

"I see," said Lissa grimly. "You sound like you'd get along great with my friend here, uh, *Chrysta*." She shot me a disgusted look.

"Really?" said Rick, turning to me with interest. "You into livin' on the earth?"

"Uh, sort of," I said neutrally.

"When she can't get to Mars," Lissa said.

Dare, meanwhile, had gone through every match in his book and hadn't gotten one lit. Casually, as if completely unaware that we'd all seen him go through his matchbook, he said, "Rick, you got a light?" Rick got a lighter out of his pack and lit Dare's cigarette.

"Cigarettes aren't natural," said Lissa combatively. "Or lighters."

"Neither are clothes, man, but society forces you to wear 'em."

"Rick, do you work?" I asked, heading Lissa off at the pass.

"Me? I'm a gardener up at the General's Palace Hotel, up on North Mountain. You know, it's far out: Even though it's, like, a formal garden, and they make us pull up all the weeds, still just to be workin' with my hands in the earth—"

"Do you know if they have any other job openings up there?"

"Yeah, they always need, uh, like cooks, dishwashers, maids. They're hirin' now, even though things don't get real busy for another month. My lady, Betsey, she's a maid up there. I'm sure she'd be glad to tell you 'bout it. Get Betsey to show you her unicorn, it's good luck."

Lissa and I looked at each other. "Her *what*?" said Lissa, speaking for both of us.

"Her unicorn, darlin'. She's got this cute li'l unicorn tattooed on her ass. It's good luck to see it. Everyone who's seen it says so."

"*I've* seen it," said Dare, inhaling on his cigarette as if it were a joint, then dramatically exhaling smoke in three smoke rings. "But then," he added, flipping his hair out of his face, "I'm lucky anyway."

Post Card

PLACE
STAMP
HERE

Chrysta Perretti
Yeller House
21 Bingleton
Excelsior Springs,
Arkansas

TO: **LISSA DANFORTH**
c/o Jake Lyles
1212 Royale Blvd.
New Orleans, Louisiana

me a lot of shit about it.

Dear Lissa,
Hey, kiddo, I miss you! Listen, I have
an address now (___) so you
have no excuse not to write. How
are you? Was there any more trouble
with the car (or Tim) getting down
there? Are things working out
like you expected? Did you get
a job or are you going to
wait till after Mardi Gras?

I have a job interview with
the kitchen manager at the
General's Palace Hotel tomorrow.
He sounded nice — but his
name is a winner: Howie Snoodgrass!

I wish you would think about
coming back here if New Orleans
doesn't work out okay. You
would like Yeller House, where
I'm staying — I'll write you

more about it later but
there's this girl there,
Joanie, who's real nice.
Say hi to Jake for me.
I miss you. See you soon,
I hope. **LOVE,** Chrysta —
yes, it is Chrysta, not Chris, so don't give

10

Coming out of the Excelsior Springs post office that morning, after mailing that first postcard to Lissa, I felt so fine. I stopped for a minute right there on the P.O. steps and looked up. Everyone had been telling me it would get terribly hot in the summer, but now, in March, it was glorious. The sky was that same brilliant blue it had been since I'd arrived in Excelsior, with just a few little cotton-ball clouds, and a light breeze was blowing, making the daffodils on the post-office lawn nod and sway wildly. I had turned sixteen back in February, in L.A.; I had a place to live and a job interview and I had decided to go back to using my real Social Security number instead of my fake ones. I drew a deep breath of pleasure, and then exhaled.

I remember that sigh very clearly, because when I let that breath out, that was the exact moment, standing there on the Excelsior Springs post office steps, that the first pain hit me.

And I do mean hit—it was exactly like being punched in the stomach, hard, except that this punch came from inside, pushing violently out, sharp and hard on the lower right-hand side of my abdomen. I gasped and dropped to the curb and sat, just doubled over with the pain, not thinking—when something hurts that much you don't think. I just sat on the curb bent over my knees.

Then, as suddenly as it had started, the pain stopped.

Puzzled, but relieved, I got up. I decided it had just been a gas pain, or something like that: nothing serious. Maybe just one of those weird things bodies do, like jerk as you're falling asleep or like when you get those sharp sharp headaches if you eat a lot of ice cream too fast. If it had been something serious, it would have persisted.

The General's Palace Hotel was on the top of North Mountain, up a long, wide, tree-lined driveway, and it really did look like a stone palace. It even had a tower on each end and balconies on the upper floors and a fountain surrounded by flowers out front. On either side I could see the formal gardens that Rick had said he worked in: rich green lawns dotted with bushes and trees, walks made out of stone with beds of daffodils and jonquils and crocuses bordering them. The air was soft and sweet with the smell of jonquils.

I climbed the hotel's big stone steps and crossed the wide porch with its fleet of lawn chairs. I pushed open the huge double doors made of some kind of heavy, dark wood with lots of little panes of glass set in them, and walked into the lobby. I just stood there for a second, taking it all in.

The carpet under my feet was soft and thick, a deep wine-red carpet patterned with large pink roses. The wallpaper was a creamy white with stripes of the same wine color that was in the carpet, and the tufted velvet sofas and armchairs (there were several of them in groups, scattered throughout the lobby) were also in wine red or rose pink. Even the air in the hotel seemed expensive, with a faint lemony-flowery smell like a cross between furniture polish and perfume.

A huge TV set, turned on but with the sound off, sat in one corner: It seemed out of place, as did The General's Whiskers Gifte Shoppe in the corner of the lobby. In the Gift Shoppe's window were things like baby-sized T-shirts that read, "My folks went to Excelsior Springs and all they brought me was this lousy T-shirt," and mugs with mottos like "If Mama says no, ask Grandma."

I walked over to the front desk. It was made of the same kind of dark old wood as the door, carved with little knobs and set-in panels of pink marble. Behind the desk I could see a switchboard, two smaller desks, and a large old-fashioned pendulum clock on the wall. Above the whole thing was a sign hanging from the ceiling by chains.

Register

it said, in this fancy old-timey script, in gold. But the best part of the front desk was the guy sitting behind it, who looked like a twenty-two-year-old Robert Redford who hadn't slept for about two weeks in a row.

"Excuse me," I said. "Can you tell me where the restaurant is, please?"

He didn't even look up from his book. "To your left down the hall straight ahead. It's closed until they start serving dinner at five-thirty, but the snack bar downstairs is open now."

His voice was reedy and condescending. Clearly he thought I was a tourist.

"I'm *not* here to eat," I said. "I'm here about a job. I was told to come by around two o'clock."

That got him. He immediately looked up and looked

me over, with curiosity. He finished his inspection and said, "Oh. That means you want Howie Snoodgrass. *Lucky* you. I must warn you that they're all *mad* back there in the kitchen."

"Mad?"

"Crazy. Bananas. Out to lunch—all of them. Don't get me wrong, some of my best friends work back there, but—"

Good vibes from him. I said, deadpan, "Well, I'll just come up here if it gets to be too much." He laughed as he waved me in the right direction. Then he picked up the book he was reading, and for the first time I saw the title. *Gay Deceivers: Homosexuals in the Straight World*. So much for cute front-desk boys, but in a way it was a relief.

I went through a pair of swinging doors marked "EMPLOYEES ONLY" and found the kitchen.

"Hello, hello?" I called. My hellos echoed in the huge cavern of pots and pans, gray but not dark, with sunlight pouring in through windows on three sides, making the room clean and light and airy despite its institutional color. "Hello, hello, anybody here?"

The place seemed empty. I wandered around. The concrete floor, painted a shiny lighter gray, was hard under my feet after the lush carpeting of the lobby. This kitchen was at least four times the size of any I'd seen: three huge stainless-steel stoves, each with eight burners. And three ovens. And four sinks, big enough so I could've sat in one of them and had the water come up to my shoulders. There were two fryers, wooden spoons the size of oars, great *big* wire whisks, and a cutting board doubling as a tabletop, as big as a double bed.

"Hello, hello?" I called again.

No sound, except for the whoosh of a huge exhaust fan. A telephone began ringing somewhere. At first I wasn't going to answer, but then I tracked it by its rings to a small, messy desk set in a corner. I couldn't find it among all the loose papers, then I saw a loop of curled black extension cord and pulled aside a cookbook that had fallen over the phone.

"Hello?"

"Well, it sure took you long enough," piped a familiar, reedy voice.

"Is this the guy at the front desk?" I asked.

"You're supposed to answer 'Kitchen,'" he said; "this is a commercial establishment, much as we'd all like to forget it."

"Well, what do you want? I mean, nobody's here."

"Ah, I was afraid of that. I've come to your rescue. I think someone *is* there. I forgot to tell you he was in the walk-in."

"What?"

"In the freezer."

"WHAT?"

"In the walk-in freezer, on the far side of the kitchen. I'll talk verrry slowly—try to understand. Go get him, tell him who you are and what you want and that I'll try and get ahold of Snotnose. Got the message?"

"Yes."

"What's your name?"

"Chrysta."

"I'm Steve—and remember, you owe me."

I found the walk-in easily. The door was propped open with a crate of lettuce, and clouds of frigid air were coming out. I opened the door a little wider, and said loudly to a hooded figure moving around in there, "Excuse me. Excuse me! Howie? Howie?" The figure whirled around, pulled off its earmuffs, and said, "What?" Then it came out of the walk-in. It was male. Tall, wearing one of those khaki parkas with the fur-lined hoods, his face was bright red with cold, and his mustache had icicles dangling from either end. His hands were padded with blue-and-orange vinyl mittens, but the thing that I really noticed, immediately after getting over the shock of seeing this ice man in the middle of spring, were his eyes. Dark, dark, dark brown eyes, with long, thick eyelashes: This guy looked right at me and he looked *mad*.

"I am *not* Howie Snoodgrass!" he said, grimly, his jawline tight.

"Well, how was I supposed to know?" I said.

"I don't know how you were supposed to know and I don't care. I just know I'm sick and tired of not being able to get anything done around here!" He banged one vinyl-mittened paw down on the cutting-board table, hard.

"Well, I'm sorry," I said hastily, all the while thinking, *God, what a yo-yo this guy is.* "I thought you were Howie Snoodgrass, and—"

"I've *already* told you I'm *not*," he growled.

"And *I've* already told *you* I didn't know that!" I said, getting mad. "Look, I don't know who you are or what your problem is, buddy, but you can just get off my case and stay off it right now, okay? I didn't know I was doing anything wrong—I made a mistake. I'm sorry, but it doesn't seem like a big deal to me."

The fellow in the parka looked up at the ceiling and then back at me. He sighed. "You're right," he said. "It's not your fault."

I didn't say anything. I knew it wasn't my fault. I also couldn't believe Steve hadn't warned me that the guy in the walk-in had a temper like the abominable snowman.

He peeled off his parka and mittens and rubbed his cold face with his free hand, then looked at me

thoughtfully. "Look," he said more gently, "I *am* sorry.
But I haven't got all day. So why don't you tell me what
you want, and if there's something I can do for you, I'll
do it and then I'll get back to work."

"My name is Chrysta Perretti," I said evenly, and
very coolly. "I want a job here cooking. I had an
appointment with Howie Snoodgrass today at two o'clock."

I could see now he was only maybe eighteen or
nineteen. He glared up at the ceiling, sighed, and said,
"Come on." He sighed another long sigh, and I followed
him through the kitchen back over toward the desk. No
longer glaring, and in a pair of jeans and a red University of Arkansas T-shirt, minus all those layers of clothes,
he looked ordinary: a skinny kid; striking eyes, but
nothing to write home about.

He sat down at one of the chairs at the desk and
motioned me to take the other chair beside it. I did.

"Well, Chrysta, I don't know what to tell you," he
said. "Howie's not here. Obviously. Maybe he just got
held up somewhere—but I can give you an employment application, at least." He pulled open a drawer
and dug through it until he found one, then gave it to
me on a clipboard with a pen. "Go ahead and fill it
out," he said, adding, "I really am sorry, Chrysta. I've
just got too many things to do—I'm not usually like
this." But he didn't smile as he said it, just kept looking
serious and tired.

He ran one hand through his hair. "Let me call Steve
and see if he can get Howie down here."

"He said he was going to call, uh, Snotnose," I said.
"If that's Howie."

He grimaced. "Steve has a pet name for everyone.
I'll check."

I glanced over the employment form meanwhile.
Name, age, date of birth, desired position, Social Secu-

rity number, experience—pretty standard stuff. The only thing I was planning to lie about was my age.

"Yeah. Yeah. She found me in the freezer," he said into the phone. "Very funny. Did you—? Don't tell me all the places you tried, Steve, just give me the bottom line. Oh, okay, thanks. Good. Thanks. 'Bye."

He hung up. "Well, according to Steve, Howie should be in shortly. So sit tight and wait while I get back to work." He paused. "Do you, uh, want a cup of coffee?"

I had the feeling he was feeling guilty about having been so grouchy to me, so I let him squirm. "No, thanks. Nothing."

But the guy didn't squirm.

"Well, if you change your mind and want something, you can get it yourself. Milk machine's over there." He pointed briskly. "There's coffee, there's iced tea, the OJ is in that refrigerator. Okay?"

"Okay."

He smiled wearily and extended his hand. "By the way, I'm Luke Beauford."

"Glad to meet you," I said, but I didn't smile back and I didn't take his hand.

Howie Snoodgrass, the kitchen manager, was *all* smiles when he walked in 45 minutes later.

"Are yuh the pretty li'l lady lookin' for a job?" Howie's teeth were very white and straight.

"That's me," I said. "I mean, I'm looking for a job."

"Ah got held up this mornin'. Ah'm usually in by nine."

His sunburn suggested he'd been held up on water skis. He was a pleasant-enough-looking man about thirty-five, fairly tall, with a receding hairline that his blow-dried brown hair could not hide. He was a little fleshy, with a jowly chin and a small beer belly which pressed

against the tucked-in edge of his blue cowboy shirt and
overlapped the belt buckle holding up his beige pants.
Several of the snaps on his cowboy shirt were open,
revealing a deep vee of dark curly chest hair decorated
with several gold chains and pendants. One of the pendants said *#1*, in solid, blocky characters; another was
one of those squiggly charms like a long, crooked tooth.
Another was a cross. He also wore several rings, including one on his pinky.

"Now, what'd yuh say yo' naaame was, honey?"

"Chrysta Perretti, sir."

"What a *pretty* naaame."

"I need a job, Mr. Snoodgrass," I said.

"Ah *admire* frankness, Chrysta," said Howie solemnly,
nodding his head. "An' yuh have jus' *showed* me frankness.
"An' init'ive.

"Call me Howie," he continued shaking my hand
with moist fleshy fingers. "Now, Ah must tell you,
Chrysta, Ah *luvvv* to work with pretty ladies, and you
are a *very* pretty li'l lady. Pretty—an' *full* a init'ive.
Now Ah'm a very happ'ly married man, been married
fo' seven years, as a matter of fact, but fo' that very
reason, Ah take a lot of pleasure from jus' bein' aroun'
other ladies, in a workin' contex'. My wife, Dolly Mae,
she's a good ol' girl, she undustands puhfectly."

I nodded, succeeding in pulling my hand away but
getting worried by the tone the interview was taking.

"But of course," Howie continued sternly, "of course,
bein' pretty is not enough, not in *mah* kitchen. Ah
expec' all mah employees to be willin' to work and work
hard, fo' *me*. Y'undustand?"

I nodded, relieved that Howie was on this track now.
I must have misinterpreted him earlier—it was probably just his style to flatter and then get to the point. Of

course he assumed being called a "pretty li'l lady" was flattering.

"Oh, I can work, I'm a good worker," I told him quickly. I told him my background, of course upping my age. "It's all here," I finished, and I handed him the filled-out employment form.

Howie's fleshy face clouded. "Where'd yuh get that form, young lady?" he demanded sternly.

"Well, uh, when I got here and there was nobody here, I hollered and finally found Luke and he, uh, gave it to me."

Howie's face got darker. He leaned across the desk and hissed, "Don't y'evah, *evah* take directions from *anyone* else in this kitchen 'cept *me*! Do y'undustand? This is *mah* kitchen, and the only person in this hotel whose a'tho'ty supasedes *mine* is"—he raised his voice—"Mistah Hugh Dewling! The ownah of the General's Palace!"

The way he said "Mistah Hugh Dewling," I expected him to stand up, salute, and start singing "Dixie." Instead, he paused, then said mildly, "Would yuh like to start on Monday, Chrysta?"

"Yes, but, uh—" I should've known that he was completely wacko, but I didn't see it because I didn't want to.

"Well, yuh come in on Monday, then, 'bout ten thutty or 'leven, an' we'll get yuh started."

"Yes, but what exactly will I be doing—?"

"Now don't yuh worry 'bout a thing, Chrysta, honey. We're goin' to make a *line* cook outta yuh. It's kind of a *creative* position, Chrysta: I b'lieve, with yo' init'ive, yuh gonna do yo'sef and olla us here *proud*! Three fifty an hour. Ah've just been *prayin'* someone'd come along that could dress up that line a little. We all clear with each other?"

I nodded, though I wasn't clear at all.

11

Yeller House, where I was staying, was an old three-
story Victorian, which had once been painted yellow
but was now faded and falling apart. There were certain
porch boards you couldn't step on or you'd go right
through, and the roof leaked. The wallpaper and ceiling
paint inside were as peeling and chipped and faded as
the yellow exterior. But you couldn't help loving the
place. It had a great feeling to it, friendly and welcoming,
and there were seven bedrooms, and a downstairs with
a kitchen, dining room, and living room, and lots of
windows everywhere—some edged with little squares
of stained glass. And the only reason Joanie Matthews
had been able to buy it so cheaply was because it was in
such bad shape.

Joanie lived there and rented out bedrooms, and it
was hard to remember she was the landlady. She was a
weaver and one of the bedrooms was her studio, filled
with looms and wool. Tall, big-boned, not too pretty,
Joanie had long thinnish brown hair and wore wire-
rimmed glasses that tilted to one side. Joanie was one of
the nicest people I've ever met. She was only about
twenty-six but you felt like she was your grandmother
because she was calling you "dear" and acting motherly
and offering freshly baked cookies. I immediately liked

her (though I knew we'd never be friends in that soul-to-soul way that Lissa and I were).

Since it was only a couple of blocks from the General's Palace Hotel, several GP employees were Yeller House residents. Tess, the evening salad girl. Rick, the gardener. Susan, the daytime salad girl, and her boyfriend, Hoot. Hoot had once been a roadie for a popular Texas rock group called Willow Tree, but he was now a carpenter. He and Susan were saving up to buy some land. Susan, who knew all about vitamins and herbs and natural medicines and home remedies, was sweet and delicate and looked about seventeen; Hoot was as big and burly as a bear, with dark curly hair and a full dark beard. He was very practical and down to earth. But I gathered he hadn't always been so earthy when I asked him how he got his name—and he told me this long story about taking acid in Austin, Texas, and winding up in a shopping mall in Houston thinking he was an owl and hooting away. *"That,"* he told me, "finished my doping days."

The whole atmosphere at Yeller House was like a dormitory in some college for misfits. And every night everyone who was around—and usually a few guests— ate dinner together (we all chipped in for food). I loved it.

The first morning on the job almost blew my mind. Howie wasn't there, but had left word that someone named Nettie would show me the ropes. She turned out to be a small, tidy, gray-haired lady. She was seated on a stool in the kitchen, her face shiny with sweat, peeling potatoes so quickly that the hand holding the peeler was a blur. Peelings flew onto the plastic garbage bag spread out on the floor in front of her, as she moved from the mountain of brown unpeeled potatoes to the peeled ones white and naked, one after the other, finishing them and tossing them into a large pot: *thunk, thunk, thunk*. She greeted me cheerfully: "Well, hello there, honey! You must be the new girl Luke told me about! Now you just hold on a minute and—" But she was interrupted by a loud banging coming from the rear of the kitchen, where a man in overalls was hammering at a large exhaust fan perched on a window. "Lord, Lester, can't you go fix something else till after the lunch rush?" yelled Nettie over the racket. "Surely there's other things broke down in this hotel?"

Lester put down his hammer. "Well, Nettie, ma'am, Howie tol' me to git in here and fix it this morning. Right in front of Mr. Dewling he said it—this morning."

"Lester, honey, that's the third time now you've told me what Howie Snoodgrass said, but you're just in the *way* here right now. Can't you see?" Another potato hit the pot.

"Yes, but Nettie, ma'am—" said Lester.

"Howie can't remember what he said one minute to the next, Lester! 'Sides, if he said in the *morning*, he probably meant nine-thirty or ten, 'stead of right in the middle of lunch. I swear you don't have the sense God gave a goose!"

"I couldn't come no earlier, Nettie, ma'am. There was frogs in the pool, dead, 'cause of the chlorine. Then, a course, I had to put in chlorine all over again. And then the air conditioning went out in Mr. Dewling's penthouse, and—"

"Oh, Lester, never mind. I ain't got time to fool with you! Just do what you gotta do and *git!*"

Thunk. Another potato hit the pot. Nettie paused to take off her harlequin-framed glasses and wipe her forehead with the back of one hand. Standing there, waiting to talk to her, I noticed something familiar about her face. But before I could figure it out, she had her glasses back on, another potato in her hand. Still peeling, she glanced toward the large wall clock: 11:35. She gasped, muttered, "Lord, Lord," then yelled, "*Cleota?*"

A strange head popped up from behind the stove; dark hair in fat rolls, wrapped up in a hairnet which went well over the yellowed forehead. The whole face was yellowy, and there was no real neck or chin, just a drape of flesh from where the face ended to the base of the throat.

"*Whut?*" said the thing in a squawky voice.

"How we doin' on the lunch line, Cleota?"

"Same's always," said Cleota sourly. "What *I* do's done."

Nettie put down the peeler and looked out into space for a second. She began counting on her fingers. "Okay, on our vegetables, we got Cleota's beans, that's one half pan, mashed potatoes, that's two, gravy is three, cornbread—Cleota, you done your cornbread yet?"

"'S in the oven," said Cleota with a loud sniff. "*I* do what I'm *s'posed* to do, unlike *some* I could name."

Nettie was back to counting. "Okay, cornbread's one full pan—so we need one more half pan on the vegetables. My Lord! We got any main dishes at all yet, Cleota?"

"Howie told *me* we were s'posed to do leftovers Monday, *an'* he said that starting today I didn't have to do *no* main dishes. Jest beans and a pan of cornbread plus my pies, which I was *fixin'* to do but I *cain't* now 'cause Lester's got hisself all in my way."

"Lord, Lord," said Nettie softly, "I'll be glad when they get our potato peeler fixed." And then, to me, "Help me get this thang, honey." I jumped, and we each took a handle of the now-filled potato pot and got it over to the sink, where Nettie turned on the tap into the pot of potatoes.

"Cleota," she said sternly and Cleota came out from behind the stove, giving me my first view of her whole body. It was just as weird as her face. She looked like a belligerent chicken, a fat, round body on short legs with rolled-down knee-length stockings. She stood with her head jutted out in front of her and her hands planted firmly on her hips, elbows sticking out like stubby little wings.

"Cleota," said Nettie, facing her directly, "don't you think you could show a little Christian kindness and give us a hand? Do you really think I'm gonna be able to train this young un here to do *all* the main dishes, out of leftovers, and be ready for the line in *twenty-one* minutes?"

"I don't know nothin' *at*all about that," said Cleota. "I jus' know that Howie told me that all *I* had to do was breakfast, cornbread, beans, and pies, which I *cain't* even do now 'cause a—" She jerked her head in the direction of Lester and the exhaust fan, which he had taken from the window. On the cutting-board table, which, I guessed, was where Cleota wanted to roll out her piecrusts, Lester had laid out an assortment of nuts, bolts, screws, screwdrivers, and hammers. Unaware of the trouble he was causing, he continued banging away, humming loudly.

"I don't give a dead crow nor a good goddamn about your pies right now, Cleota Hatfield! I just know that we got a line to get out and—"

"I won't hear no cuss words!" shrieked Cleota, squawking loudly and clapping her hands over her ears. "*Mah* Bible says, Thou shalt not take the name of the Lord—"

"Cleota, if you don't get to helpin' me on the line

right now, you are going to hear some cuss words that you ain't *never* heard before, and you and I *both* know you've heard plenty! Now stop standing around doin' nothin' and get some chicken ta fryin' and throw some pork chops on the grill—and do some kinda frozen vegetable. An' that'll take care of our line."

But still Cleota stood. Triumphantly, she said, "Well, if you 'spect me to pry apart them frozen pork chops, I'm not a-gonna do it, 'cause the last time I did I slipped with the knife and just about—"

"Cleota, honey," said Nettie, more softly, "Luke already done took out pork chops and chicken last night 'cause he thought what with a new girl and him havin' to go to Fayetteville for steaks today, this might happen—"

"But Howie says it's t'be only *leftovers* on Monday! Luke shouldna done that!"

"Cleota, just git to fryin' chicken, and be glad *some*body in this kitchen has some sense." Nettie sighed a deep sigh as Cleota, grumbling under her breath, lumbered off toward the walk-in. At last, Nettie turned to me. "Well, honey," she said, "welcome to the kitchen."

By midafternoon I had learned that "the line" meant the buffet line, which was set up on a steam table in the dining room. Customers at the restaurant could either eat off the line or order from a menu. One cook took care of keeping the line filled, and one did the stuff from the menu as it was ordered. The menu stuff was called à la cartes, which Nettie and Cleota pronounced as one word: "ollacarts." There were also two salad girls and several dishwashers.

Luke, I learned, was dishwasher and stock boy—that meant he kept the storeroom and freezers tidy, as well as keeping track of what foods the kitchen was getting low on. He gave Howie a list to order from twice a week ("Though a lot of good that does," said Nettie. "Howie couldn't find his ass if he had both hands tied to it!"). Sometimes, though, Howie just had Luke order the food, and that worked out better, according to Nettie.

She told me Luke had worked in the kitchen every summer since he was fourteen years old. There was a pride in her voice that I couldn't understand as she continued, "Luke knows more about this place than anybody 'cept me, an' I've worked here since I was seventeen. I'm sixty now, so that's forty-three years here 'cept for three years when I worked managin' the Rainbow Barbecue Pit—but Luke's got a lot more sense than I do. He's much more organized and all. When Dewling bought the place, they asked me to take on bein' manager, but I wouldn't do it. Chrysta, I just about worked myself sick managing the Rainbow: Actually, I had a heart attack, a mild one, but still I wasn't but forty-six!! Course that was the year my husband, Bill, was so sick, so I was under a lotta pressure. But when I left *that* job I said, well, I'm *never* gonna work like that! I'm gonna go back up t' the GP and I'll work for 'em hard, but when I walk out them kitchen doors each night I am *leavin* that job, it ain't a-goin' home with me. Honey, let me tell you—you can't put a price on peace of mind, and the kind of person I am, I couldn't run a kitchen and have no peace of mind. Now, Luke, I don't doubt that *he* could do it. 'Cause he don't lose his head too easy. Fact is, Luke's doin' it now in all 'cept name and paycheck."

"*I* don't think Luke has much peace of mind," I told Nettie. "When I came in here Saturday—he was *obnoxious*."

"Luke?" said Nettie, surprised. "Chrysta, honey, you must be mixin' up Luke an' somebody else. Luke wouldn't hurt a fly."

"No, it was Luke," I said. "He yelled at me for not knowing he wasn't the kitchen manager—and how was I supposed to know?"

Nettie laughed. "Well, Chrysta, honey, there are precious few that's ever seen Luke lose his temper. He's got a mighty long fuse, but it's true, when he comes to the end of it, he does blow. I oughta know—I know Luke pretty good. Now Saturday was s'posed to be Luke's afternoon off, and I 'spect what happened was old Howie dumped on Luke quite a bit, and Luke was plannin' on going to the lake. So after that I b'lieve Luke just planned on gettin' in here during the quiet part of the day and, you know, kinda workin' away his frustrations. And then you come along—" Nettie chuckled and took off her glasses and wiped her forehead again, as she had been doing periodically all day. And suddenly I knew who her face reminded me of. Who her *eyes* reminded me of.

"Nettie!" I said, horrified that I had mouthed off about Luke. "Are you related to Luke in some way? I mean, your eyes . . . your eyes are a lot alike, and . . ."

"As a matter of fact, I'm his aunt," said Nettie. She looked amused.

"Oh, I'm so sorry, I didn't mean to say anything—"

Nettie laughed again. She had a full, friendly, hooting laugh, wholehearted and completely without malice. "Honey, I *know* you meant every word! Like I say, not many has seen Luke mad, but when he is, he could try the patience of God almighty! I oughta know—I raised Luke from the time he was eight years old. His parents got killed in a car wreck. Luke's daddy was my little brother."

"Oh," I said. "Oh, God, I'm *so* sorry, I didn't know." I felt *really* bad now.

"Shucks, honey, how *could* you know?" said Nettie,

and she patted my shoulder reassuringly. "Anyway, there's nothin' to be sorry about. It happened a long time ago and Luke and I both learned to live with it. And as for what you said 'bout Luke, well, that's already forgotten, and I'm sure he deserved it anyway! Just don't hold it against him, 'cause he's usually a *real* good boy, and 'sides, you two'll have to work together now. Now, you come on out to the steam table in the dining room with me, honey, I want you to memorize how many pans it takes to fill the thang up, and how many's got to be vegetables and how many main dishes."

The *chink chink chink* of silverware being placed echoed in the large room as Nettie and I went out to survey the dining room, which was the size of a football field and as classy-looking as the hotel lobby, except for the steam table we were checking out—*it* looked like a large, canopied steel coffin, on legs, as out of place in the elegant room as The General's Whiskers Gifte Shoppe had been in the lobby.

I decided to ask Nettie the question that had been puzzling me all morning. "Nettie," I said, "if Howie Snoodgrass is as bad as everyone seems to think, why don't they fire him?"

"Fire him?" Nettie, who was shorter than me, looked up at me in astonishment. "Honey, you mean to tell me nobody's told you? Hugh Dewling—the owner of the hotel—is Howie Snoodgrass's *uncle*."

12

My life began to have a comforting sameness.

I woke up around seven each day, with the sun pouring into my upstairs bedroom window through the treetops. I slept on the narrow bed in my sleeping bag. Joanie had taught me a few yoga exercises and I'd do them slowly, stretching gradually in my sunny room, waking up quietly. After I went downstairs and had my poached-egg-toast-grapefruit routine, I might walk downtown to hang around, or pack my dirty laundry into my backpack and go off to the Downtown Laundromat. Or, if Joanie was going somewhere interesting in Frog, her green pickup truck, a lot of times I went along with her.

Joanie was quiet, low-key, and easy to be with.

She dyed the wool for her weavings herself, so sometimes we'd go out to the woods or pick leaves or berries or dig up roots for dyes. Or we might go off to the city dump to find "found objects," for her weavings: an old rusty wagon wheel, the fancy twisted broken-off leg of a piece of furniture, a broken doll. But a lot of times we'd just go out to Bear Claw Lake.

Although there are lots of lakes in the Excelsior area, many local people went to Bear Claw because it was too small for tourists to do their water ski/motor boat number. Bear Claw also had these nice rock ledges that you could dive from or sunbathe on, and it was also deserted enough so that you could skinny dip. Hippies were the only people who ever went out to the ledges. Sometimes Joanie and I would get out to Bear Claw and there would already be fifteen or twenty people all out on the rocks and in the water, some wearing bathing suits but most naked.

Bear Claw was also completely uncommercialized. You had to know how to get to it: which unmarked dirt road off Highway 23 was the turn-off, how far down the bumpy, winding, overhung dirt road to drive, where to park, and where to find the path through the woods, which you had to travel by foot for about half a mile. Joanie always showed me something along the path: ferns, wild asparagus, shiny-leaved shrubs growing in deep shade that, she said, were huckleberry bushes. Once we saw a huge woodpecker with a bright red crown, once we saw three deer, and once we saw a copperhead—a large poisonous snake common in the Ozarks, with brown diamond-shaped markings on its back—which slid across our path in and out of sight so quickly I gasped.

At times, just for a moment or two, I could feel myself relax in a way so deep that it seemed to touch my being, and I would hear myself sigh with a joy I could neither explain or express. Often, at Bear Claw, I'd have those moments. The morning when the copperhead raced by us, so smooth and dignified, I felt one such moment. That snake was poisonous, but also so beautiful—and it had no interest in harming me, it was just off on some mission of its own. I felt safe, sure that everything was all right.

Whenever and wherever Joanie and I went, we had to go early, because every day but Sunday I had to be at the General's Palace by eleven A.M. to start cooking. And as spring turned to summer and the days grew warmer and longer, and the lilac bushes on the hotel grounds bloomed and Rick transplanted box after box of snapdragons into the GP flower beds, we got busier and busier in the kitchen. More and more tourists were coming to see Excelsior.

My first busy night at the General's Palace kitchen stands out clearly in my mind. For one thing, I'd never seen anything like that much activity. Susan had gone through almost two entire pillowcases of torn salad greens. She was busily tearing up more with one hand and adding ingredients to a new ten-gallon tub of salad dressing with the other. Nettie had at least twenty-five menu "ollacarts" pinned up on the wire above the counter. She was a blur of motion, turning steaks on the grill while setting up plates, somehow keeping track of which cuts were which and how well done or rare they had been ordered.

Toby, the dishwasher, was washing and stacking, but not fast enough for the harried waitresses and busboys who slammed in and out of the swinging doors screaming, "Out of salad plates!" or simply "Cups!" Luke alternated between helping Nettie and me and scrubbing out steam-table pans. I had just refilled the line for the eighth time and put chicken on to fry when I heard someone cry "Awww!" and I looked up just in time to see a waitress stamp her foot in rage. "How many times do I have to tell that sonofabitch to order five-thousand pack, not five-hundred pack!" she shrieked. "This is the *third time* this season we've run out of coffee filters!!" At the same time several other waitresses ran into the kitchen to get coffee. "I don't believe this! I don't believe this!" I heard.

"Luke," said a pale, pale girl coming to the rear of the kitchen. She was in her twenties, no makeup, with thin, blond hair. She spoke very softly, but with authority.

Her name was Claire, and I knew that she worked at Meadow School, an alternative private school, during the fall and winter months. She said, "Luke, who should we send?"

Luke, his face red with heat and shiny wet from the grill he was standing over, looked around to see who was doing what. "Chrysta!" he said. "If we're okay on the line, run down to the snack bar downstairs—you know where that is? No? Can't miss it, just go downstairs and there it is—to get some coffee filters—oh, fifty'll get us through. Then hurry back up here, we need you. I'll keep an eye on your chicken."

I nodded, and raced off.

As I ran through the lobby, in jeans and sneakers and a T-shirt, my now-grubby white apron still on and a blue-and-white bandana tied over my head (a health regulation: long hair must be covered and held back), I thought how quickly I had learned to feel at home at the GP.

I was also thinking about Luke and Howie Snoodgrass. "How *dare* Luke send me to get coffee filters—he's not my boss, and I was busy too!" I thought. On the other hand, I had to admit Luke was there and Howie wasn't. And for him to say "I'll keep an eye on your chicken"— well, he had to be pretty on top of it to know what *any* one person was doing in the middle of all that.

But still, I just couldn't believe Howie was as bad as everybody said he was. He was always nice to me. Probably people were jealous of him because Dewling was his uncle, I thought.

By this time I was at the snack bar. I explained what I needed to the man behind the counter and was idly watching him count out the coffee filters when I heard a voice say, "Hey."

I turned around and there was that crazy little kid I'd

seen my first morning in town. Dare. He had on a black T-shirt cut off at the midriff, so that his scrawny little stomach showed. He had a package of cigarettes rolled up in the left sleeve of his shirt, and a pool cue in one hand. I wondered what he was doing here playing pool at seven on a Monday night at the General's Palace's snack bar.

"Hey yourself," I said. "Dare, right?"

He nodded, flipping his hair back. "What's your name again?"

I told him.

"Oh," he said. "How you doin'?"

"Okay." He looked at my apron. "You workin' here now?"

"Yeah."

"You like it?"

"Yeah."

"What d'you do?"

"Cook."

"Oh, yeah?" His face lit up. "My dad was a cook at a hotel for a while, in Dallas. A much bigger hotel than this. But he's really a artist."

"Yeah?"

"Yeah, he paints pictures of naked ladies." Dare unrolled his package of cigarettes from his sleeve casually. I could tell he was watching me to see if I'd react to "naked ladies," so I didn't.

"That's nice," I said in this very neutral voice. "Where's he now?"

"My dad?" Dare lit his cigarette—he seemed to have gotten better with the matches.

I nodded.

"Dallas. I think." Dare blew a smoke ring. With casual pride he added, "He moves around a lot."

I nodded again.

"Miss, I got your filters ready for you," said the counterman.

"Thanks," I told him and then said to Dare, "Well, I'll see you around."

"Okay," said Dare, and he started to walk away. Then he turned around and came back. "D'you have a quarter?"

I *knew*, I just *knew* in the way you just know things without a doubt sometimes, that Dare wanted it for the pinball machine, and I remembered my father's lectures on the value of money, how much it meant to him when he was a kid and how little it meant to me, how an allowance was a gift to spend as I saw fit but at the same time it should be valued and spent wisely, and on and on and on. I smiled at Dare. "Sure," I said, and I took a quarter out of my pocket. "Here you go." I tossed it to him and he caught it.

"Thanks," he said, flipping his hair back again. "Chrysta," he added.

As I walked out of the snack bar and headed up the stairs back to the kitchen, I was astonished to overhear Dare say to the counterman, "A glass of milk, please."

13

From then on, I saw Dare pretty often around the General's Palace. I'd give him a quarter if he'd ask for it, and we'd have one of our "How you doin'?" conversations. I'd run into him at the snack bar, and sometimes I'd see him watching TV in the lobby. Every

Monday afternoon around four there was a program on about karate and kung fu called *World of Martial Arts*, and he was *always* there to watch it. He would be completely absorbed in it, saying, "Pow!" and "Slam!" and "Whap!" as people were flipped over and pounded into the mat, his whole body hunched forward and rigid.

A lot of times I'd see Dare hanging out at the observation deck on the top floor of the hotel. From up there you could see a ring of mountains all around you in every direction, with Excelsior down below, plus the General's Palace pool and gardens directly below.

The observation deck opened into a bar which was officially named The General's Top Hat, but which everyone called The Top for short.

The Top was completely different from the other bar in the hotel, which was a real el sleazo. That bar was named The General's Boots but was usually called just Boots. (Steve from the front desk liked to say it should be The General's Armpits; The Pits for short.) Boots was on the lower level, just down the hall from the snack bar. It was dark with lots of old wood, little private booths, and a small funky dance floor. There was a jukebox with mostly stuff by Loretta Lynn, Tammy Wynette, and people like that. But a lot of nights they had live music there. Sometimes there would be a band, but often it would just be one singer with a guitar.

I was getting to know more and more about the hotel and the people who worked there. They, as much as the Yeller House people, were becoming a family to me. Steve was coming into focus, too. Like Lissa, he always had something jive to say, but there was friendliness underneath, and we became close. A couple of times we drove over to Fayetteville to see a movie together, and often we'd check out Boots together. He and Joanie, and in a different way Nettie, were my closest friends. I missed Lissa a lot though, and we wrote each other at least once a week.

Every day at the GP was more or less like my first day there; there was always some crisis at the busiest possible time. Once the power went off, around eight in the evening, leaving the kitchen and a customer-filled dining room in the dark. Another time, the bottom opened on a 25-pound package of frozen peas Cleota was carrying and they went skittering all over the floor, right in the middle of the lunch rush. "Lord, honey, Cleota done peed on the floor!" Nettie whispered to me and we both went into gales of laughter. Nettie was so *good*—just plain old good, something I couldn't remember ever thinking about someone before. I liked her so much I even put up with her endless talk about Luke.

Luke, Nettie told me, was in school at the University of Arkansas at Fayetteville—about an hour's drive from Excelsior. He was going to be a sophomore next fall. He was majoring in psychology and had a scholarship and earned all his own spending money. *Big deal*, I would think, as Nettie went on and on. Luke worked summers at the General's Palace, and in the school year came over on weekends from Fayetteville to work. *Big deal*. In Excelsior, he stayed at Nettie's house, but he had his own apartment in Fayetteville. He had been an Eagle Scout. His essay had won the Rural Electrification Program Contest when he was a junior in high school, and as a prize he'd gotten to go to Washington, D.C. He was the first Beauford to go to college. *Big, big deal*.

"Now why he wants to go into *sigh-cology* I *do* not know," Nettie must've told me a dozen times, "but I've always held that I wasn't a-gonna interfere." And then she would tell me about what a sweet, good little boy

Luke'd been, but how, after the accident his parents died in, though he was still sweet and good, "He got deep, Chrysta. *Real* deep." That was the word she always used, *deep*. "He got to readin'—you never saw a kid with his nose in a book so much! I b'lieve all that readin's why he never picked up any a my Arkansas talk—you ever notice he don't have much of an accent atall?—that an' him keeping to himself so much. He'd be up there alone in his room for hours, readin' or studyin' or playin'. I mean, when he wasn't workin'." *Of course*, I thought: *There's nothing unusual there; when people don't work, they play.* But I kept my mouth shut, and let Nettie continue for the umpteenth time, "He's always been a hard-workin' kid, helpin' me around the house, and he had a paper route first when he was nine, then he was a sacker up at IGA when he was thirteen, then—" Borrrring, as Lissa would say.

I especially didn't want to hear about Luke Beauford because there was something about him that bothered me and I couldn't put my finger on it. Not that I still thought he was a jerk—I had come to see that his behavior on our first meeting really had been unusual for him. He was polite and even friendly, though he never seemed to really let go and jive around like most of us. I even had to admit he was nice-looking in a plain, trim sort of way; and of course, I felt sorry for him, having both his parents die when he was just a kid. But still, I just didn't really warm up to him, and all Nettie's stories about how great he was didn't help things. Steve Darwin at the front desk was also a big fan of Luke's, so I had to listen to *him* sing Luke's praises too.

Looking back now, I see that Luke reminded me of things I didn't want to think about. I didn't want to think about what I'd been like, and my parents, and

Benton, Illinois. At times I felt all that had happened to another girl, someone I'd read about in a book, not me. I didn't think about my future at all, and I didn't even think about the present much: I just lived it, day by day. For me, working at the GP was just a job. Sure, I tried to do a good job and cook well, and I liked the people in the kitchen a lot—but I didn't care all that much about the General's Palace or the kitchen as a whole. I didn't care if the GP made money or not, if the dining room was good, bad, or indifferent, as long as I could get by with minimum hassle.

But Luke obviously *did* care. I'd never seen anybody so uptight at such a young age. He wasn't like any teenager I'd met on the road, and he couldn't have been more unlike my old long-ago Benton crowd. It seemed to me he was *always* in the kitchen, working away. He was there when I got there at eleven in the morning; he was there when I left at seven at night. Susan said he was still there even when *she* left, around ten-thirty or eleven. Luke did take a couple of hours off in the midafternoon but he was there at the busy times.

And then there were his lists, his multicolored lists, kept in this kind of calendar/diary book. Luke had his Weekly Special Projects (WSPs, listed in red in his list book) and his Daily Special Projects (DSPs, listed in blue in his list book). His WSPs were things he did every week, on the same day: mopping the stock-room floors and scrubbing the shelves in it on Mondays, cleaning the kitchen windows on Tuesdays, drain maintenance on Wednesdays. His DSPs were things he only did once, or once every few months, like inventory all the china and glasses. As if the world would come to an end if a Wednesday passed without drain maintenance.

Here was I, trying not to think about the past and the future, and here was good old Luke, thinking away about both. He spent all his time with his Aunt Nettie, who had raised him, and they clearly got along "like a house afire" as she put it. Bingo: his past, right there tied up with his present. He even *worked* with her! (*I* couldn't have worked with either of my parents for even one minute.) And here was Luke, Responsible Young Student in college, planning a career, Mr. Organized . . . it turned me off. I didn't think about *why* then, just that Luke was a nice but uptight grind.

There was one other person who bothered me vaguely. Dare. I remember this day in May when I ran into him out at Bear Claw.

Now, the first time I went out to the cliffs, I couldn't help looking at other people's bodies and comparing them to mine. I thought I came out pretty good; despite working in the kitchen I still didn't eat all that much and I hadn't put on much weight. And though I still thought of my breasts as too big and a general pain, I had come to see that most people considered them beautiful.

But—and this was what was so amazing—at Bear Claw I could actually be *naked*, by myself, big tits and all, and not get hassled for it or even much noticed for it. By my second trip out there, I wasn't aware of other people's bodies that way either. The cool, clear lake water felt so good on a naked body on a summer day; you didn't skinny-dip to show off or to size other people up as some other kind of sexual thing. After a while you didn't even think about yourself or other people being naked.

But that one time I saw Dare out at Bear Claw, I felt funny about taking my clothes off in front of him. Even though there were other little kids running around, hippies' kids, *they* all seemed to accept the whole thing as natural, while Dare practically had his tongue hanging out. That day, Dare had apparently gotten there just before Joanie and I arrived, and you could see he was really excited, practically jumping up and down, and nudging a bearded guy who I guess had brought him, and saying things like, "Oh, man, look at that pair of titties," in a loud whisper. He reminded me of a junior Donny Figeroa. The guy pulled him aside and said, "Not cool, Dare," so Dare shut up, but you could still see him staring and practically drooling and trying to look like he wasn't. It really bothered me, partly because I still thought Dare was only maybe nine or ten years old at the most—I mean, he looked *young*. And here he was doing this whole letch number. I didn't take my clothes off that day, and I never saw Dare at Bear Claw again.

Something about Dare troubled me, but, like I did with Luke, I pushed it to the back of my mind. I didn't want to think about that, either.

But there was one thing I couldn't help thinking about, though I didn't want to, and that was the pain. That same pain I had felt in front of the post office. Now, a month after that first one, it was coming almost every day, at least once, that incredible, punching, agonizing abdominal pain. But it always passed: That's what I told myself, and it was true. When the pain hit, I'd just stand or sit completely still, and kind of hold my breath, and wait for it to pass, telling myself, "It'll pass, it'll pass."

And it always did. For a while.

14

"Maybe it's cramps?" Joanie suggested. "It's not right before your period?"

I shook my head. I was sitting at the Yeller House kitchen table, having just finished breakfast, and she was sweeping the floor. I had finally told her about the pains, which were now coming several times a day.

"How long did you say it has been going on?"

"About three weeks."

"That *long*?" Joanie stopped sweeping and stared at me, frowning as she leaned on her broom. "Chrysta, dear! And you haven't done anything about it yet?"

The reason I hadn't done anything about it was I was afraid that a doctor might figure out that I was sixteen and report me to the hotel. I was also afraid that either the pain might turn out to be some terrible thing like cancer, or it might be nothing at all and I'd be spending money for no reason. "I wish it would just go away," I said to Joanie. "I don't like doctors anyway."

"I'm not too hot on them either," Joanie said. "But you have to listen to what your body tells you."

I didn't, though. "I'll be okay, don't worry," I said, sorry I'd told her. And I washed my dishes and went upstairs to my room to lie down until it was time to go to work.

                    *   *   *

One of the things at work that interested me was why Howie was so unpopular in the kitchen. I still had it chalked up to jealousy. Nettie said he was "as innocent an' defenseless as a little baby copperhead," and "sweet as a crocodile made of sugar."

But Howie was nice to me. He was there every afternoon when I was, usually during the hours when Luke was away from the kitchen. He'd work at his desk for a while, either going over paperwork or talking to Nettie—she pressed her lips together and did everything but hiss when he came near her, answering his questions with a short, tight "Yessir" or Nosir." Howie asked my opinion a lot and he seemed to take my answers seriously. He always told me about his plans and hopes, and he always, *always* praised me. I remember this one day in particular, when I was making beef stew.

"Y'see, Chrysta, honey," he said that day, "mah dream is to really bring about *improvement* here at the General's Palace. Ah *luv* this ol' hotel, an' Ah luv my ol' Uncle Hugh—he's been a second father to me. An' Ah want to do him an' this ol' hotel *proud*." I nodded as I dumped a bunch of chopped onions into a huge skillet in which I had melted a pound of butter.

Without breaking his chain of conversation, Howie said, "Buttah's up to one eighty-nine a pound, Chrysta, honey, use Crisco next time. Now, as Ah was sayin', to make this line as el'gant as our dinin' area out there— that's mah *dream*, Chrysta. But let's face it, Chrysta, we gotta keep our costs and our wastes at a minimum. Any ideas, honey?"

I nodded. "Well, one," I said shyly. I was proud of this idea. I had been thinking about it and hoping to be asked.

"Ah'm listenin'," said Howie approvingly.

"Well, you know those biscuits we have have at breakfast?" Howie nodded. "Well, there's a *lot* of them left over that get thrown out." I gestured earnestly toward the two giant garbage cans where all food wastes got tossed, and I looked at Howie. His face had darkened slightly. "So," I continued brightly, "we could split the leftover biscuits, brush them with garlic butter—and stick them in the oven to brown up. Like little garlic breads! I bet people'd love 'em."

Howie's tone was cold. "Chrysta, honey, Ah'm sorry, but Ah just don't b'lieve that's ec'nomic'ly feas'ble. Ah—"

I interrupted him excitedly. "Yesterday we had three pans of biscuits left over, so I tried it, as an experiment and . . ."

"The answer is NO, Chrysta," said Howie sharply. Then he sweetened up again. "But Ah'd be int'rested to hear any *other* ideas y'have. An' don' take this as criticism—Ah'd *hate* fo' a sweet thang lak yuh ta feel lak Ah was bein' crit'cal. 'Cause, Chrysta, Ah just think yuh doin' a wunderful job! Ah *knew* yuh had init'ive the moment Ah saw yuh! Ah've *noticed* yuh garnishes, Chrysta. Ah p'ticul'y lahked yuh chicken ah l'orange on the dinnah line yest'day evenin'.'"

"Thank you," I said beaming. All I had done was read a recipe book and pour a little orange juice. Though from the way Cleota's eyes bulged out of her chicken head when she saw me pouring the orange juice, you would have thought it was arsenic mixed with puree of frog I was pouring. I added, "Well, Cleota didn't care much for that chicken. She carried on to Nettie about how 'furrin' it was for a good twenty minutes!"

Howie laughed. "Way-ell, now, Chrysta honey, Cleota's just a good ol' girl 'n' doesn't know any bettah, but she's a rayel sweet lady und'neath it all, just a *rayel* sweet lady." At that, Nettie snorted loudly and marched into the dining room. Howie, in a lower voice, said, "If y'keep doin' such fine work, Chrysta, Ah may have a little su'prise f'yuh."

"Oh, yeah?" I said curiously. By now I had browned beef cubes as well as the onions. I combined them and added beef broth, salt, pepper, bay leaves, and a good shot of Worcestershire sauce.

Howie lowered his voice to a whisper, and beckoned me with a finger. "Ah'm thinkin' about makin' *yuh* assistant manager of the kitchen, Chrysta."

"Me!" I squealed, and turned to stare at him.

"Ssh, ssh," he said, putting a finger to his lips and again drawing near me, this time draping an arm around me in a confidential, brotherly way (I thought). "Now, Ah haven't made up mah mind fully yet, so jus' hold on to yuh horses. An' Chrysta—it's *five dollahs* an hour. Plus, there are certain . . . fringe benefits."

Fringe benefits? It was too much to hope for. Or was it? After all, Howie wouldn't tell me he was thinking about making me assistant kitchen manager if he wasn't really, would he? Of course, I knew I wasn't the person for it. I didn't know anything about running a kitchen, just how to cook. Luke Beauford was the person who should have the job. I mean, let's get real, he was already doing it. He was the one who cared about the kitchen running smoothly. Sure I put garnishes on the food, but basically I was just there to make a buck.

But the fringe benefits, I thought greedily: *maybe* one of the apartments! There were several employees' apartments on the ground floor of the hotel, down the hall from the snack bar. Those apartments were great—I knew, because Steve had one. And if I was given one, I would be *free*. I could live alone. Alone! I mean, I loved the people at Yeller House, but to have a place of my own! A nice place, not like that funky cabin at Henley's. A place I could decorate and fix up, and have people over to—but where I could also be alone and do my little morning routines.

I had also heard about the carriage house, the most fabulous GP employee quarters of all: two stories, a small, private building made of the same stone as the GP, down from the hotel. The carriage house had been fixed up for living quarters when Mr. Dewling bought the hotel. "A gem," Steve Darwin had called it. Howie lived there now, but he spent most of his time out at his farm by Beaver Lake, with his wife, Dolly Mae, and his pigs. He often talked about how superior home-cured pork was, which made Nettie practically choke.

But I couldn't think about the apartment just now. Now I was still a humble cook. I decided not to prattle on but play it cool.

"Well, uh, thanks, for considering me, Howie. I'll think about it. Meanwhile, listen, would you order another sack of onions?"

"Sure, Chrysta, honey," he told me. "Now, Ah have some tapes on employee motivation up at my 'partment. The ol' carriage house, y'know? Anyway, Ah thought it might be good fo' yuh to come up and listen to them sometime, prep'ratory to yo' takin' the new position. An' that way y'can look ovah what just might be yo' livin' quarters! *Now* yuh get my drift 'bout fringe benefits?"

I looked at him. Often I got the feeling that Howie was coming on to me, but then he'd always change his tune, and I'd decide I'd misread him. This time was no exception. Hastily he said, "Ah don't mean livin' quarters *with* me, Chrysta, honey! Ah've told you, Ah'm a happ'ly married man! Y'gonna havta meet Dolly Mae

soon. She's *rayel* cute! Ah mean Ah want to be spendin'
mo' time with *her*, out at our farm, so why should that
beautiful ol' carriage house get wasted? Ah thought Ah
might keep one of the 'partments down from Boots case
Ah do stay here 'ccasionally, but that carriage house
really oughta be put to bettah use—lak bein' lived in by
a pretty li'l girl like yo'self, Chrysta."

I stared at him, my eyes opened wide. I was tongue-
tied. The gem? For *me*?

"Of course Ah need to think about it a little mo', and
Ah need to discuss it with mah uncle. But—"

After Howie Snoodgrass left the kitchen that afternoon, I
was in a daze: functioning, cooking, adding the chopped
potatoes and carrots and celery to the stew, stirring it,
tasting it, but in a dream. Everything was turning out
so great! The *carriage house*? How much better could
things *get* in Excelsior Springs? I kept shaking my
head.

No sooner was he out the door when Nettie burst
back into the kitchen. "Well, if that don't beat all! Him
callin' Cleota 'sweet'! Why she's about as sweet as a
dose of cod-liver oil! An' if she's a *lady*, then I'm a
bullfrog!" Nettie shook her head vigorously. "I've knowed
Cleota all my life, Chrysta. Sweet! Why, d'you know
that before she got herself saved at Freewill Baptist at
Elm Hill, she could outdrink any man in this town?
Once she even beat up the Chief of Police! An' *that* was
when she was forty or so!" Nettie paused and shook her
head. "An' don't you feel bad about them biscuits,
honey. As much as Howie talks about cuttin' down on
waste, he don't *really* want to. Y'see, Chrysta, he takes
them big old barrels of garbage home every night, and
he's not real innerested in cuttin' down the amount."

I must've looked puzzled.

"For his *pigs,* honey! He's got about twenty-five pigs out his place! He uses the garbage from up here to slop his hogs with!"

15

The next day I got a good look at Hugh Dewling, the owner of the General's Palace Hotel. He was a tall, stern-looking man with intense blue eyes, a full head of white hair, and bushy white eyebrows. He chewed a cigar nonstop. I told Nettie I thought he looked fierce. She shook her head and grinned. "Well, he does his best to make you think so, but he's an ol' softie underneath it all. And Chrysta, don't be fooled by not seein' him around every minute—he knows *every*thing that's going on at the hotel."

When I came through the big double doors into the lobby the Thursday after I saw Hugh Dewling that first time, I wandered over to check out the big display board where they announced who was playing at the hotel's bars that weekend. At the General's Top Hat, there was Estelle Smerdly on the piano. From her photograph, old Estelle was an overweight blonde wearing a one-shouldered drapey dress and smiling as if her lips had been treated with Perma-Prest. The Top always had somebody like that: "Marvin Miner and his Mellow Music," "Hilary the Harp Lady," or "Didi-Michelle's Music Moods." They all sounded like the music you

hear in supermarkets. I don't even know why they
bothered calling it "live" music. Boots always was more
interesting.

And especially this particular day. "The General's
Boots proudly presents Luke Beauford, Original Music."
There was a picture of him: the same old tall gangly
Luke Beauford I knew from the kitchen, raggedy brown
mustache and hair, perched solemnly on a stool with a
guitar resting across his knees. There he sat, old Luke,
looking directly into the camera, not smiling or scowling,
just sitting there. If I hadn't known what an uptight guy
he was, I'd probably have thought he was sort of nice-
looking—appealing. His pose and expression didn't look
phoney at all: not macho or embarrassed or apologetic
or mean—and those huge, striking, melancholy brown
eyes looking out at me. I stared.

As Nettie says, "You could have knocked me over
with a feather."

Friday, after I got off work, Steve Darwin and I went
to go hear Luke.

I went home to Yeller House first, to shower off the
ten layers of grease I always felt coated in after a day at
the kitchen. I knew that Steve dressed up for any
occasion, and because Joanie had told me I could
borrow anything in her closet, I decided to dress up
too.

I wound up forties style: a navy-blue crepe shirt with
white polka dots, loose on top, with tucks toward the
waist, and a white sheath skirt that fit perfectly. "Oh,
Chrysta! Chrysta, *dear*! You were *made* for the forties!"
Joanie told me, eyeing me appreciatively. She fluffed
my hair out around my shoulders, shrieked "Wait!" dug
around in a box in her closet, and came up with a small

circular straw hat with a wisp of dark-blue net veiling. After she had that on me, she dashed out of the room. I heard the bathroom door open and close.

"Oh, *no*, Joanie, not makeup!" I protested, as she reappeared with a quilted, flowery traveling bag.

"Aw come on, Chrysta! Just this once, it'll be fun!"

I cringed. Makeup was from the Queen Chris, Donny Figeroa, fight-with-my-parents era. Running away had erased all that—I hadn't worn anything except Chapstick since I was fourteen or so. I thought about it. I didn't have to be scared of makeup. It wouldn't make me go back to being that person.

"Okay," I told Joanie.

"Whoo-whoo!" said Steve appreciatively when he saw me. He was duded up himself in a vintage double-breasted suit, with a bow tie and a straw panama hat. I pirouetted for him, very pleased with myself, especially with my hat. "Well, my-o-my, I *d'clare*, Miss Chrysta, I don't know *why* you run aroun' in those ol' *rags* all the time when you can look so pos'tively sinful! Pos'tively *rav*ishing!" He leaned closer and, dropping the Southern accent, said, "To what do we owe this great honor?"

"To the pleasure of your company, sir, and the desire to equal your legendary good taste." I curtseyed. I was in a great mood.

"And here I thought all this just might be in honor of Luke Beauford's debut this season at the GP!" he said teasingly.

"Luke?!" I stopped twirling and frowned at him. It hadn't crossed my mind that anyone would think I was doing this for *Luke*. Suddenly some of my pleasure at dressing up evaporated. What if *Luke* or any other people thought I was doing it for him?

"Come on, Chrysta, admit you find him as cute as

the rest of us do!" said Steve. "You know *I'd* snap him up in a minute if he was even the *least* little bit interested!"

"I know very well what you would do, Steve, but I'm not you! And I don't know *why* everyone thinks he's so great anyway. What does he sing about, how many soup bowls he inventoried on Tuesday? Or is it tender ballads about the joy of drain maintenance?"

Steve said sternly, "I sometimes think I have overestimated you gravely, my dear Chrysta. You think in terms that are *entirely* too black and white. I will have to correct this."

"What do you mean?"

"I mean that someone can inventory soup bowls or work at a front desk in a hotel *and* be a poet or a songwriter. Perhaps you'll learn that tonight."

When Luke walked out on that stage, said hello, and started singing and playing, I was floored.

His voice was deep and relaxed. It was a dark voice, brown like his eyes, gentle and strong but mellow, not strained. He was an excellent guitarist, too.

> *"There are voices all around you,*
> *but they're speaking low.*
> *Open up your heart to them,*
> *let your feelings flow.*
> *When you're dancing to the rhythm*
> *of the world that's all around,*
> *hear the music, hear the music,*
> *hear the sound. . . ."*

How could *Luke Beauford* have written those words? "Dancing to the rhythm of the world that's all around"

—Luke, with his clipboard and his list; could *he* "hear the music, hear the sound"?

"Boy he really *is* good," I whispered to Steve.

"I won't say I told you so," he said, smirking.

I listened, absorbed like everybody else: I had never heard Boots so quiet for a performer.

"This next song is a song I wrote the year I graduated from high school, when I was making up my mind whether or not to go to college. It's about leaving institutions," said Luke from the stage. "I *didn't* leave, by the way," he added, then sang:

"Well, it's fly, where might you land?
Birds fly, I know you've got your plans.
You've got your dreams to maintain you,
you've got your friends to sustain you....
You've left all your institutions—
they made you laugh, but they made you bleed.
They taught you how to be on time, but they gave
 you nothing
that you need...."

It was as if this Luke—not Luke from the kitchen, but this new stranger—was singing directly to me, putting words and music to my feelings. *I* had left institutions too, my family, my school, because they made me bleed. Listening to him moved me—I knew I was covering up the bleeding; but it was still there.

Dare flashed through my mind then, and I knew, suddenly, why I had felt drawn to him. In some way, he was like me. His whole tough act *had* to be a way for him to laugh at the institutions that made *him* bleed. Except I was sure he was still bleeding, too. And then I thought, *I'd like to talk all this over with Luke. In a deep way, asking him questions and finding out what he thinks about things.* There was obviously a lot to the guy from the walk-in freezer. I wanted to ask him how he could write a song about leaving institutions and then go into college and study hard and do the whole bit? How could he understand so clearly the way things got forced down your throat but at the same time do straight things like make lists? How could he "hear the music" and not respond?

At the end of the set, he came and sat with me at our table. Steve had gone to fool around at the bar. "Thanks for coming, Chrysta," Luke said. "Oh, I'm so glad I did!" I said. "I didn't even know you played, let alone this well. Luke, you are really, *really* good. You should make a record."

Luke put his hand over his eyes for a second. He looked pleased.

"Well, Chrysta, thanks. Thanks a lot. I appreciate that."

"I'm not just saying that, I mean it," I told him. "Your songs—in a lot of them you say just *exactly* what *I* feel about things."

Luke nodded. "I started writing songs after my parents died—my father used to play guitar, and my grandfather played banjo, and Nettie and my mother would sing along. So I grew up around that, and after they died, it just seemed really important to keep *that* alive, at least." He paused and smoothed down his mustache thoughtfully. "I hadn't been that close to my father when he was alive, you see. When he was playing music was almost the only time I ever saw him fully relaxed and happy." Luke trailed off.

"When did you start performing?"

"Oh, I didn't even think about playing for other people until a couple of years ago, I mean other than family, playing hymns and folk songs at family reunions or holidays. Not my own stuff. Songwriting was something private—like a secret diary. And now, when people tell me they liked a song of mine, or that it says something they've felt—it's strange because here I used to think I was the only one in the world who ever felt those things, so I had to get them down on paper and sing about it. But then, when I *did*, publicly, it turned out that I wasn't so one-of-a-kind after all. Performing made me feel more part of the world, like maybe everyone was more the same than different."

"Yes," I said slowly. "I remember once when..." I paused, trying to think about how I could say what I wanted to say. "... there was this time in my life when I was feeling very unhappy and lonely, but I was acting this big part, like I was tough and sure of myself, and it seemed like people, kids my age, were believing it and I was popular and in the in crowd and all that... you know?" Luke nodded, so I continued. "And I remember once wondering if maybe everyone in that crowd was playing as big a part as I was and how strange it would be if they were." Now, as Luke nodded again, *I* trailed off, flashing back to Benton but also thinking about the present, about discovering Luke was so nice after all, and how after these weeks of vaguely resenting him, here I was easily telling him a thought I had never told any-one—not even Lissa—before. And I remembered Nettie telling me a million times about Luke majoring in sigh-cology and how she couldn't understand it. But I could. I bet he'd be good, as a shrink, I thought, he's easy to talk to.

"You look lovely tonight, Chrysta," said Luke, reaching across the table and patting, of all things, my elbow.

"Oh!" I said embarrassed—I had been so intent on Luke's music that I had forgotten completely that I was dressed up. And *lovely*—what a strange, old-fashioned, corny, romantic word for Luke to use. Yet I didn't feel he meant it romantically . . . it was friendly, like Joanie's pleasure in getting me dressed up. I thought of all the times Donny Figeroa and the Benton boys had said, "Lookin' good," in that insinuating, jive way; I thought of all Howie's "pretty li'l lady" remarks. I decided that I liked "lovely," and I decided I liked Luke.

"Well, well, what have we here, a nice little tête-à-tête?" quipped Steve, returning to the table. But before he could go any further, who should pop over to the table but Dare. "Hey, pipsqueak," Steve said. "I thought you had to be at *least* thirteen to get in here."

"I'm forty, I just look young for my age," Dare said, smirking.

"No, who got you in?"

"Rick. He's my guardian—tonight." Without missing a beat, Dare turned to me and said, "Hey, Chrysta, buy me a beer?"

With a grim look on his face, Luke slid out of the booth across from me, nodded good-bye to the three of us, and walked away. Maybe he was just going to the bathroom before his next set, but I had this funny feeling that he was going to say something to John, Boots' manager, about Dare being there.

"No," I told Dare, flatly, meanwhile thinking how strange it was: Dare didn't have the faintest idea I too was under eighteen, and couldn't buy a drink any more legally than he.

"Aw, Chrysta—" Dare pleaded, but then John came up. *Yep, I thought, Luke told John. Why?*

"Out, Dare," John told him firmly. Apparently Dare knew everyone.

"Aw, John . . . Hey, Rick is here, Rick's my guardian."

"Come on, Dare, we both know that's bullshit, and

we both know I risk my ass lettin' you in here. You tell me you're not gonna hustle drinks, and what's the first thing I catch you doin', man?"

"But John—"

"*Out*. You don't get your friends in trouble, man. Not cool."

After he left, I felt confused. Sorry for Dare—who I knew must be out in Excelsior somewhere, no doubt furious—but at the same time, well, if someone bends the rules for you, you try to help them out, too, and I could see John's point. I was mulling all this over when Luke returned to the stage. And I wish Dare had been there for the first song in Luke's second set: "I wrote this one once when I was real down," Luke said, "and I heard my aunt use one of those old phrases I'd heard a million times—'Can't run from trouble'—and it just got me going.

"*Can't run from trouble—*
where can I hide?
Leave heartache, it finds me,
burning inside.
Sorrows pack my suitcase,
pain I didn't choose,
that's why I'm singing these run away blues.
Run away, run away,
distance deceives me.
Run away, run away,
trouble won't leave me.
Staying's too hard, but running won't lose
those run away, run away, run away blues."

16

"Employee motivation," said the smooth voice on the tape. "It's as simple as getting your employees to *care*."

I was sitting on the living-room floor of the carriage house, on thick, smooth, beige carpeting, my back against a large pillow in the downstairs living room, and I was wondering what I was doing there. The other downstairs room was a kitchen, and up the polished oak stairs were two bedrooms and the bathroom. I knew because Howie had told me. "We'll go up there laytah on, Chrysta," Howie Snoodgrass had promised. I wasn't sure what he meant. I felt extremely nervous, sitting there that Saturday morning, listening to Howie Snoodgrass's tapes on employee motivation. I've asked myself a lot why I walked into that situation, and I was asking even that morning. Sure, Howie *was* my boss, but I could have said no, or asked that another person come along. Couldn't I? Or maybe I still didn't want to believe that he was coming on to me, or thought it might increase my shot at assistant kitchen manager.

"The dictionary defines motive as something that causes a person to act; it defines motivate as to provide with a motive. So, when we speak of—"

"Y'want anythin' to drink?" Howie interrupted the tape. He was walking as if his balance was off.

"Just orange juice, thank you."

"Y'can have a screwdrivah if y'lak," he offered.

"A screwdriver, a screwdriver," I said nervously. "Now what is that again?"

Howie chuckled. "Why, aren' y'cute," he said.

"No, I always forget. The, uh, names of drinks. And what goes in them."

"Yuh don' have t' play inn'cent with *me*, Chrysta, honey." He was drawlier than usual.

"I'm not playing anything, Howie, I just asked—I just don't drink that much outside of a beer once in a while—"

"A screwdrivah's vodka 'n' orange juice, Chrysta, but I got plenny a beer—Bud, Moosehead, Lite—Dolly Mae, she says she needs to watch her weight, but obv'usly that's not *yo'* problem, Chrysta. Now, honey, whud'll it be?"

"Orange juice," I said firmly. Howie scowled and disappeared into the kitchen. The tape droned on. "A behavior that is discouraged and punished tends to stop. A behavior that is . . ."

Howie returned and flipped the tape off. "Here'sy'-orange juice, Chrys'honey. But Ahbrahy'beer casey'-changey'mind."

He must've been boozing it up long before I showed, I realized. It was only nine-thirty or so. I seemed to remember hearing that early boozers were the hardcore alcoholics. Or maybe Howie had just done it this once—just for me. He put the tray down on a table, and dropped onto the couch near my cushion.

"The tape is very interesting," I said politely, skittery with nervousness.

"Yeah, employmotivashuns ver' impor'an', ver' impor'an'." He pushed himself along the couch so he was closer to me, and I moved back.

"B'les geddowna business, Chrysa."

Howie made another flopping move down the couch
in my direction. I looked up, judging the distance to
the door. I was *scared*. Think, Chrysta. Business. "Yes,"
I said. "The tapes mentioned that—"

"Y'know thassnot whutamean, Chrys honey. Abou
geddin downa business. Y'know Ah've bin ver' 'tracted
t'yuh since th' mom'nt Ah laid eyes on yuh, y'know
that? Ver' 'tract'. Course y'know that, girl lak yuh."

Echo: *You come on hot, but you're so cold when it
comes right down to it!* . . . Donny Figeroa. Of course,
back in those days, I *did* flirt and try to act sexy, so I
could understand Donny's point. But now—I had never
flirted with Howie.

I stood up. "I don't have any idea what you're talking
about, Howie," I said. "And I'm leaving now."

"Now, Chrysahoney, don' run off, we c'n have us
some reeel fun, and, uh, y'don' wanna geddon m'bad
side, do yuh?"

I made a leap for the door, just as Howie began
scrambling after me. He tripped over the coffee table
and kicked it, knocking the beer onto the rug just as I
reached the doorknob and turned it.

It was locked.

Howie staggered to his feet and came toward me.
"Now jussa min', young lady, yo' not goin' *nowhere* jus'
yet—"

"Howie, leave me alone, don't touch me, I—"

Frantically I tried the door again, pushing against the
handle, twisting it. *I didn't want this.* Was there one of
those little buttons on the knob? No. Howie had locked
it with a key. Trapped. Not in Excelsior, safe Excelsior,
where you can go out after dark alone, where it's safe,
where people leave their keys in the car . . . No! Not
here.

Howie had the look now, the look that had flashed on and off his face so quickly so many other times. Why had I refused to recognize it? "'Sno use, Chrysahoney, s'locked, s'why don' y'jus' relax an' enjoy y'sef?"

"Howie, keep away, I'm warning you—" *Think straight, don't panic. A back door? Maybe I should make a run for it. After all those months of hitchhiking and staying safe, now, to be raped in my new hometown by my boss. But* think *Chrysta, you've got to—*

Suddenly, I heard footsteps on the driveway and coming up the house and a pounding on the other side of the door. "Coming! Just a minute!" I screamed as loudly as I could.

"Don' ansah it, Chrysa, honey! We're goin' hafuuun! Reeel funnn!" The pounding continued.

"Just a minute!" I screamed. "Howie, come open this door, please, there's someone here!"

Howie staggered toward me, his face red.

"I'm sorry!" I yelled through the door. "Howie seems to be having a little trouble opening the door, don't go away!"

Howie growled at me and shoved me out of the way. He fished around in his pocket for the key and finally opened the door.

Luke.

He looked directly into Howie's flushed, angry face, glanced at me, took in the beer spilled on the rug, and said in a calm, neutral voice, "We have a reservation for fifteen for lunch, sir, physicians' wives, a private party to be served at The General's Top Hat."

"Well, she's busy, she can't he'p you, she's takin' th' dayoff."

"Oh no I'm not," I said quickly, stepping toward Luke and making it across the threshold.

"Well, sir, I didn't come to get Chrysta. I just came to ask you what you want served. Or do you want to leave it to the cooks?"

"You simple hillbilly sumbitch," said Howie, enraged. "Buttah wooden melt in y' mouth, would it? Do Ah wanna leave it to th' cooks! Ah'm gon' have yuh fired f' this, y'ovahstept y'autho'ty too many times, y'arr'gant—Interruptin' me'n m'own house 'sif y'owned th' place—"

Luke raised his eyebrows, gave Howie a look that silenced him, and turned and walked off.

I had to run to keep up with Luke as he strode toward the hotel. "Wait up!" I said. "Luke! God, I'm so glad you got there when you did!" I was trembling; I couldn't catch my breath. "Oh God, Luke, thank God you got there!"

Luke didn't say anything. He was scowling.

"Luke?" I said. "He can't really get you fired, can he?"

Luke shrugged angrily. "He's a fool if he does—I keep his damn kitchen running for him." Then he turned to look at me. His mouth was pressed into a hard line, and his eyes narrowed slightly. "Well, I suppose I have to apologize for breaking up your little party," he snapped.

I stopped dead still on the path. I couldn't believe it. "*Party?*" I said.

Luke kept walking. Suddenly I got furious. I ran after him.

"Now *you* wait a minute here!" I grabbed at his shoulder and pulled him around.

"Just what do you mean by apologize? *What* little party? What is that supposed to mean, huh?" I demanded.

Luke looked me over, his lips pressed together, and without a word turned and started toward the kitchen again.

"Luke, *what* is going *on?*" Everything was crazed, tilted.

He turned again, looked directly at me, then sighed and sat down on the grass. I sat down next to him.

"Maybe *you* better tell me what's going on, hunh, Chrysta?" He sounded tired.

"Isn't it obvious?" I said. "You walked in there. You saw what was happening." I stopped and took a few deep breaths to try and calm down. Then a thought hit me that nearly knocked me over. "In fact, Luke, you've seen for a *long* time, haven't you? Haven't you? I mean, your hints about Howie— Why didn't you just come out with it and tell me? Luke, you knew him better than I—you could have warned me!"

Guardedly, Luke said, "Well, frankly, Chrysta, I wasn't sure if you wanted or needed to be warned."

There was something I wasn't getting.

Luke continued, his voice rough. "Oh, come on, Chrysta, I can't believe you didn't know what was going on. I mean, the *only* time he showed up was when you were in the kitchen, other than late at night if he'd been smoking dope and arrived to chow down on Cleota's pies."

"I thought—"

"Wait, hear me out, Chrysta, I spent a lot of time wondering whether or not I ought to say anything to you. But I knew you didn't like *me*—not before you heard my songs, at least."

"Luke—"

"No, wait. You had a right not to like me—I was a jerk that first day you showed up! You didn't know Howie or *me* and I figured you thought it was just sour grapes, me wanting to be the manager so I was bad-mouthing Howie. And then I saw you getting all buddy-buddy with Howie. I thought, Umm-ummm, since her brain is obviously larger than peanut sized, she *sees* what he's like—and she's out to use him. For her own benefit."

"What!" I said, standing up, looking down at Luke, who remained seated on the grass. "Now you listen, Luke! How can you think that *I* would want to use that creep? Like that? I mean, that I would use sex to— Are you *kidding* me, Luke? I *never* saw what Howie was like—not till this morning!"

"Well, what was I—?"

"No, no, *you* wait, now it's your turn to listen, Luke! I—oh, I haven't been honest with myself. I guess that's it. Yeah. I saw, but I told myself that— Oh, never mind. God, I am so . . . But if you hadn't showed up when you did—"

Luke looked at me, quiet and neutral.

"All right, now I see that he was trying to get me into bed. I mean, my God, how stupid could I be? Everyone's prejudiced against poor little Howie because his uncle— God! Dumb! Dumb! And I could've seen it all along if I'd opened my stupid eyes for a change!" And suddenly I sat down again, hard, on the grass, drew up my knees, put my head down, and cried. Lissa was right; I was unrealistic, silly, and romantic about Excelsior. Completely, stupidly, dangerously unrealistic. I was a fool.

"Chrysta—" said Luke, gently taking my hand, "I'm sorry, I didn't—I mean, I had no right to assume that—"

"No, no," I said, tears still rolling down my face. "I am *dumb*. I am incredibly stupid. It would have served me right if . . ."

Luke looked at me, put his hand on my shoulder, now comfortingly. "Well, I've screwed up again," he said. "Not you, me. I've made a bad situation worse for you." He shook his head. "My God, I'm sorry, Chrysta, I just read the situation wrong, completely wrong, and I'm sorry. *Please* stop being so hard on yourself. You're not dumb, *I* am. I *do* believe you, one hundred percent, and I should've warned you about Howie. And not jumped to conclusions. It was wrong of me, and stupid, and, and...I like you, Chrysta, and I'm so *glad* I'm wrong; I'd hate to see you mixed up in something like that. And I'm so *glad* you're safe. I just wish I hadn't been too pigheaded to talk to you about all this straight on before, so you didn't have to face that."

"What is it Nettie's always saying, Luke? About foresight?"

"'Hindsight knows better than foresight'?"

I nodded.

"Thanks," said Luke. "Thanks, Chrysta." He smiled at me, then pulled a handkerchief from his back pocket. I took it. I had never met a man who carried a handkerchief. It was as old-fashioned as the word "lovely" had been the night before. I blew my nose.

"Look, let's go to the hotel, in the back entrance. You go wash your face off with cold water and we'll start cooking lunch. Okay?" Luke smiled at me, and we went off to work together.

17

You can't run from trouble, Luke's right. You deal with it, or it deals with you.

The Sunday after Howie went after me, Benton went after me. Or caught up with me.

I woke up in the morning with the pain again, and it didn't stop. It was a steady throb, with flares so sharp they took my breath away, pain I could hardly speak through or think during, just hold on.

I didn't want to tell Joanie. "Look, I just don't feel like going out to Bear Claw today," I told her, trying to sound cheerful. "I've been working real hard. I just want to lie around here today."

"Okay," she agreed, and then, "You sure you're okay, dear? You look pale, Chrysta."

"Just tired," I said.

But by nighttime, I couldn't fake it any longer. Around ten-thirty, doubled over in pain, I knocked at Joanie's door.

She was lying in bed reading. She looked up and gasped. "Chrysta! What is it! What happened?"

"That pain," I said, and it was an effort. "It's back. It hurts. *Oh, God, Joanie, it really hurts.*"

Joanie was already out of bed, pulling off the bathrobe and pulling on jeans and a shirt, "Come on, kiddo," she said. "We're going to the hospital."

In a flash we were into Frog, with its dive-bomber motor and its shrieking gears. *Twists, curves, oh that hurts, we will be there soon, of course, it's just a few minutes away, hang on, just because you asked for help doesn't give you the right to lose it entirely.*

Emergency room. Bright, bright lights. *Do you have medical insurance what seems to be the problem date of birth get the doctor here answer the questions Dr. Besum footsteps down the hall I'm lying on the form, hey I'm not really that old, but I'll let you find that out. I have a fever? Oh, I'm not making it up, this must be*

*real. Gynecological exam, the table flat and narrow,
climb up, climb up, the lights hurt my eyes, here I am
again, knees up, feet in those metal stirrups that aren't
shaped like feet at all, how silly to drape that sheet over
me.* "Now, now, dear, don't worry, this will be over
soon, this is going to feel a little cold," *the metal thing
that they crank to pry you open,* "I don't believe I've
seen you here before, you're not one of my regular
patients, are you?" *Can he tell by looking at me there?*

Joanie has one hand on my shoulder, she looks so
worried, her glasses glinting, the light is so bright, then
that prod and I jump and lurch, finger prodding,
poking, digging into that tender place red-hot with pain
that place that place that has been hurting so badly and
won't stop now, stop it stop it!

"Easy, easy, I'm sorry to be hurting you," says Dr.
Besum, straightening up, probing again. Joanie says,
"Here, Chrysta, hold my hand." I grip, tears running
down the sides of my face, out of the corners of my eyes
and down over my temples into my hair because I am
trying to lie flat except *enough enough enough you've
found it, that's it, it hurts hurts, hurts, isn't that
enough?*

"I'm sorry, uh, Chrysta," *poke, probe, stop, please
please stop.*

Then—he straightens up, I hear him pull off his
rubber glove, a sucking sound, and I hear him toss it in
the wastebasket, and then I am unclamped, lips close
together, and he walks up to where he can look down in
my face. He is kind, an older man with rimless glasses,
gray hair, small and tidy. The emergency-room lights
blinding bright above and behind him. I would trust
him, if I had any trust or feeling or thought or anything
besides the pain, the nurse with him, neutral and

white, but kind enough, all this concern and I am the center of it. All my life, my body forcing me to center stage.

"...growth the size of a grapefruit," he says.

Alarm bells going off. Must listen. Must understand Listen. Can't drift, this is important.

He is talking to Joanie. "You'll go back and pack her an overnight bag. Bring it here. She's not leaving."

What? I don't want to stay. I'll be trapped—they'll get me, they'll find me. Hospital: An institution ... I'll bleed. Soothing voice, "...no, no, definitely not cancerous. Probably some kind of cyst or possibly an ectopic tubal pregnancy. Acute pelvic inflammatory disease, chronic for some time. Infection. Abscess. High fever. Won't know what it is till we get in there."

I don't hear the connecting, soothing words, just the dangerous, important words. *Till we get in there.*

"...going to stay here tonight... don't want you leaving... pain killer plus antibiotics immediately... an intensive program, if that doesn't do it... take effect within twenty-four hours... or ... have to operate."

They gave me something to sign. The nurse helping me to a sitting position, her arm supporting my back. A surgical release form. *Next of kin.* "My parents are dead," I told them. They wrote it down. I always thought I'd say that if I had to. Now I've said it.

Other relatives?

"Lissa Danforth, care of Jake Lyles, twelve twelve Royale Boulevard, New Orleans." I remembered her name and address right through the pain.

Relationship to patient? "Sister."

A day and a half later, I had surgery.

18

The nurse said, "Cough, please, Miz Perretti."

Out of the fog, the blur of drugged sleep starting to recede into only pain, belly like a hot iron was being held there, that voice floated.

"Now, Miz Perretti?" it reprimanded me. "Now you gotta cough, honey, or your lungs'll fill with phlegm and you'll get pneumonia."

Pneumonia? My mind closed again, and I sank back into the cushion of agony and anesthesia.

That voice again, persistent as a mosquito in my ear. "Now you gotta cough, Miz Perretti."

I could no more have coughed than I could have flown to Mars. I had never had surgery before, not even my tonsils out. I had no idea. How could I know what it feels like when they cut you open, snip you open and take out big chunks of your body, and sew you back together? My head ached, my throat ached, I was nauseous and very thirsty, but all of that was shadowed by that great throbbing unhealed hole gashed into me. Time didn't exist, nothing existed except this pain.

"Cough, Miz Perretti. Now I gotta make you cough."

I made a scratching noise in my throat. *Agony.*

"Again."

I repeated it.

"Again."

I repeated it.

"That's good now, just one more time."

I wanted water, to drink and drink and drink deeply, but the pain was too much for me to hold my head up. Nothing but hurting, *throb, throb, throb*, and thirst.

Later. Who was holding the cup?

I opened my eyes at last and saw knees covered by a loose brown skirt. Someone was sitting by my bed. I followed the skirt up to the waist, to the chest and shoulders and face. Lissa!

I jerked involuntarily and gasped with the flare of hurt across my abdomen. It must have shown in my face.

"Pain," I whispered. I think that's what I said. It was so hard to form words, to say them. "How'd you—?" I asked.

"Ssh, ssh, don't talk," said Lissa, her voice soft. "I'm here, it's okay. They think I'm your sister."

And I went back to sleep.

"Well, well, how's the patient?" It was Dr. Besum, all smiles. Lissa was still beside the bed.

"Okay," I whispered. I tried to sit up a bit, but fell back down.

"You had quite an abscess in there, little lady," said Dr. Besum, unbearably cheerful. "Your left ovary was eaten up with it, and your tube. We got the infection out of there, and we got your appendix while we were at it, and we did a lot of scraping. We got all the infection, plus left ovary, left tube, pieces of right tube, appendix. You're doing just *fine*. I don't mind telling you, I was worried when you came in." He leaned over and patted my hand. "If you had waited any longer . . ."

"But what caused it?" I asked. An effort, a huge effort. But I could talk today—right through the pain. Astonishing that I could form words.

Dr. Besum hesitated. He leaned over the bed, closer to me. "Chrysta, dear, I suspect you have been sexually active for quite some time, is that correct? Perhaps a little—indiscriminately?"

My heart gave a wild, fluttery leap of fear. I looked out the corner of my eye at Lissa. I could feel her there, looking at me, direct and strong, willing me to be strong.

"Yes," I said, whispery with pain.

"Well, I suspect what happened is that some time ago you had gonorrhea, probably without knowing it—it's very often asymptomatic in women. And you didn't get it cleared up then. You've probably had a low-grade infection going on in that area for years, and for some reason it just flared up acutely now."

I was silent. I could see the bottle so clearly, lying on a blue-and-white square bandana in my drawer. The left-behind pills that *he* took. I had rotted away inside, secretly, my body in silent agreement with him. Congratulations, Dad. You finally won.

Lissa spoke then. "Dr. Besum," she said seriously, "will my sister need to notify everyone with whom she has had sexual relations since that time?"

"No, no," said Dr. Besum. "By the time it's gotten into the tubes that extensively, it's long past the infectious stage."

As he left the room, Lissa whispered to me, "Well, at least you don't have to write 'em all, thank God. I mean, think of the postage!"

And I laughed. I did, right through the shock.

"I leave you alone for one minute and look at what

happens to you!" said Lissa, shaking her head. Then our eyes met and she said, "Oh, Chris, I'm so sorry. I'm so sorry."

"Chrysta," I corrected her.

"You're improving," she said. "Shithead."

The next morning, the pain was still there, first and overwhelming. But there was clarity now too. No one was in my room—no nurses, no bustling, and no Lissa. Sun through the window. I patted my stomach, cautiously; it was swathed in gauze. I tried to sit up, a little, fell back. My butt hurt! "Turn over, Miz Perretti," the remembered voice in the middle of the night, delivering that relieving sting in the butt, floating through the pain but not stopping it.

A flower arrangement, sitting on a chest of drawers, who had sent that? Daisies and that white cloudlike stuff—baby's breath—and ferns, and yellow chrysanthemums. On my inner arms at the elbow crease, bouquets of a different kind: bruises blossoming purple and yellow. They had taken blood, of course. *What else had they taken?*

A question that left me with a fear as physical as the pain in my abdomen, a fear that soaked and weakened every muscle in the body.

Lissa was there when I asked, later that morning, during morning rounds.

"Dr. Besum, what does this mean to my—I mean, can I still—I can still have kids, right, can't I?"

Dr. Besum frowned, drumming his fingers on the guard rail. He didn't say anything. He didn't look at me.

"Dr. Besum? Well, can I? Will I ever be able to have kids?"

He sighed. "Chrysta," he said, still looking away,

then glancing at me, then away again, "I tried to save as much of the right tube as I could, but—"

I looked at him. Lissa, on the other side of the bed, was staring at him, her hazel eyes huge and round, her electric hair swarming out around her.

"—well, I won't say it's impossible, Chrysta, because, well, what they're doing in reconstructive surgery these days is fantastic. But with that tube severed like that, the egg will just have no way to— You understand? Of course, I *did* save the right ovary. You'll still have periods, you'll still be producing hormones, you won't have to take estrogen . . ." His voice trailed off.

"So I can't have children," I said flatly.

Pain all around.

19

Oh Luke, Luke, I know you say I have to write it out, so I can stop carrying it around, but it's too hard, I can't do it, if I start talking about it, I might never stop, only it wouldn't be talking or writing, it wouldn't be words, it would be crying sobbing howling.

Wait. Stop. I know that's the point. So that I don't keep feeling that way inside. So that I work it out. But what if I can't work it out? What if there are some things that just can't be worked out?

It turned out the chrysanthemums were from the Yeller House crew. I got lots of gifts, and lots of visitors,

Yeller House people, kitchen people, people I knew from just around town or out at Bear Claw. It should have made me feel good but it didn't. It didn't make me feel anything. Except physical pain, and guilt. That old Randy Newman song, "Guilty," kept going through my head.

The pain I doubt will ever heal. I'm sorry, Luke, I just don't think it will.

One of the toughest things was the advice my visitors gave me. Tender, well-meant, think-positive advice that made me screaming crazy angry.

Not that I ever showed it.

There are desires and hopes so deep that they're like breathing or hair growing or blood pumping. They're part of you, much deeper than thought, always and automatically there, beyond anything you can explain or make sense out of.

"It's not the end of the world," I got told. "You can adopt." As if I hadn't already told myself that obvious fact, my brain lecturing my screaming heart like a parent lectures a child. I'd thought about adopting; I'd taken in animals all my life and loved them. I knew that someday I could and probably would do the same for kids. In a hazy, day-dreamy, back-back-back of my mind way, I'd always figured I'd adopt two or three kids someday and then have one of my own. Just one. To know what it was like.

To feel it moving inside me, to watch my belly get rounder and rounder, firm and full with a baby. Of course, I'd have natural childbirth, and he'd be there—the one I had been looking for, found. Lover and friend and partner, the one I had gone to the Lamaze classes with, seen the movies with, done the exercises with. In my labor, his hand would be on my shoulder or massag-

*ing my back. We'd be together, sharing the build-up,
the excitement, me pushing and working, him encouraging,
sharing the climax when our child—is born! Our kid!
Made of both of us, grown in me, but separate now, its
own person: miraculous.*

My deep secret, how long had I had it? My fantasy.

And now, even if I ever did find someone to share my
life with, having a baby would stay a fantasy.

"Look, most people wish they'd never had their kids.
Anyway, it's not such a big deal." Well-meant advice,
cutting me surely as Dr. Besum's scalpel had slid
through my belly and opened it, pulling me apart.

*You think I don't know that? Listen, folks, I'm the one
who ran away when I was thirteen, one-three, got that?
You think I didn't know I wasn't wanted? Wasn't loved?
Or if I was, IF I was, it was so tangled up in everything
else?*

If *I'd* gotten pregnant, if *I'd* had a baby, I wouldn't
have been like my parents. I would have *loved* my
child. I would have let my child know I loved her. Or
him. I wouldn't have tried to force my daughter or son
to be my way. I wouldn't have pretended I was doing
something for my child if it was really for myself.

"Chrysta, your worth as a person, your worth as a
woman, isn't dependent on your ability to bear kids."
So earnestly said: "Just because society tells you you
have to have kids . . ."

My wanting to have kids—which I'd never even
admitted to myself till the surgery *forced* me to it—
God, it went so much deeper than doing what *society*
told me to do. I didn't give a flying fuck about what
society said! I'm the one who dropped out of high
school to pursue a promising career as a drifter,
remember? But my *own* drifter, not society's and not

yours, pal. If I want to have a kid, and if I mourn not being able to, it has nothing to do with society. And worth? My worth as a person, a woman?

I am not sure what my worth is based on, if anything, though I know it's not big tits or the ability to get knocked up. In fact, I may be without worth, unworthy, worthless—that's an opinion my father held. But if I did have "worth," it wouldn't be because I had a nice perfect set of ovaries and could breed with them. You insult me, thinking I'd think that.

This pain at having most of my reproductive organs ripped out has nothing to do with the *outer* world. Not that you could have known my inner world, since *I* didn't even know it until the surgery took me on a guided tour of my own desires, hopes, and dreams. By destroying them.

And my worth, maybe, is that I survived. I'm a survivor. I lived through my parents' abuse, I lived through running away, and I'll live through this (but is that working it out, Luke—just knowing you'll survive?).

A survivor, independent, and self-reliant. And I was, truly, on the road, in Excelsior. But . . .

Deep, way below all that, lay part of my mind and feelings, more like breathing than thinking.

And now Chrysta scrapes the bottom of herself and comes up with: *I'm strong, because I had to be. And I don't want to always have to be. I'm looking, but I haven't found. Looking for . . . ?*

Does it undo my triumphs?

I've never said I wanted to fall in love and have babies someday, never said it even to myself, till now. But I do. Or did. Can't now. Can't. Too late.

It was a good thing I landed in the Excelsior Springs Hospital. It turned out they had some kind of government grant, and in return they had to offer "assistance to the financially disadvantaged," and I was one. So I didn't have to pay the usual fee for a stay in the hospital, which with drugs and all would have come to about $3,000, an amount which staggered me. Instead, I was cheerfully told by the accountant, I would have to pay "only" $1,750 to the hospital plus Dr. Besum's fee, "only" $980. Considering that the most I'd ever had at one time since splitting was $600 when I left Big Sur, it was pretty depressing.

I thought about skipping out on the bill. But I knew I wouldn't. Partly it was just I wanted to stay in Excelsior, but there was something else, that the surgery made me see. "You can't run from trouble." Nettie's saying and Luke's song came to me, lying there. The VD, hidden all those years, had resurfaced because I hadn't taken care of it. That guy who picked me up hitchhiking, Mr. Jenkins, had said, "You've got to take responsibility for yourself in the world *as it is*." The words kept coming back to me as I lay there. As did the fact that I was going to be in hock to Excelsior Springs Hospital and Dr. Besum for the rest of my life. I could just see it, five dollars a month for the next 95 years. But you can't run from trouble.

Except—someone took up a collection for me. If you think this didn't blow my mind, think again.

As Lissa said, "This belongs in *Little House on the Prairie*, kiddo, not real life."

I was pleased and insulted and completely blown away, not in that order, when I found out. After I'd been in the hospital a week, one morning when Lissa was there, Joanie and Luke had visited me with $360. "And there's more too," Joanie said proudly. I freaked.

"Are you behind this, Joanie?" I demanded. "Or is it your bright idea, Luke?"

"I'm not behind anything, Chrysta," Luke said, puzzled. And Joanie added, "A lot of us care about you, Chrysta, and—"

"Oh, God," I said, shaking my head. Another thing to deal with. Sure it would help solve the money problem, but it put me in debt to everyone. Good old no-favors Chrysta. "Joanie, Luke, I appreciate this, but I don't want it. I can pay for it, I already have it planned—I—"

"Oh, cut the crap, Chrysta," Lissa snapped at me suddenly. "Just stop doing that whole number, okay? It bores me to *tears*. I can't believe you're not down on your *knees* thanking Joanie and Luke and Excelsior and your luck."

"I can't take it," I said. "I can't. I'll give it back."

"But Chrysta—" said Joanie.

Lissa cut her off. "You asshole, who are you going to give it back to? Are you going to cremate it and scatter the ashes over Excelsior?"

Luke added, more gently, "Nobody kept a list, Chrysta: fifty cents, Jane Smith; Tom Jones, two twenty-five; you can't give it back."

"It would've taken a hell of a lot of fifty centses to make up three hundred and sixty bucks, you guys, and I don't know that many people here. I mean, I just feel like, oh, I bet Susan and Hoot gave more than they should have, I know they've got some savings but it's for their house in the country, and—"

"Maybe they *liked* giving you money, Chrysta, maybe it made them feel good." That was Luke. And Joanie added, "Please, Chrysta, dear, I didn't know you'd get so upset about this."

"She—is—NOT—upset," said Lissa, glaring at me. "God, I don't believe you, jerk. You're just too much." She shook her head. "People love you, get it? L—O—

V—E? Like valentines? Just because your parents hated you doesn't mean the whole world has to hate you. You're incredibly stupid."

But Luke finally put me at my ease. "Look, don't take it so damn personally, Chrysta! People just kind of look after each other here. It's no big deal. I've lived here all my life, I've seen it done a lot. One of the kids I went to school with got cancer; people raised a lot of money for his medical expenses. *Thousands* of dollars. And when Larry Evans, the mechanic—you know him? —when he had to move his garage because the building got sold, about five or six bands—Gaskin's Switch, Flying Heart Band, Friendly Power Trio, I played a few songs solo—we got together and threw a boogie with a three-dollar admission tab for him. Billed it as Thank Heavens for Evans and raised him twelve hundred dollars."

I listened. I didn't know what to say. Luke said, "All it means is you're part of Excelsior Springs, Chrysta. This is your home now."

And corny as it sounds, tears sprang to my eyes.

Lissa was at the hospital with me every, though not all, day. She was staying at Yeller House, having grudgingly conceded that though she still thought Excelsior was a "dinky little town out in the sticks" there was "a lot going on." She filled me in on her New Orleans life: She had worked briefly at a strip club but quit and was now waitressing. She had a new boyfriend, Peter, who played trumpet in the streets. I brought her up to date, too. When I told her about Howie her face darkened. "That bastard. I hope he gets his ass nailed." She shook her head. "You shouldn't have to deal with that."

"Look, I'll have to get a job somewhere else, that's all."

"I say nail his ass," said Lissa grimly.

Nettie came to visit a few times. Once, trying to keep a straight face, she brought a card from Cleota. It was one of those real tacky ones, with the 23rd Psalm on it in fancy script.

"Nice sentiment, considerin' the angel of peace it comes from, don't you think, Chrysta, honey?"

"Nettie, don't make me laugh, *please*, it hurts too much."

Nettie ignored me. "Yes, that ol' picture a Christian tolerance told me, as she gave me this *nice* card, 'At least she ain't *here* a-pourin' *orange juice* over the chicken!'"

Luke stopped by to see me too, quick, friendly visits.

But one day, on one of Luke's visits, a line was crossed, a line between friendship and something else.

He came in with his guitar in one hand, a bunch of very scraggly flowers in the other. "I thought I'd play you a song or two today," he said.

"Fine."

The late-afternoon sun coming through the window gave Luke an elongated shadow. That was the only moment there was: late-afternoon sun, Luke and his shadow. And, of course, the pain. I watched Luke and his shadow from my bed.

"You know Dare? That, uh, little waif hippie kid who hangs around the hotel?" I nodded. "Well, of course you do. He heard you were sick and he tried to come visit you, but they wouldn't let him in because he was under fourteen. So he sent you these." Luke waved the bedraggled bouquet of wild sweet peas, Queen Anne's lace, and a few snapdragons and zinnias, doubtless ripped off from the hotel's garden.

"I'm surprised," I said. I couldn't imagine Dare dropping his tough-guy act long enough to send anyone flowers. "Nice."

Luke continued, "Yeah, he tried to tell 'em he was sixteen, but they laughed him right out of the place. Pissed him off, I'll tell you. He's just twelve, you know, and with that baby face of his he looks even younger. Anyhow, he sent these with me."

Again I thought about my real age, sixteen, and how I would only *just* have been allowed in to visit someone in the hospital. Poor Dare.

"Well, thank him for me," I said.

Luke brought the flowers over and set them in a glass on the small table next to my bed. The colors were bright, impatient against the white room. I looked up to see Luke looking at me.

"Chrysta, I've been thinking about you a lot lately," he said softly. "I'm *so* sorry this had to happen to you."

"'S okay," I said. "*Had* to happen? I still haven't figured that one out."

He shook his head, reached up, and smoothed his mustache with one hand, such sadness on his face, and kindness in his brown eyes. Luke never offered me advice, never tried to make light of what I was feeling.

Now he said, too quickly, "Well! I brought my guitar; I thought some music might cheer you up."

"That depends on what you sing," I said, only half joking, thinking of Randy Newman's "Guilty," which was still going through my head often.

Luke laughed. He knelt to unbuckle his guitar case.

"No, I'm serious," I said. How could he know about me and Randy? And then, to my surprise, I told him. Immediately, he sang a few bars of it:

"Oh, I'm guilty
Yes I'm guilty
And I'll be guilty all the rest of my life
'Cause I never do

What I'm s'posed to do
Nothin' I ever do seems to turn out right."

"I'm surprised you know it," I said. "That doesn't seem
like your kind of song."

"'Guilty,'" he said, "is one song everybody knows."

He tuned his guitar and began to sing softly, standing at the foot of my bed, rocking slightly back and
forth. One of his own songs:

"You say you're frozen in your life,
frozen in the ice of your days.
You think you're cold and you're still,
enclosed by your will and your ways,
and you've been waiting for someone
with that special touch of fire,
to take you from this place...."

I too was waiting, waiting for someone. But unlike
the girl in the song, I hadn't been frozen. I had acted,
moved, left, saved myself—sort of. I had survived.

"Luke, you're *so* good," I said. Then I added, teasing,
"I thought you were going to cheer me up, though.
That one makes me want to go drink Lysol."

"Oh, I forgot," he said. "Usually I just play whichev-
er song comes into my head. I guess that wasn't too
cheerful, huh? Let's see now—"

"Wait," I said. "Luke, who was she? The girl who
was frozen in her life?"

He pulled up a chair and sat, guitar across his knees.
He sighed. "There was this girl I used to go out with in
high school here; she was from Berryville. Real sweet
girl, bad scene at home. She couldn't wait to leave
home, but she wasn't going to do it the hard way, like
find a job and move out or figure out some way to go to

college. She was just going to find someone she could marry and then she'd live happily ever after. I was on the list of possibilities." He grimaced. "She wound up marrying a guy who works in the chicken plant. She's eighteen now. They have twins." He stopped abruptly.

"No, go on," I said.

"That's about it, really. After that, I got myself involved with a hippie girl here in Excelsior. I was crazy about her. I'd see her on weekends. She was a couple of years older than me, and . . . She was my first real lover, if you want to know the truth."

Again, Luke stopped.

"Well, what happened?"

"I'm not boring you?"

I shook my head.

"Well, I don't tell this to many people—" Luke hesitated, then smiled wryly. "But it turned out she had somebody else at the same time. *Several* somebodies. . . . I'm sorry, Chrysta, I keep forgetting I'm supposed to cheer you up."

"This girl—did you like her a lot? Did you love her?" I asked. Lissa and I had talked about love and being in love, but I'd never had this kind of conversation with a boy. I felt excited—like I was on the edge of grasping something that had always been just out of reach.

"Oh, I was crazy about her. But looking back and trying to understand it later, I think it was just sex. Just turn-on. She was a *fox*! And her being my first and so experienced, and me an innocent seventeen, I couldn't get enough. Would you like to hear a song about *her*?"

He sounded so eager, I smiled. "Sure."

"It's not cheerful either."

"That's okay."

"In fact," he said happily, "it's one of my most depressing songs.

"I still keep that old coat you gave me,
though my reasons have all changed.
I used to wear it to get back at you,
my cloak of bitterness, my faded coat of hate.

"And I laughed when I told Stephen,
it was the only good thing that I'd got
from all those hours I thought I shared with you,
from all that time we had lost.

"We were lovers, never friends.
I'm old enough to know that's no good.
I thought the passion might just hold us,
but I knew it never could."

When he stopped, he said, "Wait, don't say anything. Here's a cheerful one."

He began "Rainbow Blues," that John Sebastian song that goes "I'll paint rainbows all over your blues." But he wasn't five lines into it when a skinny, witchlike nurse with dyed black hair in a hairnet rolled in.

"This is a *hospital*, young man!"

"I know," said Luke softly. "I'm sorry if I was too loud."

"Too loud!" the nurse snorted. "There's a man who's in the next room who's *critically* ill! He's dying!"

"And *heaven* forbid," said Luke, "that he should hear *music* playing when he dies!" She sniffed and exited, but Luke and I, we looked at each other and smiled.

20

"Howie's on probation, Howie's on probation!" Steve Darwin sang as he danced into my hospital room the next day.

"What, what? Did he get busted?" I tried to sit up, but it still hurt too much. "Crank this bed up and tell me what you're talking about."

"Not until we've had our din-din," he chided me, then dramatically pulled the foil from a paper plate. "Voilà! What 'ave we 'ere? For ze dinner tonight, for mademoiselle, we 'ave ze rice aux brown, salade chez Maison Yeller, and ze quiche spinach."

"Lissa must have cooked," I observed. Quiche was Lissa's one fancy vegetarian dish. I had eaten her quiche ten times in our three weeks together in L.A.

"You are right, Mademoiselle Lissa eez ze chef." He changed voices. "Now eat up, lambikins, and let Stevie tell you the news. First off, our precious kitchen lost close to eleven thousand dollars this summer—they just did the books."

I put down my fork. *Eleven thousand dollars?*

"It's *easy* to blow eleven grand if you know *all* the wrong things to do," said Steve. "And do them. I'm surprised it isn't more. It would've been if Luke hadn't been covering Howie so well."

I nodded slowly, remembering the biscuit hassle. "But eleven thousand dollars!"

"Don't look so surprised—Howie was a *genius*, you know that," Steve reminded me. "Remember the T-bones he put out to thaw on top of the unused fridge behind the salad area and then forgot to tell anybody about them and they spoiled? A case. And a case of thirty-five T's alone is two hundred and ten, two hundred and twenty dollars. And when you think of the leftovers that got thrown out, and the fresh vegetables that stayed in the walk-in and rotted—"

"I guess I can see how Howie did it, then," I said slowly. "It's just hard to believe. Eleven thousand dollars."

"Well, you *better* believe it," said Steve. "Hugh Dewling is watching Howie like a *hawk*. One false move and—" Steve drew his finger across his throat.

And the next day, as if to prove it, I had my most surprising visitor yet. Hugh Dewling himself, the grand old man, came to see me.

"Chrysta, you've been working in my kitchen how long?" he asked, pulling up a chair next to my bed and making himself at home.

"About two months," I said, wary. I recalled Nettie telling me that he knew everything that went on but was just an old softie.

"Well, I'm conducting a little investigation," he said, eyebrows drawn sternly together. "We've had a considerable shortfall this year and I intend to get to the *bottom* of it!" He banged his hand emphatically on the bedside table. "You see, Chrysta, I am a very wealthy man and I got that way by an *unceasing* determination to get to the bottom of things. And I'm not afraid to get my hands dirty."

I nodded, wondering if there was something in the

air at the GP that made everybody connected with the hotel wacko, like that dust from pigeon droppings that caused Legionnaire's Disease at that hotel in Philadelphia that time.

"And the mismanagement of the kitchen is a matter which I *personally* must investigate."

"How come you don't have a Southern accent like Howie does?" I asked, suddenly. Oh, great, act like an idiot, Chrysta; you're only talking to Hugh Dewling, who owns the General's Palace, just say any old thing that comes into your head.

Hugh Dewling seemed taken aback. "I, ah, oh, yes, Howie. I attended Columbia University in New York City, that's why I have no accent. I suppose you know Howie is my nephew."

I nodded.

"Well, makes no difference. Got to get to the bottom of things. Nettie Carlisle said I should talk to you. Said you could tell me about the day-to-day operations of the kitchen as well as she could. She also said that you could tell me, quote, something about Howie that I ought to know, unquote."

I remained silent. So Luke had told Nettie about the carriage house episode.

"Of course," added Hugh Dewling, "I am talking to *all* my employees in my efforts at investigation."

"What do you want to know exactly?" I asked warily.

Instead of answering me, Hugh Dewling lit a cigar, applying the light several times and exhaling clouds of gray smoke. "You know," he said, "that Nettie Carlisle is quite a woman. *She* should be running the kitchen. Offered her the job, but she turned it down. No ambition. Mind if I smoke?"

"Yes," I said. It was a little late. The whole room was already floating in a vile mist.

"Oh!" said Hugh Dewling, startled. He hunted for an ashtray. "Why didn't you say so earlier?"

"You didn't ask me earlier."

He glared at me, got up, and went into the bathroom to put it out, returning with the cigar, now unlit. He chewed on it as he continued.

"So I asked Nettie Carlisle if she'd kinda keep an eye on things, let me know if—things were working out. Well, she said, 'No sir, if yer askin' me to be a stool pigeon, I will not.' Spirited. Which tickled me, to tell you the truth. I like that about these Ozark people. Blunt. Then I said, 'Well, Nettie, if I check in with you once in a while, will you let me know your opinion?' 'Yessir,' she said, 'I'll do that much. If'n you ask me the questions, I'll give you the answers.'" He paused again, to chomp on his cigar, as he gazed thoughtfully out the window. Suddenly his eyes focused and he looked straight at me. "That's like you. No answers unless I ask the questions."

"Well, I don't know what kind of things you're interested in." I was hedging.

"Bull-dookey! I'm interested in recouping the eighteen thousand five hundred dollar shortfall it appears that my nephew has managed to run that kitchen into in just four short months; is that clear?"

"It's clear," I said. I couldn't wait to tell Steve Darwin that his figures were off by $6,500.

"Sorry I, ah, raised my voice. I got carried away."

"So did your nephew." The minute I said it I couldn't *believe* I had. No tact.

"Just what the hell do you mean?" bellowed Hugh Dewling. "Are you going to sit here all day, or are you going to answer my damn questions?"

"*Ask* your damn questions, then."

"You're spirited too," he said. He looked at me contemplatively. "I like that. You a good cook?"

"People tell me I am."

"What do *you* think?"

"I think, yes, I'm pretty good. I do a lot of the sort of foreign stuff. Chicken à l'orange, swedish meatballs, uh, lasagna—"

"You know how to make cheese enchiladas?"

"Yessir."

"I'm crazy about greaser food. You make cheese enchiladas for me sometime, then we'll see how good a cook you are."

"Okay." I was starting to like crazy old Hugh Dewling. I could see his game was to try to intimidate you, but he liked it if you stood up to him.

"Well, Chrysta Perretti, what do you think of Luke Beauford?"

"Sir?"

"How does Luke Beauford measure up?"

"Oh, he's a real hard worker, Mr. Dewling. I mean, he's officially a dishwasher, but he helps everybody in the place, he helps the cooks, he does stock—he refills the waitress station when it's busy out front."

"Does he get along with everybody pretty well?"

"Well, yes, he does—except for with your nephew—"

"Forget Howie's my nephew. So Howie and Luke don't get along?"

"Right."

"*Why?*" Hugh Dewling leaned forward, narrowing his eyes, chomping his cigar. He looked like a detective in a movie hot onto a clue.

"I don't really know," I said, fidgeting.

"Take a guess," said Hugh Dewling. "Forget Howie's my nephew and take a guess." His eyes glittered.

"All right," I said recklessly. "Howie's jealous of Luke because Luke's better and works harder and just stays more on top of things. And everybody in the kitchen knows what's going on and likes Luke better."

"Damnit, *now* we're getting somewhere!" said Dewling triumphantly, pounding his fist on his knee. "No one, not even Nettie Carlisle, would come out with it. They all think that since Howie's m' damn nephew I wouldn't want to hear the truth! Hell's bells, anybody in *my* employ has to work his tail off, nephew or no!" He chomped his cigar a few times and then removed it from his mouth. "What," he asked slowly, "was the something Nettie Carlisle told me you'd tell me that I should know about?"

And I told him.

The next day Luke brought me a memo, folded into an envelope. *General's Palace Hotel, from the desk of Hugh Dewling*, it said at the top. Then, in scrawly handwriting, *Please call me when you're out of the hospital and ready to work again. Get well soon. H.D.*

"Good news?" Luke asked.

"I think so," I said cautiously.

"I thought it might be," he said.

21

I spent ten days in the hospital, and a month after that at Yeller House recovering. I got tired easily, and I slept a lot, but I went for a walk every day, and every day the walk got a little longer. Still, I was surprised at how long I hurt. The bleeding grew less and less and finally I quit wearing a Kotex. Finally I went out to Bear Claw, and for the first time I felt embarrassed being naked there. They had shaved me between the legs and the hair was just beginning to grow back. And just above where my pubic hair would have ended was a thin, bright-red line, curved up a little at the ends, like a kid's crayon-line drawing of a smile.

("Poor Chrysta," Lissa said when I lifted my skirt one day to show her the scar. I'd been crying, and she said, "Crying on the outside, smiling on the inside.")

Since the surgery I was more than ever two people; one who laughed, jived, worked, gradually recovered; one who didn't. Just like always, only more so.

One month and eleven days after the Sunday night when Joanie had driven me to the emergency room, I called Hugh Dewling and set up an appointment to see him the next day.

His office, on the main floor of the hotel, looked out on the carefully combed green grass and the flower-bed-circled fountain. The seasons had changed while I was sick. From spring tulips we had gone to summer zinnias and petunias.

Hugh Dewling sat with his back to the window, facing the door. He was behind a huge, heavy, antique-looking desk. My feet sank into a dark-red oriental carpet as I walked in.

"Sit down," Hugh Dewling said, indicating one of two red leather armchairs. I sat.

"Are you better?"

I nodded.

"Hearty? Capable of hard work?"

"I think so, sir."

"Thinking so's not enough."

"I'm sure then."

Dewling stared at me thoughtfully, his crazy eyebrows drawn.

"I have often thought," he said, "that I would like to write a book on the use of intuition in managing." He stared some more. "You can make your cost projections, your ROI's—that's 'return on investments,' Chrysta—but finally, you've got to use your intuition. Hell's bells, I'm a wealthy man, Chrysta. I didn't get that way by being a fool, you get my gist?"

I nodded.

"I take pride, Chrysta, in knowing every single one of my employees by name. They may not *know* I know 'em, but I do. Now I love people, Chrysta, God bless 'em, but you can't take your eyes off 'em for a minute. Can't tell a damn thing by blood, either."

He cleared his throat and fell silent. I shifted in the red leather chair, which was sticking to the backs of my legs.

"Now, when I hired that bastard, 'scuse my French, Chrysta, but I know you young people swear all the time, because he was related to me, *I didn't listen to my own intuition and I violated good common-sense business practice!*" He shook his head.

"My nephew's a lying, cheating, womanizing sonofabitch. Wouldn't mind that, but he can't do a job either, haw! That's a joke there, Chrysta, laugh. But that little old Nettie Carlisle, now *her* nephew is hard working, decent, has ambition and spirit. Pluck. It's the goddamnedest thing. Howie is a thirty-three-year-old teenage cheat; her nineteen-year-old is a *man*. Who can do a *job*." He paused and buzzed his secretary. "Send in Luke Beauford from the kitchen, please."

Luke came in, in jeans and a T-shirt with a white apron still tied over it. He was grinning.

"Beauford, siddown," barked Hugh Dewling.

"Yessir." Luke plopped into the other red leather armchair. Its cushion gave a wheezy sigh.

"You remember what I told you when I called you in here the day I fired Howie?"

"Yessir."

"Well, tell Chrysta what I told you. Lemme see how good a memory you got, Beauford." Dewling was trying to look stern, but you could tell he was enjoying himself.

Luke turned to me. "Well, Chrysta, after Mr. Dewling met you, he called me in and told me he was going to fire Howie, and asked me would I be interested in being kitchen manager and did I think you'd make a good assistant. I said yes to both questions, but explained I could only do it till early fall because I intended to go back to school. Well, Mr. Dewling wasn't too pleased with that—"

"Don't mince words, boy," roared Dewling. "I told you your ass was where your head ought to be if you could turn down an offer like I was making you!"

"Right," said Luke mildly. "Well, he asked me if I'd still come over weekends during the fall and I said I would, like I did last year. Then he asked me if you had any plans to—I believe the phrase was 'go gallivanting off to school or some other damn fool place this fall or winter,' and I said no, as far as I knew you didn't but I wasn't sure. I said I thought you liked Excelsior Springs and were planning to stick around. And he said, well, how about if he made me kitchen manager and you assistant kitchen manager, with me more or less training you all summer. Then, in the fall, you'd be *acting* kitchen manager during the week when I was in Fayetteville."

"I don't believe this," I said slowly.

"We'd both get a lot more money than we're making now. *But* we'd have to prove we could turn the kitchen around, at least break even by the end of the season."

"But . . ." I said. "Well, this is all very . . . nice, but, uh, I don't know the first thing about running a kitchen. I'm a good cook, but—"

"I told Beauford here," put in Hugh Dewling, "that I was aware of that but I was willing to take that risk."

"But *why*?" I said, looking from Dewling to Luke and back to Dewling.

"Intuition," said Hugh Dewling, "and common sense."

"But wait, you haven't heard the rest," said Luke. "If you and I work out here together, Mr. Dewling wants to send you to kitchen management and chef school over in Fayetteville, at the Vo-Tech, during the winter when the hotel's closed."

"Now I *really* don't believe this," I said, dazed.

"You don't have to decide now," Hugh Dewling told me. "Decide at the end of the season. Work here till then. A good kitchen manager is goddamned hard to find, y'see. If you import one from one of the big cities they want an arm and a leg to come to an out-of-the-way place like Excelsior Springs. I want to get someone who *likes* Excelsior and is willing to stay here, and someone who likes the old hotel. Someone spirited. I'm taking a long shot, Chrysta. I think you might do it for me."

"I don't believe this," I said. I stared out the window at the fountain.

"Give her the bottom line, Beauford," barked Dewling.

"Well, right now, you're making about five hundred dollars a month take-home, like I was as dishwasher. Mr. Dewling is prepared to pay me fifteen hundred take-home as kitchen manager and you a thousand take-home as assistant, *if* by the end of the season we have the kitchen breaking even. He's also offering you the carriage house to live in. If things work out and he sends you to school, he'll pay all your school expenses plus six hundred dollars a month to live on, with a guaranteed job as kitchen manager next season, with me as *your* assistant."

"My God," I said, staring first at one of them, then at the other. "I just don't believe it."

"Tell her to stop saying that," said Mr. Dewling. "I hate all this negative thinking."

"Stop saying you don't believe it," said Luke. "Mr. Dewling believes that you have to think positively."

"But if you knew how badly I need money," I said, still dazed. "I mean after the surgery and all . . ."

"You've got a lot to learn, young lady," said Hugh Dewling sternly. "Never tell your employer you need money. You get paid what you're worth, not what you need. I'll expect you to work your tail off for me. If you don't, I'll have no qualms about booting you out. Remember that."

"Yessir," I said.

"So think about it," said Hugh Dewling.

22

When I told Lissa about it, she said, "And so Chrysta moved to Excelsior Springs and lived happily ever after."

"Makes you think I might've been right, eh?" I said, gloating. "About getting good vibes from Excelsior?"

"Girl, let me tell you, you have the most *bizarre* luck of anyone I've ever met. One minute you're at death's door. Next thing, a rich old geezer decides you're hot, puts you on the fast track, and makes you a career woman. You are the only person I've ever known who made *my* life look boring."

"Make you want to stick around?" I asked, teasing, knowing that now I was better she'd return to New Orleans any day. To my astonishment Lissa replied, "Well, I'm thinking about it, kiddo, believe it or not. If I can figure out a way to get Peter up here, I might just do that. You make it sound so *exciting*."

It should have been happily ever after. I moved into the carriage house, the most beautiful place I'd ever lived in in my entire life, and *mine*. I kept it very clean, and I had morning routines I loved—yoga exercises, poached egg for breakfast, and watering my plants. I had an angel-wing begonia and some Wandering Jew Nettie had given me when she divided her houseplants, and I spent thirty dollars of my paycheck one week to buy two beautiful hand-thrown pottery planters at The Springs Pottery, downtown. Gleaming and alive in their ribbed, shiny pots, those plants made me feel the carriage house was *home*, not just a place to stay. I loved them.

My body had recovered from the surgery, and now, with time alone and quiet and my own space, my head and feelings began to slowly recover, too. I missed the atmosphere at Yeller House, but of course I could visit.

Lissa had taken my room there temporarily, and I still spent lots of time there. But it was so good to come home to my own clean place and be by myself.

I worked at the kitchen during the same hours I had before, but with an extra hour in the morning when Luke and I worked together. He showed me about doing stock, ordering, and estimating costs. He asked me to come up with a regular rotating biweekly menu for the buffet line, so we could order the same ingredients day in and day out and standardize our recipes. I did, and I enjoyed it.

Luke liked my garlic biscuit idea—and the biscuits were popular in the dining room, too. We started making a cake each day, in addition to Cleota's pies, and we got the waitresses to fix a fancy dessert tray and wave it in front of the customers, saying "Care for any dessert?" Most tourists seemed to find it irresistible. We pulled in a lot of bucks with those desserts. On them alone, in the first two weeks of our regime, we pulled in $1,293. As I became aware of the figures—the bottom line, as Mr. Dewling called it—I saw how Howie had managed to blow all that money. I loved running a kitchen, and it was a whole different number from just cooking (though I still enjoyed that, too). I began to think that I really would take Mr. Dewling up on his offer and go to Vo-Tech in the winter.

It ought to have worked out. I ought to have paid my dues by that time: gone through my bad stuff, started learning to be happy.

But I hadn't, and I didn't.

23

The heat of August hit, all at once. One night I walked downtown to sit out on the bench. I was depressed. It was hot, sticky, about to rain—and my scar twinged and ached. *I'm an old lady at sixteen,* I thought. *My body feels it when it's going to rain.*

And there was Dare on the bench. It was the first time I'd seen him since before I went into the hospital.

"Hey, Dare! Thanks for the flowers! How've you been?" I said, sitting down.

"Okay." He looked scruffy, as usual, but he seemed a lot less lively. He swung his legs back and forth listlessly, his shoulders slumped over. He had a long stick he was scratching back and forth on the sidewalk. He wasn't smiling, but it wasn't that put-on tough, unaffected punk act either: This was real. He looked the way I remembered feeling those last years at home.

"What's wrong?" I said.

"Nothin'."

He continued playing with the stick, now running it down a crack in the sidewalk. His dirty hair hung down, an uneven curtain around his face. He looked pitiful.

"I'm kind of down tonight, too," I said. "My scar really hurts, I think because it's going to rain. It makes me feel like I'm an old lady."

Dare glanced at me with a flicker of interest, then went back to fiddling with his stick.

I continued, "And the scar hurting reminds me that I can't have kids anymore. Because of that surgery. I didn't know how much I wanted to have kids till I found out that I couldn't."

"Why would you want to bring 'em into this shitass world?" He paused, swung his hair out of his face, then sat up a little straighter. "Say, you got any weed on you?"

"No," I said.

"Cigarette?"

"No."

"Well, d'you have a quarter?" Dare knew I was always good for a quarter. But not that night.

"No, Dare, I went out of the house without any money."

"Oh." He went back to scuffing his feet on the pavement. I wished there was something I could do for him.

"Hey, listen, Dare," I said, getting an idea. "You know I'm cooking up at the hotel—well, sometime, if you want, I could get you a meal up there."

He straightened up and looked at me real excited. "You mean, like, in that big, fancy dining room?"

"No, no, just in the kitchen." He looked crestfallen, so I added, to make it more of a big deal, "You know, like behind the scenes with the people who really *run* the place. Like an *insider*."

He brightened up again. "You think I could?"

"I think *maybe* you could. We have a policy about nobody on kitchen staff eating for free until after we pull the line—that means take the food from the buffet back into the kitchen. If there's enough of what's left over to *save*, then the kitchen staff's not allowed to eat it. But if there's three quarters of a pan or less of something, we can eat it, free. I have to check, but I think I could feed you on the leftovers."

Dare grinned—and elbowed me in the ribs conspiratorially. "But I guess, even if there's no leftovers, since you work there you could always slip me something, eh, Chrysta?"

I straightened up indignantly. "Since I work there, Dare, I try to see that the rules are *kept*, not broken!"

"Oh!" Dare seemed surprised. Then he looked at me. "Hey, could you get me some food *tonight*? Like *now*?"

I felt terrible. Here I'd gotten his hopes up and—

"I'm really sorry, Dare, I'd like to, but like I said, I have to check it out. Come up around nine some night and I— Or come over to my house now if you want, I could fix you something."

"Never mind," said Dare. He sounded so disappointed. "It don't matter anyway."

"Listen, does anyone know anything about that kid Dare, who hangs out around town a lot?"

Rick, toking on a joint, nodded as he inhaled, then, passing it to Joanie, exhaled and answered, "Well, I know a little about him. What d'you want to know?"

It was around nine-thirty at night. We were all sitting comfortably around the remains of Lissa's good-bye dinner at Yeller House. She was going back to New Orleans the next day, to persuade Peter to come back up with her. If she succeeded, she'd be back in a week or two, with all her stuff and Peter's loaded in the back of the old Chevy he owned. If she didn't, we might not see her again for a while. So Joanie, Rick, Steve, Susan, and Hoot had made her a special send-off dinner.

They'd waited till I got there to cut the cake: a honey-carrot cake with cream cheese icing.

"Well, where does Dare live? Whose kid is he?" My meeting with Dare the day before had bothered me. Looking back I'd realized that *all* my meetings with Dare, from the first time I'd met him, had bothered me.

"He's a pretty far-out little dude in some ways," said Rick. Lissa sighed exaggeratedly; she still had trouble with Rick's "hippieisms," as she called them. Rick never noticed Lissa's sighs, though, and her sarcasm went right by him. "He's pretty fucked up though. Mellow till you get to know the kid, but he'll shore rip y'off in a hurry, if y'don't keep your eye on him."

"Yeah, but what's the *story* behind him?" I said impatiently, passing the joint without toking to Lissa, who drew deeply.

"Well, let's see. He used to stay with Fran Winters; I think he still does sometimes. She lives out not too far from Ozarka Lake—you know her?"

I shook my head.

"As I understand this—I may not have this straight—Fran used to be friends with a girl named Ginger. And Ginger used to live with Dare's daddy. In Dallas."

"Was Ginger Dare's mother?"

"Oh nooo. No-no-no-no-no," said Rick. "Ginger was just, like, one of Dare's father's girl friends." The joint came around to him, and he toked again.

"*One* of?" asked Lissa. She looked pretty, in a flow-ered halter-top dress. "Already I can tell I'm not going to like this guy." Hoot got up and began to clear the table.

"So Dare's daddy, his name was Darrell too, Darrell, uh, Wilkie I think it was—"

Hoot, standing at the sink, put down the plates and

turned, staring at Rick. "Darrell *Wilkie*?" he said, astonished. "From Dallas, right?"

"Right," Rick nodded. "Right, right."

"Was he, uh, kind of a short dude, muscular, dark hair—?"

"I don't know, I never met the fella, this is all just what I heard from Dare and a little bit from Fran."

"God, I bet it's the same dude. I know him, I'm sure it's the same Darrell Wilkie. Now ain't that something? I just bet it is. How many Darrell Wilkies can there be in Dallas?"

"D'you know him from school or what?" asked Susan, her head tipped to one side.

"No, from when I was roadie for Willow Tree. I used to take care of gettin' their dope for 'em, used to buy cocaine for 'em—that was, like, one of my duties. And I got it from a dude named Darrell Wilkie. In Dallas. Seems to me like I remember there being a real young kid around that apartment, yeah; now this was five or six years ago . . ."

"Well, Dare would only have been six then," I put in.

"Right." Hoot shook his head. "I just bet it's the same dude. Darrell Wilkie. Amazing. I don't remember a Ginger, though. Seem's to me like Darrell Wilkie's lady at that time was a girl named Mary Ann . . ."

"Oh, he went through *lotsa* girls," said Rick. "Least that's what I got from Fran and Dare both. Now Dare, of course, he's real proud of it, always tellin' me about this chick and that chick that his father made it with." Lissa and Joanie both grimaced. "Pardon the expression, ladies, *chick*'s just how Dare puts it. Fran was pretty down on Dare's father. She said he made a career of livin' offa women, between dealin' coke and ever' so often workin' as a cook. Though he called himself an artist. She felt like he really ripped off her friend Ginger, and she was one in a long line."

"Anybody want more cake?" said Hoot. "If not, I'm going to put it away. It's drawin' flies." He stood up with the cake. "I'm sure it's the same dude," he added, shaking his head, as he opened the drawer where old plastic bags were kept. "He *was* kind of a prick."

"But that doesn't explain how Dare got here. From Dallas and his dad to Excelsior and Fran Winters," I said.

"Well, I'm getting 'round to it, hold your horses, darlin'," said Rick. "'S much as I understand, Dare got into some kind of trouble at school or with the police— anyway, his daddy felt like he had to get Dare out of Dallas in a hurry. And he remembers this friend of Ginger's—he and Ginger have long since broken up, 'member—this friend of Ginger's, Fran Winters, who used to get along real well with Dare."

"Holy shit," said Lissa, shaking her head. "That poor kid. Give your son to a friend of a friend, that's a great solution!"

"And so, anyway, he, the daddy, Darrell Wilkie, he 'members this Fran," continued Rick. "And he remembers she moved away from Dallas to do a back-to-the-land trip somewhere in Arkansas. He checks it out, finds out where, drives up to Excelsior, and more or less just lays Dare on Fran."

"No phone call first?" I asked. "He didn't write a letter or something first?"

"Are you kiddin'?" said Rick, laughing.

"A letter," said Hoot, "would *definitely* not be that dude's style."

"I knew it the minute you said 'one of' his girl

friends," said Lissa, tightening her lips. "Oooo, I hate guys like that. Peter Pans. Never grow up. Babies making babies. I've known a million of 'em."

"You're not exactly Miss Responsibility yourself," I teased her.

"You can bet if I had a kid, though, I'd be responsible," said Lissa fiercely. She was dead serious. "And you would be too."

Joanie, who had been listening intently, nodded, pushing back her wire rims. "Me too," she said. "It's different when you've got a kid."

"And it's always the *girl* who gets stuck with the kid, you notice?" said Lissa vehemently.

"Oh, come on," said Hoot. "Don't generalize, Lissa."

"Not always," said Susan slowly, "but most of the time. Look at how many single mothers there are in this town, Hoot."

"*I've* sure seen 'em around here," said Lissa, grimly wrinkling her eyes, somewhere between disgust and pity. "All over town, draggin' ass. The single-mom cakewalk. They have long hair, and a long skirt on, and the kid is always in the damn backpack, and they have this sort of spaced-out, distracted, *sad* kind of look—"

Me, I was silent. I was thinking about being a mother, and about having the option of being one taken away from me, about if I would have been a good mother—I was thinking about Dare, too.

"I just have this one thing to say," said Rick mildly, looking up from the joint he was rolling. "Dare's father may be for shit, but I've never heard *nothin'* about his mama."

Almost a week later the latched screen door at the back of the kitchen rattled one night. "Chrysta!" hissed a voice.

I looked up, clipboard in hand. I had just checked off all the ingredients for Swiss Steak—which we call Swiss Mistake.

I put down my clipboard, walked over to the door, and peered out into the dark.

"*Dare!*" I said. I immediately unlatched the screen. "Hey, Dare, I'm glad to see you!"

"You are?" he said as he came in, blinking in the light.

"Sure," I said, and without thinking about it, I leaned over and ruffled his hair—he was such a cute kid. He didn't seem to mind.

"Remember—" he hesitated—"the other night when—" He stopped.

"When I said I thought you could come eat here? Yeah, I remember." I'd asked Luke and he'd said it was okay.

He grinned that terrific wholehearted grin that had won me over the day we met.

"Well, can I, like, eat here *tonight*?" His eyes were wide, looking up at me expectantly.

"Well, sure, uh, like, hey, man," I said, teasing him.

And that's how I first started feeding Dare.

Nearly every night just after nine there'd come this little whisper from the screen door, and I'd let him in and I'd fix him a plate of leftovers. I'd be finishing up the kitchen chores, and he'd gobble the food up and go back into the night before I could say very much. But I felt so drawn to him, though I couldn't have said why.

Finally, one night, I said, "Hey, Dare, if you'd like to earn your meals you could come around eight-thirty and help out, you know? Help pull the line, bus tables, maybe, stack the clean dishes."

Dare looked at me, suspicious.

"Okay," he finally said, with a long, dramatic sigh as

though he were committing to building a pyramid, or some other unbearably difficult labor.

24

August was pretty busy, but everyone told me there would be a slowdown the first few weeks in September, at back-to-school time. Then—bang! October would hit. October, when the leaves changed. Every day more tour groups called to reserve lunches or dinners. Soon the reservations calendar on the desk was completely filled up for October.

I remember one day in September standing at the sink, rinsing cabbages and looking out the window at the pool and the tourists lounging there. There was this teenage girl there with dark hair, who looked a little like me, my build and coloring. She was wearing a tiny bright-pink bikini and sunglasses, lying on a deck chair, sunbathing. A boy with longish hair pulled himself up out of the pool, came over to her, and sat down. I could see her laughing. Was he her brother, boyfriend, somebody she'd just met? One by one I rinsed each cabbage, the water cold on my fingers. An older couple—her parents, I guess—arrived. The father paunchy in his trunks, the mother wearing one of those skirted one-piece suits. The three of them discussed something. Then the girl got up and went with them. Was she as normal as she seemed?

I kept thinking, all that morning, *I could've been that girl by the pool.*

My parents. I had left them in September, almost three years before.

I always thought about my parents around this time of year. I'd wonder if I should call them, if I ever would. I'd run the whole thing, Benton to Excelsior, through my mind. But I'd come up with: *no way.* Why should I forgive them, or offer them a second shot? Didn't they do enough to destroy me the first time around? I'm better off on my own.

Another thing happened one September day. I saw Luke coming out of the stockroom, a fifty-pound sack of potatoes slung over his back. And something about him—the concentration on his face, the way his shirt stretched across his abdomen—made me catch my breath. *I used to think he was so plain,* I thought, *but he isn't, not at all!*

I felt this little tug inside me. He'd be going back to Fayetteville the next week to school. *My God,* I thought, *how will I ever run this place on my own?* But it wasn't just the kitchen without Luke I was worried about. It was *me* without him.

September, with days so brilliant it hurt, the sky such a vivid blue, the leaves turning. And Dare. Claire, the pale girl who waitressed evenings at the General's Palace dining room, told me more about him. During the day she taught at Meadow School, where a lot of the hippies' kids went.

She and I were at a table in the dining room one day, having a coffee break.

Out of the blue, she said, "I wish I knew what to do about Dare."

"Why, what's wrong?"

"Well, you know he doesn't read, and—?"

"Dare? Doesn't *read*?" I couldn't believe it. Dare was so sharp. Also, I had always thought he was like me. And I had been reading everything I could get my hands on at his age: It had been my salvation and escape.

"Well, he's dyslexic," said Claire. "It's a reading disability. He sees words the wrong way."

"Oh," I said. *The poor kid,* I thought: not to have parents around, not to have enough to eat, not even to be able to read. My parents had been bad news for sure, but at least they had kept me fed and clothed and educated. And until the last few awful years, Dad had been my friend. Dare hadn't had any of that.

Claire continued, "Well, Dare came to me last summer. He said, 'Claire, I want to come to Meadow School and learn how to read, but I don't have any money. Would you let me come anyway?' Of course I said yes. And he showed up the first day, seven-thirty in the morning, on time and everything. He's got guts, I'll say that. Well, lunchtime rolls around. The other kids pull out their brown bags. 'I'm not hungry,' says Dare. For a week he pulls that. Finally I start bringing an extra sack lunch for him. 'Okay,' he says. Not thanks. Like he's doing me a favor taking it! He'll never admit he needs help— which is one reason I was touched that he came to me about learning to read. It's not his way, to ask for help. He had to overcome a lot to do that."

I nodded, knowing how hard it had been for *me* to ask for or accept help.

"So yesterday I go to the school in the morning, get there at seven-fifteen to open it up, right? I turn the key, push open the door, and there's Dare, lying on the floor asleep in a corner with a rug pulled over him. Turns out he's been jimmying one of the back windows open, crawling in, and *sleeping* there since school started, but until yesterday he'd woken up before I got there." Claire paused and shook her head. She picked up a spoon from the table, started drumming it, and put it down again.

"Wasn't he staying with a woman named Fran Winters?" I asked.

"He was, but it didn't work out. I don't know why, and I haven't asked. Press a kid like Dare and he's liable to get antsy and disappear."

"Right, right." When had *I* stopped being scared, stopped running? When I moved to Excelsior? At some point I had crossed a line. I wasn't an adult but I didn't feel like a scared kid anymore.

"I just don't know what to do," Claire said, drumming the spoon again. "I just wish I knew somebody who could take him in."

"I could," I said suddenly. I didn't even stop to think about it. "I could take him in."

25

"You think you'll be comfortable?" I asked Dare.

"Yeah, sure," he said offhandedly.

Dare looked around the soon-to-be-his bedroom, on the upper floor down the hall from mine. "This *is* pretty nice," he added. He looked more bedraggled than ever. The room was really a perfect all-American boy's room— walls with wood paneling, a single maple bed with a golden corduroy bedspread, a small maple desk. It looked like a JCPenney ad, only the model wasn't dressed yet. I imagined Dare cleaned up, in a new pair of jeans without holes, a new pair of sneakers without holes, and a new T-shirt without holes.

"You've got Hugh Dewling to thank for all this," I told him. "He's letting me live here, and so indirectly he's letting you live here too."

Dare sniffed, tossing his hair out of his eyes.

"He's taking a big chance on me, letting me live here," I said.

"So?" said Dare, shrugging. "He gets something out of it."

"Oh, sure," I said, "but so do I."

"Then you're even," said Dare. "*That's* no big deal."

Yes, it *is* a big deal, I wanted to say, because you don't meet all that many people in life who are willing to take a chance on you, even if they *do* get something out of it.

But that sounded dangerously like my father, guilt tripping away, nagging you to appreciate something before you'd even seen what you were supposed to be appreciating.

So I just said, "Anyway, Dare, it's Hugh Dewling's place, and I want to take care of it." I paused. "And it's also *my* place for now, and I like keeping it clean and pretty, to come home to after work. . . ." I paused again. "And now it's going to be *your* place too." Dare cocked his head to one side and eyed me warily. I plunged in. "Anyway, before we go get your stuff at Fran's, we better talk about some things."

"Talk about what?" said Dare, suspiciously. "I just want to live here."

"That's fine," I said soothingly. "That's good, I want

you to live here, very much. But we have to decide on some—"

"Rules?" suggested Dare, in an I've-heard-it-all-before-so-let's-get-it-over-with tone.

"If you want to call it that, yes." And then I went over the things I had come up with after I'd told Claire I'd take him. No dope in the house. He could keep his room the way he wanted, but the rest of the house had to stay neat. He had to be in by ten on school nights. He'd help out with household chores. I tried to give him the reasoning behind each "rule." But it didn't seem to sink in.

Dare agreed, not asking questions, but nodding and saying, "All right, all right," sighing lots of weary sighs. Finally I said, "Hey, kiddo, I'm not trying to put anything on you for the hell of it, it's just that—"

"I said all right, I'll do it!" said Dare harshly. "Just tell me what I have to do to stay here and I'll do it!" Boy, I thought, taken aback, I thought he'd be *happy*—I was offering him a chance to earn his own way, like with helping out on the chores, instead of having to accept charity. But then he looked up at me and said—sincerely, I thought—"I *do* want to stay here with you, Chrysta, I really do."

And somehow, I had no doubt then that it would work out: because we both wanted it to. I knew there'd be a lot to work out; but he needed to be loved and cared for, and I was going to do my damnedest to give that to him, the way nobody had given it to me until I met Lissa and came to Excelsior, the way Lissa's friend Michael had given it to her, the way Nettie gave it to Luke. I was going to be *good* to Dare, and I was going to give him as much time as he needed to heal. I was going to save him.

What I didn't see was that *I* hadn't healed yet. Or that Dare's case was terminal.

On the ride out to Fran Winters's, bumping along in the back of Joanie's pickup, Dare began to test me in a lighthearted way. We had to yell to be heard above the din of the engine and the rushing air as the truck raced along the highway.

"NO DOPE?" yelled Dare, teasing. "DID YOU TELL ME NO DOPE?"

"THAT'S RIGHT, PAL!" I shouted back. "NO DOPE AT THE HOUSE! YOU CAN SMOKE IT ANYWHERE ELSE, NOT THAT I COULD STOP YOU, BUT NOT AT HOME! OKAY?"

"OKAY!" Dare shouted back. "BUT *WHY*?"

"FIRST OF ALL, YOUR BEING THERE, DOPE OR NO, ISN'T LEGAL!"

"WHAT?"

"LEGAL!" I shouted more loudly. "I DON'T THINK IT'S REAL COOL LEGALLY FOR AN UNDERAGE RUG RAT LIKE YOURSELF TO BE HANGING AROUND WITH ME WHEN THERE'S NO PAPERS OR WHATEVER. I DON'T WANT TO INCREASE OUR RISKS! GET IT?" Especially when *I'm* underage, too.

"OH!" Dare was grinning. He was in a great mood. "YEAH! BUT NOBODY'S *EVER* MESSED WITH ME, YOU KNOW! I'VE NEVER HAD ANYTHING SERIOUS WITH THE LAW!"

"WHAT?"

"I CAN ALWAYS TALK MY WAY OUT OF IT! I'VE NEVER EVEN COME CLOSE TO BEIN' BUSTED AS A STAT OFFENDER!"

"A WHAT?"

We came to a stop sign and Joanie slowed. We

continued in normal voices. "Stands for *status offender*,"
said Dare, rubbing his throat.

"Oh, right, right." Now I knew; what runaway didn't?
And I was not only still a runaway . . . but getting ready
to adopt one. He had no idea that we were in the same
boat. *In the same boat*. The phrase made me think of a
photograph I had seen in a newspaper once, of a bunch
of Cambodian refugees crammed into a little boat, but
nobody, no countries, would let them land.

"You know, like, something that wouldn't be a crime
if you were over eighteen or something. Man, they
throw you into jail for nothin' just 'cause you're a kid. It
sucks." Dare jutted his chin out angrily.

"You're right," I said. "It does. But still, that's why
no dope at the carriage house."

"Sure," said Dare.

"Plus," I said, "it's Mr. Dewling's house, and I know
he wouldn't want dope around."

"He wouldn't have to know. He's never around."

"But *I'd* know, Dare. It would bother *me* that I was
doing something in *his* house that—"

"How do you know he'd mind?" giggled Dare. "Hey,
for all you know, Chrysta, he might even be getting
stoned in the penthouse every night." Dare mimicked
toking a joint and wiggled his eyebrows up and down.
"Can you see old Dewling . . . ?"

"Listen, if he *does* get stoned," I said, "it is on
brandy and cigars. To each their own."

"So what's the difference?"

"The difference is that in his mind I'm sure one's
okay and one's not."

"You ever ask him?"

I raised my eyebrows at him, pretend stern. "Young
man," I said, "marijuana *happens* to be illegal."

Dare made big round innocent eyes at me. "It *is*?

Gee, Chrysta, you shoulda told me! I never woulda
done it if I'd—I mean, all these years that I been
smoking—"

All these years that I been smoking? How long could
a twelve-year-old kid have been smoking dope, anyway?
Then I remembered what I had heard about Dare's
father dealing. Probably all his life. He probably had
marijuana tea instead of milk in his bottle. If he ever
had a bottle.

"CAN I PUT STUFF ON MY WALLS?" We were
back in motion, and shouting into the wind again.

Just like any ordinary kid, I thought. What would it
be, KISS posters? I smiled to myself. "I THINK SO.
DEPENDS HOW YOU PUT IT UP. LIKE SCOTCH
TAPE WOULD BE OKAY, BUT NO TACKS."

"WHAT?"

"TACKS! TACKS WOULDN'T BE COOL, BUT
TAPE'S OKAY!"

"HOW 'BOUT GLUE?"

I looked sharply at Dare to see if he was joking. He
was.

"I'LL GLUE *YOU* TO THE WALL!" I yelled.

"THEN YOU'D HAVE TO LOOK AT ME ALL THE
TIME!"

We rode in cheerful silence for a few minutes, bouncing along in the sunshine. I'm sure Dare's throat was as
hoarse as mine, but I felt good anyway.

"WHAT ABOUT GIRLS?" Dare shouted suddenly.

"WHAT?" I shouted back.

"GIRLS!" yelled Dare. "CAN I BRING GIRLS HOME
TO SPEND THE NIGHT?"

So much for Dare's being just like any ordinary kid.

"CAN'T WE FACE THAT WHEN THE TIME
COMES?"

"WITH ME," Dare shouted proudly, "THE TIME

MIGHT BE TONIGHT!" He was grinning. "I HAVE TO GIVE 'EM NUMBERS! THEY'RE STANDING IN LINE!"

Unh-hunh, I thought, *sure.*

"IT PROBABLY DEPENDS ON THE INDIVIDU-AL GIRL, DARE!" I shouted. Careful here, Chrysta.

The truck turned down a dirt road toward Fran's house. We were moving more slowly now and could talk in normal voices.

"Dare," I said slowly, "about your having girls over . . ." I paused. "It can have—can be a lot more heavy, or lead to something a lot more than you think at the time."

Dare shook his head and said gravely, "Oh, *no,* Chrysta, I know all about *that!* I'd use a rubber!"

Fran Winters's ramshackle house was surrounded by an overgrown fenced-in yard shaded by oak and pine trees. The roof sagged. A black-and-white cat lounged on the messy porch, perched on top of a lopsided chair that had one leg broken off; other than that, the place seemed deserted. It was quiet out there, peaceful: no sounds at all except the wind in the trees.

"Mm," I said. "Well, I wonder where Fran Winters is." I had wanted to talk to her, or see if I could learn any more about Dare, and find out why it hadn't worked out between him and Fran.

"Oh." Dare sounded surprised. "Oh, she's in Austin, Texas, now."

"What?" I said. "You *knew* she wouldn't be here??" I couldn't believe it—here I'd taken time off work plus asked Joanie to drive us out here, and now no Fran.

"Yeah." Dare flipped his hair back, unconcerned. "She's from there. You think I would come out here if she *was* here? She's a real bitch."

Joanie and I exchanged looks.

"But Dare, dear," said Joanie gently. "How can we get your stuff if she's not here?"

"Easy," said Dare. "Open the door, walk in, and take it. She doesn't keep it locked." He sniffed contemptuously. "Who'd want to rip off *this* dump?"

"But Dare," I said, "we can't just go barging in—"

"Sure we can," Dare said. "It's my stuff. And it's not locked."

Joanie and I looked at each other again. The place was uncannily quiet. It was spooky, I decided, not peaceful.

Dare's stuff was stashed in a corner behind a long, sagging couch. The room had a low ceiling and was covered with a faded, grayed wallpaper that was peeling off to reveal other layers of wallpaper. The linoleum was the same way: The surface layer was yellow, but here and there you could see patches of a green-and-white-checked pattern that was underneath. A dusty houseplant, its leaves drooping a little, stood in one of the two dusty windows. The room was shadowy, even with the windows, because the house was under so many trees. Yeller House was falling apart too, but it was cheerful and full of good vibes. This place gave me the creeps.

Dare said, "That's where I slept," nodding his head toward the couch as he leaned over it to pull out two pillow cases, each about half full. One pillowcase was plain white, grayed by the dust and cat hairs from the floor; the other had a picture of Snoopy on it.

"Let me check to see if I got everything," Dare said, dumping out the pillowcases' contents: four or five T-shirts, a red sweater, two pairs of jeans, a pair of corduroy pants, two bandanas, and one sock; also a large book, which Dare showed us proudly. It was called *The Martial Arts*. "See that?" said Dare, flipping through the pages, mostly pictures, until he stopped at a photo of two Orientals, one in the air and about to hit the mat hard, the other crouched over. "And that?" Two men, each with a heavy stick, fighting, their sticks crossed. "And look at this, isn't this boss?" Two wrestlers, one choking, eyes bulging out. All the men wore white karate pajamas. "I *love* this book," said Dare. It was obvious; the book was well worn, its corners frayed. "My dad gave it to me," he added. Suddenly Dare shouted "HAH" so loudly Joanie and I jumped, and he sprang into a karate pose: legs apart, knees bent, both hands up. Then he relaxed. "Don't worry, I don't really know anything," said Dare. "I wish I did, though."

The other pillowcase contained only two things—a plaid winter coat, and an old beat-up stuffed animal that had once been a bear.

"My mom bought me the coat," Dare said. "I mean, she sent the money to Fran and she bought it for me. But she probably spent a lot of it on herself, that bitch."

Joanie and I looked at each other. Dare caught the look. "Yeah, every so often my mother sends some money for me, to whoever I'm staying with. I guess now you'll get it, hunh?"

"Dare," I said slowly, "where does your mom live?"

"Florida, I think," said Dare, now stuffing his things back in the pillowcases. "I think. They lived in upstate New York, but then they moved a couple of times."

"They?"

"Yeah. First my mother and father, then my mom and John, the guy she married. My *stepfather*." Dare said "stepfather" in this sarcastic way. "Anyway, Fran-the-bitch Winters has her address. And my dad's. You ready to go?"

"No," I said. "Let me leave a note for Fran. Where's some paper?" I wrote it on a paper napkin:

Dear Fran,

Dare is staying with me now. I live at the carriage house behind the General's Palace Hotel. I'm a cook there.

I would like to talk to you and also get Dare's parents' addresses. So please call me at 555–3041. That's at work. I don't have a phone at home.

Thanks,

Chrysta Perretti

"*Now* are we ready to go?" asked Dare impatiently.

"Wait," said Joanie. "Where's the kitchen?" Dare pointed and Joanie went and returned with a mason jar full of water. As Dare and I stared, she watered the plant on the windowsill. She caught us staring and said defensively, "Well, who knows when Dare'll be back? Or Fran? I don't want the poor thing to die." That was Joanie, right there, in a nutshell.

Bouncing home in the pickup, after seeing that ratty house, I realized that Dare's life as a kid was *completely* different from mine. I wish I could have remembered that straight through.

26

A few days later, Steve and Dare both showed up at the dining room at five-thirty. "Dare," I said, "you know you can only eat off leftovers, after the line's been pulled, unless—"

"Chrysta, my love," said Steve, "not to worry. I am taking this little pool shark you have made the mistake of adopting over to Ville de Fayette, and so I take responsibility for feeding him beforehand. In short, I am picking up the tab, so cool your jets."

Dare had talked Steve, who was going to Fayetteville to see *Close Encounters of the Third Kind*, the Special Edition, into taking him along.

"Is that okay?" asked Dare. "You said ten o'clock was okay on school nights."

"Well, if you go to sleep as soon as you get home," I said. Dare breathed an exaggerated sigh of relief.

Steve said, "Well, Dare, all I can say is, if I see something cute in Fayetteville, don't cramp my style."

Dare looked up at Steve, his green eyes deep and earnest. "Oh, no, Steve," he said seriously. "I can dig it. I'd never do that. I went everywhere with my dad and I never cramped *his* style. He's bisexual."

I went back to the kitchen to clear my head. What next? Was it all show, like me toughing it out with my father?

Nettie was smoking a cigarette near the waitress station. Since it was early, there were no "ollacarts" yet.

"Nettie," I said suddenly, "do you think I've gotten in over my head, taking in Dare?" Nettie had met Dare; he was hanging around the kitchen a lot now.

"Well," she said, grinning, "little boys aren't easy, Chrysta. I never had any of my own, you know, just raised Luke. I wouldn't take a million dollars for Luke; but I wouldn't raise *another* kid, *especially* a boy, for a million dollars either! It's not easy, Chrysta." She eyed me speculatively. "What got you to thinkin' along these lines, honey?"

"Dare's always telling me these . . . *things*," I said slowly. "And I know some of 'em are true. I mean, I know he had a really bizarre childhood. But I don't think *all* the things he says are true. I *know* sometimes he's got to be fibbing to shock me or something. But why should he do it with *me*? He knows I'm on his side. I don't understand it. I thought I did, but I don't. And I can't just come out and say 'Dare, are you telling me the truth?'"

"Well, Chrysta, it's like this." Nettie took the last drag on her cigarette and stubbed it out. "If I say the sun was out today, that's true and we both know it. If I say it rained today, well, that's a lie and we both know it. But there's a whole kinda place in the middle where I can say the sun was out but it was a little chilly, and it's a matter of how it appears to me, y'see, not really true or false. In a kid's thinkin', sometimes, 'specially a kid like that Dare, things get all mixed up. There's what's true, and what he'd *like* to be true, and what he'd like other people to *think* is true, and what other people *do* think is true. Y'see? And it gets all mixed up. For any kid, but 'specially one that's been shuffled around much as he has. Like you say, he probably *is* tryin' to impress you or shock you or somethin'—most kids want to do that. But there's also probably *some*thin' to it, bless his heart. He's had a pretty tough life. Kids like him sometimes go too far, and—and— But Dare does seem to like you, Chrysta. And in my opinion, you're saving him. That's what I think. So when he says those things, you just kinda take it with a grain of salt."

What Nettie said made sense. "Nettie, how did you get to be so smart?" I asked her.

Nettie threw back her head and laughed. "Me? Ah, go on! An ol' hillbilly like me?" Smiling, she shook her head, then looked at me directly. I was struck, as always, by how much she and Luke looked alike when they gave you a straight-on look. She turned for a second to reach for a coffee cup, and walked over to the coffee machine. "See, Chrysta, each crop a kids thinks they invented the whole ball of wax. That's part a bein' young. You take me. Now my father—Luke's grand-father—was pretty strict. And I ran away at fifteen to get away from him." Matter-of-factly, Nettie filled her cup.

I stared at her.

"Now, don' look so surprised! Yep, I ran away with a plumber, a kid about twenty, when I was fifteen. We went on up to Missouri to get married. I put a piece of paper in my shoe that I wrote 'eighteen' on, so when the judge asked me 'Are you over eighteen?' I could say Yes and be tellin' the truth! Now ain't that just kids today?"

I was stunned, but I managed to say, "Well, kids today probably wouldn't bother putting the piece of paper in their shoe."

"They probably wouldn't bother gettin' married either!" said Nettie, and hooted. Then she leaned forward and added, seriously, "And I think that's not a bad thing, either, to tell ya the truth. They ought to make gettin' married real, real hard, and gettin' divorced real, real easy, 'stead of the way it is now. Marry in haste, repent in leisure, like they say."

By the time Luke went back to school in Fayetteville, Dare and I had a pretty good routine set up. At least I felt like it was good. I'd get up first, and do my yoga, and have a little quiet time to myself. Then I'd go in to wake him up.

Waking up Dare was strange, even before things got bad between us. No matter what time he'd gone to bed, he just didn't want to wake up.

"Dare, Dare," I'd call softly, standing at the foot of

the bed. I began as gently as I could. But he never heard me when I spoke softly. "Dare!" More loudly now. "Dare! *Dare!* Hey, DARE!" I'd lean over the bed, and shake his shoulder a little. "DARE! WAKE UP!"

And all of a sudden, bang, he'd sit up, awake, and burst into tears. Or maybe burst into tears and then sit up awake. I'd plunk down on the bed next to him and put my arms around him. "Hey, Dare. It's all right. You're here with me, everything is okay. I've got breakfast going, you're going to see Claire and everybody at Meadow School, then come over to the kitchen or do whatever you want. It's okay, it really is." And I'd wipe away his tears with a bandana and gradually he'd give this little smile, sort of peering out from under the tears, and finally a bigger smile, and then he'd be awake and he'd go off to shower while I finished breakfast and made his lunch for school.

It was an emotionally draining way to start the day, for me almost as much as for Dare. But I remembered how Marshall, my dog, used to come and wake me up mornings and how that helped me face everything. I wanted to wake up Dare with that much love.

By the time Dare got to the kitchen, he was usually cheerful, at least when we first lived together. His clothes were clean, since I did his laundry with mine at the Downtown Laundromat. I had bought him a new pair of sneakers, socks, a sweater, a couple of shirts. Sometimes, he'd have those on and sometimes he'd wear his old stuff. I never hinted that he throw his old stuff out or mend it or have somebody mend it. And I never asked him to cut his hair either. Looking ragged and beat-up was part of his trip, like his one earring—a different one each day. He must have had about fifty. I

didn't have pierced ears, o I never gave him any, but
Joanie had given him several.

We'd talk over breakfast; not much, but some. I'd do
him scrambled eggs and toast and orange juice or cereal
and milk with sliced bananas. And always cocoa, nice,
hot, made-from-scratch cocoa. Dare loved anything
chocolate, and though he knew I thought sweets weren't
healthy food, I didn't want to lay some heavy number
on him about it. It seemed to me he needed to be
spoiled a bit, to have someone pay attention to what *he*
thought and what *he* liked—the way I'd wanted my
mother to do. So cocoa at breakfast it was, and often a
slightly stale but still-good piece of chocolate cake from
the kitchen in his lunch. Oh, I got to know all of old
Dare's food likes and dislikes. He loved hot jalapeño
peppers, mostly because he could show off about how
many of them he could eat at one time. Most people
just take tiny nibbles of them, washing each nibble
down with a bite of food; but Dare would eat five or six
or more whole with a meal. He hated green vegetables.
He liked salads only if they were swimming around in
an ocean of blue-cheese dressing. He was wild about
pomegranates—you know, that red fruit with all the
little seeds? He liked pancakes. And one day, at breakfast,
he told me shyly that his mother used to make chocolate pancakes for him.

"*Chocolate pancakes?*" I couldn't imagine anything
sounding worse.

"Yeah, unh-hunh. On my birthday and Christmas,
sometimes other times, too. It was when I was real
little, but I still remember it."

"And they were *good?*"

"Yeah, yeah, *real* good."

"Chocolate pancakes," I said, musing out loud. "I

wonder how she did that. Maybe just put cocoa in the pancake batter?"

"I guess," said Dare, shrugging. "I don't know. I was little. I just know they were *real* good."

I decided I would make Dare chocolate pancakes for his thirteenth birthday, which, he'd lost no time in telling me, was on November 17. He dropped a few hints about a radio, too.

Okay, Dare, I thought, *I got the message. Radio and chocolate pancakes. Sure thing—you bet.*

I was even looking forward to it.

27

It's hard to remember when I started to sense trouble. First, Dare's stuff began seeping out of his bedroom and spreading all over the carriage house. A jacket here draped over a chair; a sock poking out from under the couch there, a sneaker on the kitchen table. I'd say, "Dare, could you pick this up, please?" and he'd say, "Oh! Sure, sorry," in this surprised way, like he'd completely forgotten. But after a while it got to be "Yeah, yeah, yeah, all right, okay," and then "Why do you have to be so uptight about one little fucking T-shirt?" And pretty soon I didn't have a nice clean place to come home to. Even if I'd picked up that morning, Dare managed to come back from school to do a quick trash-out of the whole house. There were his dirty dishes in the sink, the bathroom rug wadded up and the bathtub lined with soapy scum, the plastic boats he liked bathing with beached in the mess. The lampshades in the living room would be askew, there'd be footprints on the couch, and a copy of *Hustler* magazine, open to the most gross-out photograph, lying on the coffee table. (I'll bet Dare was the only *Hustler* reader in the world who still played with boats in the bathtub.) I resented it, and we fought.

For a while, I was patient. *After all,* I'd think, *any time people live together, one is more of a slob than the other. It's ordinary. And he's never had a home. Maybe he's testing me, to see if I'll throw him out like everyone else did.*

Even when a joint fell out of the pocket of his blue-jean jacket once at the Laundromat, I handled it calmly.

"Dare, we agreed—no dope in the house."

"You didn't *find* it in the house, you *found* it in the *Laundromat*." Tauntingly.

"Come on, Dare—don't be a smart-ass."

"Well, you *said* I could smoke, just not at home. And somebody gave it to me, okay? And I forgot to get rid of it before I came home. Come on, Chrysta, lighten up."

"Try," I said carefully, "not to let it happen again. Okay?" He had said "home"—a first. Was he starting to feel secure at last?

It had been about a hundred million percent easier living alone than with Dare. I had less time to myself, and I was doing a lot less reading—which I missed. But there were a lot of good days and fun times, too. Once we took the bus to Fayetteville together, on my day off, and I bought him a new pair of jeans and some cowboy boots and then we went to see a movie in the mall, had pizza, and came home. Several times, on my days off, we went on picnics, often with some of the Yeller House people or Steve Darwin.

And we'd have fun in the kitchen, too, just teasing and jiving around. Once I gave him this bowl to lick that had had chocolate cake batter in it, and he smeared some on my face and I smeared some on his, and we wound up madly chasing each other around the kitchen, chocolate batter on our faces, and Nettie was doubled over, laughing and dodging us. At those times I was sure *something* must be getting through to screwy little 12-going-on-36-year-old Dare. If I just loved him enough, and hung in there, maybe he stood a shot at making it in life somewhere outside of a juvenile delinquent home. For it was becoming clear to me, watching Dare swing from ordinary kid to real little S.O.B., that he was at some kind of crossroads. He could go either way: get it together somehow, or go down the tubes. And it made me realize that I, too, had been at a crossroads during my last months in Benton and my first months on the road. But since coming to Excelsior, and particularly since the surgery and my new job, I had made my choice, finally: I *was* getting it together. I wasn't going to go down.

But the scene at home with Dare started to deteriorate after he'd lived with me about a month. By the end of two months, it was so bad even I had to admit it couldn't go on the way it was.

Around this time, several things happened. One was I got a letter, addressed to me c/o General's Palace Hotel Kitchen:

Dear Chrysta,

I am writing because of your note I'm still in Texas but the lady who is feeding the cat noticed it on the table and sent it to me here with my other mail mostly bills.

I am glad you have Dare some body needs to God knows + I hope you can handle him no one else has been able to and many people have tryed. I don't know what he has told you of himself he lies a lot but his parents divorsed when he was 3 but when his Mom remarried he didn't get along with his stepfather + wond up burning down a chicken house when he was 9. His Mom couldn't handle it + sent him to his Dad Darrell Willie who is a real turkey and after that it was one thing after another. His father finly brought Dare to me because we used to get along in Dallas I lived near them + Darrell was with my girlfriend Ginger for a while I felt so sorry for Dare in Dallas + tryed to be his friend. But that didn't work but any better than anything else did for Dare he is to messed up a kid + he wond up calling me names threatening to burn down the house + throwing rocks at the windows he broke 4 and having crying fits I couldn't handle it ether. Until I got your note I thought he was staying with Dizzy this guy in Exc. Sp.

I am in closing names and adresses of his parents and I will probably run into Darrell when I am in Dallas + I will say you have Dare now sooner or later his Mom + Dad will contact you probly + make promises like they make every one who takes care of Dare which they will not keep because they are also so spaced + untogether + messed up people.

Good luck and be careful. Dare is so messed up that he could just do anything. He can be swert some times but be carful seriusly I mean that.

Yours Truly,

Fran Winters

*   *   *

Dare had started to come home later and later every
night and we had hassle after hassle about it. It wasn't
long before he had stretched his curfew to past midnight.
Then one school night he stayed out to one A.M.

I went in as usual the next morning at seven-fifteen.
"Dare, honey, try to wake up. Wake up. Wake up,
please. Dare? *Dare! Dare, it's time for school!*"

He woke up, he cried, he sat up and looked at me.
But instead of the smile underneath the tears like he'd
had when he first lived with me, there was only that
sullen expression he'd had for the last couple of weeks.

"I don't want to go, Chrysta," he said, rubbing his
eyes. "I don't feel well. I got a sore throat."

I put my hand on his forehead. No fever that I could
tell. But whether he was sick or not, I felt I shouldn't
force Dare to go to school. He'd only cut, sooner or
later, if he hated it. I knew, having cut permanently.

If Dare had known how to read and write, I wouldn't
have tried to get him to go at all. I mean, I was a
dropout, and I'd done okay. But if he couldn't at least
read and write, how could he hope to survive? And
going to Meadow School had been his idea.

"All right, Dare, you can stay home today if you're
sick. On one condition. You *stay* here, all right? All day,
and tonight. If you're too sick to go to school, you're too
sick to run around. Do you agree? All day and tonight?"

"Yeah," said Dare, lying back in his pillow, throwing
one arm across his forehead. "Yeah. Gee, Chrysta, I
really don't feel so good. Thanks for lettin' me stay in."
His voice was weak: a dramatic delivery.

"I'll bring you supper over. You can go downstairs
and get your lunch, okay?" He nodded. I stroked his
head. Despite all our hassles, I cared about Dare. "Do
you want to have some breakfast now?" I asked him.

"No, no," said Dare, again in his invalid voice. "Maybe, in a while, I'll go downstairs and have a piece of toast and some tea. But I don't think so. I *really* don't feel well."

Lay it on thick, Dare. Tea and toast? I admired his acting ability, but I was hurt. He could have leveled with me. I wasn't the enemy. But maybe, to Dare, everyone was the enemy.

I went off to work. It was a typical crisis day, no time to think, even for a second. Susan greeted me: "Oh, Chrysta! We're out of flour!"

"We're *what*?" I said. "How can that be? Fadler's came Wednesday and we got four fifty-pound sacks!"

"You go look out at that dining room, you'll see how it can be," said Susan grimly.

I went through the swinging door and gaped. Breakfast was usually our slowest meal of the day; but that day the forty-five-table dining room was packed, and people were waiting in line to be seated. The fall rush everyone had told me about had hit. We were almost out of grits, there was only about a quarter pan of biscuits left, and only a few little dried-up-looking chunks of scrambled eggs. There was plenty of bacon, but that was it.

I raced back into the kitchen.

"Cleota!" I yelled. "You're supposed to keep an eye on the line! What are you doing baking pies, when that line's just about empty and we still have an hour and a half of breakfast?"

Cleota put down her rolling pin and turned and glared at me, her hands on her hips and her weird little face thrust forward. "Don't yell at me, Chrysta Perretti! Ah can walk *right* outta here and leave you flat! Ah'm a lot older'n you and Ah deserve *ree*-spec'! It says in *MAH* Bible that—"

That's the kind of day it was, *all* day. At dinnertime

Dare called. We didn't have a phone at home, and I could tell he was calling from the hotel snack bar, 'cause I could hear the pinball machines.

"Greg and Dizzy and Carlos came by—they invited me to this party tonight." There was a pause. "And *I'm* going!"

Greg and Dizzy and Carlos were all low-life Excelsior hippie types, constantly stoned or drunk, hanging out full time, full of original lines like, "Hey, man, you got a place I could crash?" I hadn't realized Dare had lived with Dizzy until Fran's letter, though of course I knew they knew each other. Everyone in Excelsior knew each other.

"Wait a sec, hang on," I said to Dare. I leaned against the wall by the desk, one hand against my forehead. In the corner of the kitchen where I stood, I could see activity in every part of the huge gray kitchen: the uniformed waitresses buzzing like strange insects around the waitress station as they made coffee and iced tea; Tess and Susan carrying bowls of green salad, Jell-O salad, cole slaw, out to the salad bar; Nettie traveling back and forth, potholder mitts covering her hands, carrying trays full of steaming food out to the steam table in the dining room. I shook my head to clear it, to focus on Dare, to find the right thing to say to him and the right tone of voice to say it in. Had I been this hard on *my* parents? But my parents had been harder on me than I was on Dare, surely. *Surely*.

"Well, but Dare? I thought we agreed this morning if you felt sick enough to stay home from Meadow School—"

"Listen, Chrysta, I feel all better," Dare interrupted me. "Some friends of mine dropped by and invited me to a party and *I'm GOING to go*."

"I'll be down to the carriage house in a second—why don't you meet me there?" I said and hung up.

Dare was waiting, sitting on the steps to the carriage house, angrily tapping his foot and jabbing a stick back and forth in the dirt. He looked as if he had been crying. His eyes were rimmed with red, and his lower lip stuck out.

"Dare, I brought you some cake. Chocolate." I held it out, a peace offering. Shades of my mom. But Dare *liked* cake, especially chocolate. *It's different, I'm not like her, I'm NOT!* "And I'll run down with dinner around seven-thirty. It's lasagna." I paused. "I've got to get back to the kitchen, but can we talk a little now? And then more when I bring dinner?"

"I don't want your cake," Dare said, narrowing his eyes. "And I don't want your lasagna. And I ain't gonna be here at seven-thirty, I already told you. I am going to a *party,* and you can't stop me. I don't have anything to say to you anyway."

"Well, that's too bad," I said, stung. "'Cause *I* want to know what's going on. What's bothering you, Dare?"

"Nothing is fucking *bothering* me, Chrysta! Some people asked me to a party and I'm going! You can't stop me! And I don't have anything to say to you."

"Well," I said, "in that case, you'd better listen, 'cause I have a few things to say to you."

"So?" Dare shrugged. "I don't care what you have to say."

"Dare," I said, taking a deep breath, "you don't see it, but I'm working very hard at the kitchen—"

"I don't care about the lousy kitchen! And I AM going to that party!"

My father, slamming the door each night and saying, "Phew! What a day!" floated through my mind. I had nearly said the same thing to Dare.

"Dare, we had an agreement this morning about your staying home from school. Didn't we?"

"I was sick *then*! I'm *better* now! Some friends came by and asked me to a party and I'm *gonna* go, Chrysta."

"Dare, when you moved in, remember the rules we agreed on?"

"You can take your rules and shove 'em!"

"And you'll go to your party, smoke weed, lie about how many girls you made it with, and boast about your father! Right? And then come home here to crash?" I knew I had to stop, and I did. But just that second of my losing it was enough to throw Dare into a frenzy. He stamped his foot and started screaming.

"I hate you! I *hate* you! I'm *going*! I *AM*! And you *can't stop me*! Those are *my* friends, and if *I* want to *party* with them *I will*!" Tears of rage were streaming down his face. It was amazing how quickly my anger vanished and turned to pity. I started remembering the day I yelled all those things at my mother, when I told her what a selfish glutton she was, and how later she let Marshall out—all that came back to me. I remembered how I had felt, screaming at Mom, but how I just couldn't stop. That was probably how Dare felt, screaming at me.

"Dare," I tried again, "Dare, listen! Okay?" I raised my voice so he could hear me above his own furious sobbing. "Just try and hear what I'm telling you. You've got to *give* a little, not just take! A lot of people have told you the same thing in different ways. We're not trying to hurt you but it really is *true*, Dare. You think we're all making it up? Some of us *love* you, Dare, some of us just don't want to see you ruin your life! Because, let me tell you straight, Dare—you are on the way to doing just that! But you can still—"

"*I hate you, you selfish bitch!*" exploded Dare. "*It's MY life and I can do what I want with it! You don't know anything about me! Just shut up and leave me alone! Leave me alone!"* He turned and started walking up the path away from me, kicking the dirt, yelling all the way. *"I hate you! You're as bad as all the rest! I haaaaaaate youuuuuuuuu!"*

I watched him walk away, his last piercing scream ringing in my ears. I sat down on the carriage house steps and put my head in my hands for a minute or two. I kept flashing on my mother's face in the kitchen the morning of my birthday, and my father's as he doled out the pills. Then I'd see Dare again. I had this terrible weight in my stomach, and I was trembling all over. I sat there and waited for the feelings to pass, but they didn't. So I got up, finally. I had to get back to the kitchen.

All the staff had overheard Dare. "All you can do is the best you can," said Nettie sympathetically, shaking her head and patting me on the shoulder. "We got a full dinin' room out there again, too. Well, Luke's here at least, that's something good."

"Yeah," said Susan. "God, I'm sorry about Dare, Chrysta." She sighed. "You've been trying so *hard* with that kid!"

"Well now, it may yet work out," said Nettie. "Don't jump ship until you're shore it's sinkin'. But even if it don't work out, Chrysta, you done the best you could. And that's more'n most people can say—about anything."

"Yeah," I said tiredly. "Thanks! I haven't given up yet."

"That's m' girl!" said Nettie. "Luke's in the storeroom, said he needed to see you when you came in."

"Okay," I said.

And that's when everything changed. I still don't know why it happened at that particular time and place, not that it matters.

In the stockroom, with its one dusty window, with its

burlap sacks of potatoes and its red net sacks of onions and its brown paper sacks of sugar, with its shelves lined with #10 cans, each with a bright label (red tomatoes, purple beets, yellow corn), in neat rows—in the middle of all that, everything changed.

I said simply, "Luke, what am I going to do?"

We looked at each other, his eyes dark, fringed with those long lashes. Neither of us spoke. Then wordlessly he put out both his hands, and I took them. He drew me to him, and then our arms were around each other and we were pressed together tightly.

My face, turned to one side, was pressed against his chest. I could feel his ribs through his T-shirt, and I could hear his heart beating.

After a while he said softly, "Why don't you go home and get a little rest?" He lifted one hand and stroked my head gently. "After we close, I'll see if I can't find Dare and at least make sure he's okay. Then I'll stop by to give you a report, okay?"

28

Groggily I sat up in bed.

"Chrysta, I found him," I heard Luke calling downstairs, knocking, and then pushing open the door of the carriage house. "I found him!"

I checked my watch. It was after eleven P.M. I had crashed since six. I put on my bathrobe and came downstairs.

"Where was he?" I asked, yawning and disoriented.

"Carlos's. That's where the party was. I'm glad you got some rest." Luke stopped a full six feet from me. Suddenly I was full awake as we stood there, both awkward, me in a bathrobe.

"Oh. And?"

"Well, he was okay, stoned, but not completely crazy stoned. Subdued, for Dare." I thought about the way I'd felt getting stoned the night of my thirteenth birthday. I'd been subdued, all right. Luke continued, "He put up a fuss when I walked in—'Did *she* send you?' *She*. You're the heavy, Chrysta."

"I know."

"I said, 'No, man, I sent myself.' And believe it or not, Carlos stuck up for you. He said, 'You better be nice to that lady, Dare, she's taking good care of you.'"

"I bet that went over big with Dare."

"Yep. He said the hell you were taking good care of him, he was taking care of himself."

I sighed and sat down on the couch. Luke sat down too—all the way at the other end.

"Carlos told him he didn't know a good thing when he saw it, so Dare dropped it and went back to staring into space and toking on whatever came his way." Luke paused, then smoothed down his mustache. "I agree with Carlos, by the way."

"Thanks."

We had been glancing at each other, quick glances and then away. There was a pause. Then Luke said, "May I?" as he indicated the space of sofa between us.

I nodded, and Luke moved next to me. I looked down at the floor, though I could feel him looking at me. Slowly Luke touched his hand to my chin and turned my face toward him. I knew he was going to kiss me and I felt scared. I kept telling myself it was silly, this was nothing I hadn't done before.

But it was.

When Luke kissed me, it was like when you jump off the high dive on a hot day and you haven't hit the water yet—but you know you will.

What I mean is: I was turned on. I desired Luke. An old-fashioned word, *desired*. And I thought of Luke telling me I looked lovely that night at Boots, and I thought of Donny Figeroa and some of the other men and boys I'd known. Dare flashed through my mind too, and Nettie and Mr. Dewling. But all those thoughts, coming and going, were melting quickly into this desire. A strange, strong, sweet power, a pull.

I love you, Luke.

The words came into my mind; there was no time to push them away. I didn't say them out loud, but hearing them inside me made me tremble, made my heart beat even faster. I was scared—but so happy, too. So that's what all this was about! *I loved Luke*. I marveled: How long had I loved him without knowing it? And then I just melted into his lips, his mouth, his arms tight around me.

And when we pulled away and looked at each other, it was somehow even more intense than kissing. I looked away, down at the floor.

"Chrysta," said Luke, very, very softly and again he tipped my chin up so I was facing him. "I've hesitated, because, well, I thought you might feel, with me being nineteen and you being twenty-four, that—"

"Luke," I said, "I'm not really twenty-four. I'm sixteen."

And then I told him the whole thing. The truth.

*   *   *

Later, upstairs:

"Chrysta? Are you protected? Are you on the pill or something?"

In the dark, my hand on his spine, I could feel each vertebra. Oh, how I loved him!

"I can't have kids, remember? So I'm okay."

"Oh, God, I forgot! I'm sorry, Chrysta, forgive me!"

"It's okay."

"God, you've had a rough time." His voice soft and resonant in the dark, near my ear. Why were we whispering? His long arms wrapped around me, his long body pressed into me. I loved him. I loved him!

"Ssh, ssh," I said. "Everything's all right now."

Around one o'clock that first night Luke spent with me, I woke up, hearing Dare come in, and I sighed. Luke lay sleeping beside me, one arm flung half over me. The touch of his warm sleeping skin, the sound of his deep, regular breathing, filled me with joy.

Maybe now, I thought, *with Luke in the picture, things will work out with Dare. Luke and Dare have always gotten along. Maybe Dare'll listen to Luke, because he's male, where he wouldn't listen to me.*

I went back to sleep filled with loving Luke, and also filled with hope. Hope for Dare. Hope for the three of us.

In the morning, when I woke Dare with his sleeping-angel little-boy face, it was the usual, only more so. I called his name, stroking his arm gently. He cried out, then bolted awake, in tears, and grabbed me, clinging. Then shame flashed on his face. The tears stopped and he let go of me.

"Dare, sweetheart, don't cry! Maybe if you talked to someone about it—"

Already his face was sullen. "I *don't* goddamn *cry*, Chrysta. I just hate waking up, that's all."

"Okay, Dare," I said. "See you downstairs. By the way, Luke's here."

Dare glared at me, but didn't say a word. But by the time he staggered down to breakfast, he was ready.

"What are *you* doing here?" he demanded, scowling at Luke.

Luke put down his coffee mug and said mildly, "I stayed here last night."

"Oh," said Dare, eyeing him warily.

"Listen," said Luke, "my car's up at the hotel, and I have to run into town and do some errands. You want me to drop you off at Meadow School?"

"Yeah, that'd be all right," said Dare, gulping down his eggs. Later Luke told me that for most of the ride Dare didn't say anything, just stared straight ahead. Then, as they approached Meadow School, Dare suddenly asked, "Did you sleep on the floor?"

"No," Luke told him. "No, I didn't sleep on the floor, Dare."

There was a pause, Luke said. They drew up to Meadow School, and Luke stopped the car. "You know, Dare, there's room for both of us in Chrysta's life."

Luke said that Dare, getting out of the car, looked at him, and said, "Yeah, yeah, yeah, yeah."

29

So Luke and I fell in love and became lovers. Everybody, *everybody*, except Dare, seemed happy for us.

"Well, to tell you the truth, I kinda expected it," said Nettie. "You're both good kids, an' bein' together so much . . ." She paused, twinkling mischievously. "Just don't up and get married, least for a while. Why mess up a good thing, honey?"

And Steve, giving me a peck on the cheek in congratulation, said, "I can't *think* why you didn't gobble that boy up *months* ago."

And Joanie was thrilled. "Oh, Chrysta, *dear*, I'm so happy for you!" she said, opening her eyes wide behind her askew wire rims. "*And* for Luke, of course!"

But things with Dare went from bad to worse. To the pits. Steve had told me once that the phrase "the pits" got its meaning from heroin addicts who were really far gone—so far gone that they had collapsed almost every vein in their bodies and the only place left where they could shoot up was in their armpits. Well, I felt like I had tapped into just about every vein I had trying to work it out between Dare and me, and I was running out of veins. And here I was in the middle of so much happiness with Luke, wanting so much to give some happiness to Dare too, and it wasn't working.

* * *

I wrote Lissa a long letter about it, and she wrote me back an equally long letter—one that got me thinking.

Sweetcakes,

Well, I'm glad you decided against life as a nun! I was worried that if you saved it too much longer, moths were going to fly out of it the first time you used it! Sorry to be gross, but I guess you're used to it from me by now.

Chrysta—I'm so happy for you. REALLY. I felt funny telling you about Peter & how much I care about him, because you didn't have anybody & also when I saw you last you were hurting so much & I didn't want you to be jealous of me or to feel like I was leaving you for some trumpet-playing dude in New Orleans. Well the truth is I love him. We sit around and jive all night laughing our heads off sometimes. We're good *friends*, not just two people balling each other because we're horny or whatever.

& so I'm really happy you have Luke. I wondered if something might not be up (no pun intended). I mean he hung around the hospital so much serenading you with the guitar. (I got serenaded with a trumpet. It fits, doesn't it.) But I didn't want to say anything. I never got to know him real well, but he seemed nice. A little straight for my taste, to be honest, but then you get straighter by the day yourself.

I can see why Dare would be a big problem, specially now. Dare has probably been a problem since he was born. But what can you do? I mean you've tried your best but he may just be beyond help. At a certain point you me Dare or anyone has to stop looking at how bad their life has been &

start making it better. Now I don't understand why some people can & some people can't do that. I mean Dare just may have to fuck up & there may not be a dam thing you can do about it. He may not be able to get his shit together.

Anyway Chrysta I haven't been there as far as having a kid to look after goes, but you can't let Dare or anybody else fuck up your life. You have to help others like Michael helped me, but if they can't accept it too bad. You have to let go. There's so little happiness in life that when it comes along, grab it. That's what I say. Anyway when you're happy you can help people a lot better than when you're lonely or depressed. Right? Take it from me.

I would tell Dare straight out that there's certain things he has to do or else you're going to kick him out. & that's it. Clean up & no dope & whatever. And if he doesn't do it too bad. He's got to learn sometime. Or if he can't learn then let him deal with that. Even if it lands him in juvey home or wherever. You can't protect him from life. Nobody can protect anybody from life though people always try when they love somebody. But you can't. You can't protect someone from themself either. Not even that, unless THEY want to. It's sad. That's why I say grab the happiness you can.

Well you know I hate writing letters and this is turning into a dam book. Why don't you ask Luke about all this, he's the one studying to be a shrink. Tell Luke hello and tell him I'm glad he appreciates quality.

                    love and kisses xxxxxxxooxxxxxx,
                                        Lissa

30

Luke had a whole other life in Fayetteville, about an hour's drive away. He had a tiny upstairs apartment in a big old house near the college, furnished with a combination of Salvation Army stuff and things from Nettie's attic. During the week he threw himself into his studying—the way he threw himself into everything. Wednesday nights he'd call me, and most days he'd send me a postcard. (That was another old-fashioned thing about Luke: besides letters and postcards being cheaper than phone calls, he *liked* them better.)

I rarely saw him in the middle of the week, because I was so busy with Dare and the kitchen. Sometimes it seemed so awful and unfair that, after having waited all this time, waited even when I didn't know I was waiting, for someone I could love who would love me back, that we couldn't be together all the time. But most of the time it just seemed like such a miracle that we had found each other in the first place that I couldn't complain because all the details weren't 100 percent perfect.

Besides, as I still had the kitchen in its very busiest time to run, and I had Dare to look after—I was pretty busy myself. But then I worked out a plan.

Monday was my day off at the hotel. Luke had three classes on Monday, but they were all in the morning. So one Monday after we had become lovers, I took the bus over there early in the morning, and walked from the bus station to his apartment. We spent the afternoon there together, just quietly in the living room. That was one thing about Luke and me—we didn't have to be always actively jumping around doing something or talking or going somewhere. We could be together quietly doing separate things but be connected with each other, the feelings there without being expressed. To be sitting across the room from him, reading, in his clean, light living room, to be able to look up and see him, book on his knee and pencil in hand, notebook balanced on the fat padded arm of the chair he was sitting in, his face serious and wrinkled in concentration as he underlined and made notes: This filled me with elation. Every so often he'd look up and catch me watching him and we'd smile at each other and it was as if the room was filled with light. Sometimes, of course, *I'd* be reading and feel him looking at me.

One Monday we made love in the late afternoon, in Luke's tiny bedroom, on the old four-poster bed his father had been born in, one of the pieces of furniture Nettie had saved from when she sold the farm. It was a beautiful, solid bed, covered with a blue patchwork quilt Luke's grandmother had made. The late-afternoon light, warm and golden, poured into the bedroom window on us, and Luke's long skinny body, with just a few curls of light-brown chest hair, was so dear to me. And then, as we moved and stroked and kissed each other, to feel that tenderness grow into something else, into desire and finally that sweet and breathless explosion—I knew, at last, why everyone made such a big deal about sex. Yet, I thought, they had it all wrong. This wasn't "sex," an isolated thing between two bodies. This was something full, as warm and golden as the October light streaming in on us.

"Oh, Luke, I wish I was the first for you! I wish we could be the first for each other!"

"What's important," he said, "is that we're the *last* for each other."

I felt too small to contain all I felt.

Later we showered, made dinner, and stopped at the Safeway for me to pick up a pomegranate for Dare, and then Luke took me to the bus station, and I went back to Excelsior. In the middle of our love, we went on with our ordinary lives.

When I got back, Dare was waiting for me. I couldn't have been more surprised. He had been getting in at ten since the night of the big blow-up, the first night Luke stayed over, but only just *exactly* at ten. Sometimes I thought he must sulk around in the dark outside and wait until he heard the bells from the Catholic church chiming ten, so he could walk in at *exactly* that moment. It was hard to tell if he was testing me or making an effort to go along with the rules. Probably both.

"Where've *you* been?" he demanded the minute I walked in the door.

"What is this, Nazi interrogation night?" I came in and set my purse down and looked at him. It was hard to believe that soon he'd be thirteen. "I went to Fayetteville. I told you I was going."

"Yeah, yeah, yeah, yeah. You go see Pukey Lukey?"

I just gave him a look.

"All right, all right, I'm sorry," he said. "It's just that I missed you."

I must've looked totally astonished.

"No, Chrysta, I did, I did! I went up to the hotel after school and you weren't in the kitchen, and when I ate dinner there wasn't hardly anybody I knew and—"

So this, I thought, is how children make their parents

feel guilty. Or was this for real? Somehow, it was just a little too thick. Like toast and tea.

"Dare," I said, getting an idea, "want to go to Fayetteville *with* me next week?"

His eyes got wide. "Could I? Could we? Like last time? Do you think we could?"

I winked at him, and then leaned over and ruffled his hair. "Not like last time, *better* than last time. Be good this week and I'll see what I can work out, kiddo." Between that and his glee at finding the pomegranate in his sack lunch the next day, it was the best week we'd had together in a while.

What we worked out was that Luke would leave his Volkswagen (a black one, second-hand, that Nettie had gotten for him for a high-school graduation present) at the bus station so that when Dare and I arrived, we could tool around Fayetteville together, and not meet Luke until the late afternoon, which would give Luke time to go to classes and do some studying.

First Dare and I went by Sears, and I bought him a new pair of jeans and a Dracula mask. We had a great time trying on all the masks and chasing each other around the Sears toy department. I picked up a paperback book for myself at a bookstore next to Sears: *Cat's Cradle* by Kurt Vonnegut, which Steve had told me I would like. Then we went to lunch at the Pizza Hut. I had salad, and Dare ordered pizza with double cheese, sausage, black olives, and lots of hot jalapeño peppers. We walked around the square and window-shopped.

Dare asked for a chocolate milk shake at a drugstore we passed, but I said, "Wait, it will interfere with the surprise I have planned." Dare began madly trying to guess what it could be. "A movie? Something else to eat—pomegranates?"

"Nowhere close, kiddo," I told him. "You've gotta wait."

My big brainstorm surprise was that there was this karate school in Fayetteville, House of Chong, that I'd heard advertised on the radio. They had a deal where they'd take you on a tour of the whole building and tell you everything they had to offer and even give you a *free lesson* just for coming by. Of course, it was just to get you to sign up, but still, I knew Dare would go ape over it.

And I was 100 percent, dead-on right. We were lucky, because the guy who showed us around was nice and friendly. It was one of those places that had a phoney Chinese look to it outside—plaster dragons, and all in red and black—but inside it was just an ordinary gym, with tumbling mats and parallel bars and ropes and a trampoline.

But to look at Dare, you would have thought he had died and gone to heaven. The guy showed us through and then he asked Dare if he was ready for his free lesson and Dare nodded—he was too excited even to speak. They got him these little white karate pajamas, and he put them on. First the guy gave him this lecture about how karate was an *art,* and the only time a karate master should use it for self-defense was if someone's life was threatened, either his or someone else's. One phrase stuck in my mind: "The man of real power need never *show* his power."

Then the guy showed Dare one kick and one "stance," as he put it. It wasn't very much, even for a free lesson, but Dare didn't seem to mind. The guy let him jump on the trampoline after, and Dare was thrilled with that, too. Even after he changed back into his own clothes, he wanted to stay to watch other people work out, and so we stayed, till five-thirty. I read my Kurt Vonnegut book as Dare watched people flip each other over and practice handholds, kicks, and stances. I had never seen him so focused on anything. He was totally intense, watching; his whole small body was rigid with excitement. He had one hand knotted up into a fist and he kept pounding it into his other hand. "POW!" he'd say, or "MAN, look at THAT!" Not loudly, almost under his breath. It was like when he watched *World of Martial Arts* on television at the GP lobby, only more so.

After that we drove over to Luke's. Dare was in a great mood. He didn't come down from the House of Chong karate school for hours. He kept saying things like "Oh, wow, Chrysta, that was *great*! Did you see when that guy threw the other guy over and then they had to do it over again *four times* because the teacher said that they—" I nodded, pleased Dare was happy.

Of course, when we got to Luke's and I saw Luke standing there so tall and rangy and handsome, when he gave me a good solid hug, but only a quick one 'cause Dare was there, I couldn't help feeling a pang of regret that Dare was along. But that passed quickly. Luke asked Dare all about House of Chong and how he'd spent his day and so on. And Luke made dinner for us, chili con carne and nachos, one of Dare's jalapeño-laded favorites. Jalapeños *twice* in one day—Dare was in fine form.

I remember I was washing lettuce and Luke was setting the table when Dare called in to him, from the bedroom, "Hey, Luke, who are these people on your wall?" He was talking about a few photographs, and even though Luke had told me about them, I followed him into the bedroom to hear what he'd say to Dare.

"Well, this here—" He pointed to a large white farmhouse with porches on both stories. "This is where I lived till I was six years old. A farm. You can't see it from here, but just about a quarter mile in front of here is the White River. Sometimes my mother and dad and I'd take a picnic down there in the summer, if my mother could get my father to stop working for a few minutes. And Nettie—you know, Nettie from the kitchen, Dare, she's my aunt; she lived over this way about a mile or two, with the man she was married to."

"That your parents?" Dare pointed to another photograph. The picture showed three adults and a child sitting on the white steps of a porch. One of the women in the picture was Nettie, caught—characteristically—laughing. The other woman was light haired with a sweet, pretty face, huge eyes, and a shy smile. She looked a little like Luke. Luke was sitting between the two women one step down from them. He was a cute, funny-looking kid, big eyed and alert. Luke's father, a tall, rangy man, sat a little apart from the women and the boy. He had a stern face; unsmiling, the jaw set.

"That's them, all right," Luke told Dare. "My folks."

"They still live around here?" asked Dare. I couldn't believe he was asking all these questions. I was so pleased.

"Nope," said Luke. "They're dead. Got killed in a car wreck when I was eight. Nettie raised me."

"I wish my parents were dead," Dare said conversationally. "I know for sure I wish my stepfather was dead. I wouldn't mind puttin' a bullet in him myself."

I was speechless, just speechless. I looked over at Luke to see how he was taking this, but he didn't look back at me or catch my eye. He was staring at Dare.

"You know, Dare," said Luke, slowly, "that's a funny thing. I used to wish almost the same thing about my father sometimes."

Did I gasp out loud? Dare turned to Luke.

"*You* did?" he finally asked.

"Yeah," continued Luke. "My dad was a hard, hard man. Real strict. Used to punish me for anything, it didn't matter if I had really done something wrong or not. Sometimes he'd spank me, but more often he'd take a belt to me."

"Your mom try and do anything?" asked Dare, head tilted to one side.

"Well, she tried to stick up for me. And my Aunt Nettie tried. But he didn't listen much." Luke paused. "But he wasn't terrible all the time. He played the guitar, and he taught me how to play on this little old Montgomery Ward child's guitar he got for me. He had a lot of patience with me when it came to music. But he had a bad temper otherwise. So like if he'd locked me up in my room and said, 'No dinner' *after* beating my butt for something like interrupting him in the middle of a sentence—well, sometimes I'd just pray for him to die. So my mother and Nettie could raise me."

"Oh, Luke," I said. I felt so sad for that little kid Luke had been! I couldn't believe he had carried all this around for so long, and that he'd never told me. It would take a long time before Luke and I really knew everything about each other. Maybe we never would. Maybe two people can just try.

"So you see," Luke said, leaning against the bed and looking at Dare, "when he *did* get killed, Dare, I thought that maybe I had made it happen. By wishing for it. And that God had taken my mother, who I *really* loved, along with my father. As kind of revenge on me for having bad thoughts. It wasn't till I started growing up that I began to understand I hadn't made him die."

I suddenly flashed on when Luke came to visit me in the hospital, before we fell in love, and how he had said, "'Guilty' is one song everybody knows."

"Oh, wow, man," said Dare, and he actually put out his hand and touched Luke's arm. I couldn't believe it.

But that day was our last good time together.

31

Three days later the kitchen phone rang and it was Claire, Dare's teacher at Meadow School. She sounded urgent, and furious.

"Chrysta! You've got to come and get Dare," Claire said. "One of the other kids, Jamie, said something to him that ticked him off, and Dare went after him, freaked out. He was kicking and punching and screaming and yelling that he'd karate him. Jamie's got a bloody nose. . . . We had to take Dare outside and just about sit on him."

I didn't know what to say.

Claire's voice softened. "I feel terrible about this, Chrysta, but I have eleven other kids to think about, and school can't just stop while Dare has a temper tantrum. He's had other temper tantrums before, Chrysta, but he never went after another kid *so* violently before. We just aren't equipped to handle that."

What am I going to do! I thought. *Where will he go if he can't go to Meadow School? What will happen?* I panicked; "Why me?" I wanted to scream.

Instead, I said out loud, "Okay."

"I feel terrible, Chrysta," said Claire. "When can we talk?"

"How about at five o'clock, when I take my afternoon break, before you start working?"

"Okay. I'll be there."

"Listen, Claire?" I paused. "Do you know what Jamie said that set Dare off?"

There was a long sigh on the other end of the phone. "Dare and Jamie were arguing about something and Dare said something about Jamie's parents, who are going through a very sticky divorce right now. And Jamie told Dare that at least he, Jamie, had real parents, but that Dare didn't. That you weren't Dare's *real* mother, that you just took him in because you felt sorry for him. And that you were a rotten whore because you were screwing Luke. I'm sorry, Chrysta."

When I managed to speak I said, "But who is this kid Jamie? I don't even *know* him! How could he know all these things and—and twist it up that way?"

Grimly, Claire said, "Well, before Dare decided that Luke was all right *this* week, he went through a period of blabbing all over the school. Jamie was just repeating what Dare said last week."

"Oh my God."

"And Jamie got decked for it. You coming?"

"Yeah, I'll be there in a minute."

Nettie minded the kitchen for me while I went to get Dare, and she lent me her car to go pick him up in. It was a huge 1963 Pontiac, as big as a boat. I could hardly see over the front hood as I steered around Excelsior's curves.

"They gonna kick me out?" Dare asked tonelessly, jumping into the car almost the second I pulled up. I went in to see Claire. She pointed out Jamie—a dark-haired seven-year-old holding a bloody handkerchief to his face.

"I don't know," I said tersely when I got back in the

car. "Claire didn't say anything about it. She and I are going to talk this afternoon."

"She's a bitch," said Dare. I shifted into second to climb the grade up to the General's Palace, and the gears made a horrible grinding sound. "God, Chrysta, can't you even drive a car?"

I shot him a look.

"All right, I'm sorry," he mumbled.

I didn't say anything.

"I *said* I'm sorry!" he yelled.

"Great, Dare, you're sorry. You want me to applaud? I get dragged out of the kitchen in the middle of doing lunch because you tried to deck some kid who is only *seven years old*! Dare, that's a *rotten* thing to do. Claire didn't tell me over the phone that Jamie was five years younger than you. I didn't find *that* out until just now."

"If you knew what he said to me—"

"I don't *care* what he said to you, Dare. He is *seven years old*. You don't mash a seven-year-old's face into the floor! Not for any reason! It's a good thing his nose isn't broken!" Of course I did care what Jamie had said, especially because it had come from Dare the week before. But that was too complicated to even begin to deal with yet.

"Aw, Chrysta, lay off."

"Why don't *you* lay off, Dare? I thought you *wanted* to go to school!"

"Crap." Dare pressed his lips together, and sat up enough to stare fixedly out the window.

"Well, Dare, I have to know. I'm going to talk to Claire this afternoon. Do you or don't you want to go back to school? If you don't, then what do you plan to do?"

"Just get off my case, okay? I'll think about whether or not I want to go to the lousy school. I'll think about it today, Chrysta. All right? Now will you get off my case?"

"All right," I said. "But remember that guy at the House of Chong? Remember he said about how a man who knew karate should never, never abuse it? He said—let me see if I can remember it exactly—I think it was 'The man of real power need never *show* his power.' And he said a karate master is always calm, and in control of himself, remember?"

Dare made a noncommittal gesture with his head, then said, "Aw, who gives a shit?" So much for trying to communicate with Dare on his own level.

I parked the car and we got out. We agreed that Dare would spend the day at the carriage house, and I'd come by around four o'clock to talk with him before Claire came over.

But at four, when I raced over with a slice of Cleota's chocolate pie, Dare was *gone*.

He didn't come home at all Thursday. Always before, when we'd fought, he'd come home late, but still before morning. By Friday night he still hadn't shown up. His stuff was there, but I was seriously worried, and I couldn't concentrate at work. Nettie said I should sit tight, that Dare would surely be back. And she was right. At three o'clock in the morning Saturday there was a loud knock on the door.

I was furious. The months of abuse, mess, worry, trouble, interruptions, and middle-of-the-night wake-ups had finally gotten to me. "Look, Dare," I said after letting him in. "*Enough!* I'm not going to spend the rest of my life fighting with you. I'm through arguing about the rules here. I'm telling you, Dare, how things are gonna be around here. No dope in the house, keep your stuff picked up, and help out with the chores. In by ten on school nights. Or you're *out!* That's *it!* And *you* decide whether or not you want to go to Meadow School instead of piddling around. If you decide against it, and you want to go on living here with me and eating at the hotel, you better have some good plan for how you intend to spend your time during school hours. Is that clear?"

Dare didn't say anything. He was furious. He sat on the couch bouncing one knee up and down real fast, with his lips pressed together.

"Dare," I said, "if you stay here, you gotta put something *into* the place. You can't just take, take, *take* all the time. You're using me, and you're ripping me off. You're ripping *yourself* off too, Dare, don't you see?"

"Chrysta, get off my case. I'm sorry I split without tellin' you first. I just had to get away."

"Well, Dare, this house is *my* place to get away to, and I can't stand to have it trashed all the time! And I can't stand all this fighting with you!" I stopped. Sometimes I couldn't believe how much like my own parents I sounded, not the words, but the emotions behind the words. "Dare, I worry about you when you just disappear for days on end! Don't you see that? I love you! I care! But I've reached my limits. I need your help."

"You want to kick me out?" This was said so casually, as tonelessly as when he'd asked me if Meadow School was kicking him out. Yet I could see so much fear in Dare's green eyes that I tried again.

"Dare, from the very first time I met you, on the bench with Rick, I just felt there was something special about you. I don't *want* to kick you out. I want what's best for you. *And* what's best for me. But I can't go on with the situation like it is. It's too hard. Can't we change it, make it better?"

Dare looked up. His eyes were liquid with tears. He had gone from angry to sad.

"But Chrysta, what about what *I* think is best for me?"

"What *do* you think is best for you, Dare? Do you *know*? I mean, if I just had a *feeling* about what you wanted, then maybe I could—"

Dare, tears rolling down his face, was silent.

I went on. Steeling myself. Remembering Lissa's letter.

"You need to decide whether or not you want to go on living here, Dare. You have to *decide*, to make a choice. I *want* you to stay here. But if you can't live with my conditions, you *have* to move out. It's your decision to make, and *you* have to make it."

"But that's like kicking me out," Dare said, glancing up at me with his wet eyes.

I steeled myself further.

"No, Dare, it isn't. Don't put that on me, kiddo. I'm not asking anything you couldn't do if you decided you wanted to. And Dare, you won't find anyplace, anywhere, in the whole world, where you can just do what you want and get taken care of and not have to do anything in return."

"People are so fucking selfish, man," said Dare.

"It's your choice, Dare," I said evenly. "I'll give you to Thursday to make up your mind."

It wasn't until the next day, when I was back in the kitchen, that I glanced at the calendar and saw that the day I had picked for Dare's deadline, the coming Thursday, was his thirteenth birthday.

32

On Sunday I was breading chicken in flour to fry, as Luke did paperwork for the end-of-the-season inventory. I loved the weekends, when both of us were in the kitchen. It was less frantic now; the tourists had dwindled down to half as many as we'd had three weeks before. It looked like we were going to do better than break even; we were going to recoup Howie's entire loss.

I heard the phone ring, and I heard Luke's "Hello, Kitchen." There was a pause and then, "Just a minute, I'll get her.

"Chrysta? It's for you!"

"Just a sec." I walked to the nearest sink and washed the flour off my hands, then headed for the desk. Luke, his head over the mouthpiece of the phone, said, "I think it's long distance," as he handed it up to me.

Puzzled, then with a sudden wave of panic—maybe my parents had caught up with me after all these years?—I lifted the phone slowly to my ear. "Hello?"

"Yeah, ah, hello. This Chrysta Perretti?" The voice was male, low, deep, somehow greasy.

"Yes?" I said. Luke got up and gestured to the seat at the desk, but I remained standing.

"Ah, this, this is, uh, Dare's *father.* Darrell Wilkie,

Senior, you know? Fran Winters told me Dare's living with you now."

I sat down hard in the chair. "Oh," I said. Luke mouthed "Who?" I put my hand over the phone and mouthed "Dare's father." Then I said into the phone, "Yes, Dare is staying with me. What can I do for you?"

"Dare still around?"

"Yes, Dare's *still around.*" I felt this huge rage boiling up in me.

"That's good, that's, uh, good. He, uh, doing okay?"

What do you care, you dirty, rotten—"Well, he's having some problems, but basically—"

"Yeah, Dare, uh, usually has problems, but he usually, uh, manages to look out for himself."

"*He's had to,*" I said pointedly.

"Well, listen, I just wondered about, uh, how he was. I, uh, haven't heard from him in a while."

"He hasn't heard from *you* in a while. Not since I've been looking after him, and that's been since September."

"Well, Dare knows that I ain't much into writin' letters."

"Yes, you've made that clear to him."

There was a pause. Then the voice again, crawling and probing. "Whoa, lady. I mean I 'preciate your taking care of the kid and all, but nobody *asked* you to do it."

Like father, like son. I said coldly, "Did you call to speak to Dare? I can go get him."

"Yeah, yeah. It's, uh, like, his birthday sometime this week. Thursday? Thought I'd come up from Dallas and spend some time with him."

"Oh, I know he'd like that," I said, genuinely now. No matter how much of an S.O.B. this guy was, Dare adored him and looked up to him. He'd be thrilled about a visit. "Hang on. I'll go get him."

Dare's face when he picked up the phone was a

combination of awe, rapture, and complete concentration. His voice, when he spoke, was soft, "Hi, Dad." Pause. "Yeah. Yeah. All right, I guess. Yeah, she's all right." I walked back to the pile of chicken pieces I'd been breading, so I wouldn't overhear any more of the conversation. Luke, putting on his parka to go into the freezer—like on the first day that I met him—smiled at me, and I smiled back.

"Chrysta?" called Dare from the desk a few minutes later. "He wants to say good-bye to you." I washed my hands again and hurried over.

"Yeah?" I said.

"I, uh, just wanted to, uh, say," said that sleazy voice, blurred slightly over the staticky hum of long distance, "how much I enjoyed talkin' to you. I'm, uh, lookin' forward to meetin' you when I come up Thursday for Dare's birthday. You got a nice voice. Maybe we can get together, and, uh, get to know each other a, uh, little better."

"Don't count on it," I said. "*Dare* will be glad to see you. *I* have other plans." I hung up, so furious at the come-on I was shaking.

But Dare was standing by the fryer, waiting for me. He looked so ecstatic that I almost forgave his sleazy dad. "Chrysta," he said, his eyes shining, "my dad's gonna come visit me on my birthday! My dad! He's coming! He's coming!"

Oh God, I thought, *I hope it works out for him. I hope it works out for* me.

I went over and over the situation, talking with Luke that night, before he went back to Fayetteville.

I remember at one point I wailed, "It's no use, Luke, I've just messed it up! I haven't done *one thing* right with Dare!"

"But Chrysta, you've tried. Don't you see how admirable that is—how brave? Very few people would have done it at all."

"Well, but if I haven't helped Dare, what difference does it make whether or not I did an admirable thing in trying?"

Luke sighed. "You love him, Chrysta, you've tried your best, and I know, I just *know*, there's been some effect, way down deep inside him somewhere. Maybe when he's twenty he'll get arrested for assault and battery—but maybe without your having taken care of him he would have murdered the person. Or maybe you've laid the groundwork, so that when the next person who tries to help him comes along, he—or she— won't have quite as hard a time. Who knows? All I'm saying is don't be too harsh on yourself. You can never see how things are going to turn out. No one can."

He's right, I thought later on, after Luke had left for Fayetteville. Warm in the afterglow that was mixed into the bittersweetness of our Sunday night good-byes, I thought: It might *still* work out. It might.

Maybe Dare's dad wanted him at last.

33

Before I got Dare up on Thursday morning, I put his wrapped gifts next to his plate. Steve had gotten him a *Close Encounters of the Third Kind* T-shirt. Nettie had a blue sweater for him. Luke had gotten him a

pocketknife, a Swiss Army one, with about six little
doodads on it: a screwdriver, fish scaler, nail file—even
an ivory toothpick that you pulled out of this little
groove. I knew Dare would go ape over the pocketknife.

And from me there was a clock radio from Sears, the
fancy deluxe digital model. A radio because he'd asked
for one; a clock so he could start getting himself up in
the morning—if he decided to stay. If he didn't, well, at
least he'd have something good from me to take with
him. "Eighty-two dollars?" Luke had said. "Chrysta,
don't you think that's an awful lot?" But I was glad I'd
spent enough to get something sturdy.

At breakfast he was cheerful, though more subdued
than I would have expected. His eyes widened with
pleasure at the sight of the presents, and he was
obviously pleased at the chocolate pancakes I had
concocted. As I stood by the stove, dropping the batter
onto the skillet, he said, "Hey, those smell just like the
ones my mom used to make! You *did* it, Chrysta!"

"Aren't you going to open your presents?" I asked
him.

"Which one is from you?"

"The blue one with the red ribbon."

"I'll save that till last, 'cause that'll be the best."

I was making the pancakes in shapes, which was
something I had forgotten my mother did for me when
I was little. Were there other good things I'd forgotten?
I made a bunny with one big drip for the body, one
medium drip for the head, one little drip for the tail,
and two small pointy drips off the tip of the spoon for
the ears. I was afraid Dare might think it was babyish,
but he laughed, and ate the chocolate pancake bunny, a
dragon, and an R2D2. I made some plain old round
ones for me and sat down next to him to eat. Chocolate
pancakes were a lot tastier than they sounded.

"Will you read the cards?" he asked me.

"Okay. Let's see, this is from Steve: It says, 'To Dare—who is definitely a close encounter of the *weird* kind. May your birthday be a special edition. Love, Steve.'"

He tore the present open and was pleased by the T-shirt. "Oh, *wow*, Chrysta, man, you should've gone with us! See this guy *here*? When he comes out of the UFO, and he's real small and scrawny with these weird little eyes and . . ."

Nettie's sweater gift was slightly less of a hit.

"You'll be glad this winter, though," I told him. "And that blue will really show off the color of your eyes. You're going to be a real ladies' man, you know, Dare."

"Going to be? I *already* am!"

The pocketknife left him speechless with joy as he folded and unfolded the various gizmos. "*Luke* gave this to me? I can't believe it! Boy, I can't wait to show my father this!"

"What time did your father say he'd get here?"

"Around two. He said around two or two-thirty. And now it's time for—your present! You give good presents, Chrysta."

He tore into the gift wrap. "Oh, *wow*!" We took it up to his room and I read the directions and he figured out how to set the alarm. We plugged it in and turned it on. Because Excelsior's in the mountains, there weren't that many stations, but he could still get AM from Berryville, Fayetteville, Rogers, and Springfield, and FM from a few other cities. We pulled the radio, still plugged, into the closet, so we could check out its glow-in-the-dark features. It was interesting, I thought, that Dare could read numbers but not words. We set the alarm and listened to it go off; we set the "Wake to Music" and listened to *it* go off.

But through all this there was the sense of sadness, and a tension. Dare's decision was hanging over us, and yet we were trying so hard to act happy.

Finally I said, "Well, it's about time for me to go to work. What do you plan to do today, Dare?"

"Well, I thought I'd go drop in at Meadow School for a while, then come back up here and wait for my father."

"Oh," I said, and added cautiously, "I told Claire today was the day you were going to decide whether or not you wanted to go to Meadow School regularly, and whether you wanted to live here with me. And she was very nice about it. She said it was good you were going to make up your mind, because she couldn't have you just floating in and out."

"After my father gets here, I'll let you know," he said. I guess maybe Dare was dreaming about that reunion even more than I was.

At two o'clock Dare was sitting on the carriage house steps, waiting.

At four, he was still there.

At four-thirty Claire called me to say Dare hadn't told her his decision, but that she was a little worried about what she'd do if he decided *yes*. She said that that morning Dare had been bragging about his father, and finally Jamie made some crack about how come if his father was so great he just dumped him up here in Excelsior, and Dare went after him again. "We saw it coming, so we were able to head if off, this time," said Claire, sighing. . . . "Still . . . I don't know. I'm between a rock and a hard place. If we *don't* take him, especially if he decides he wants to come back, where's he going to go? But we have *eleven* other kids."

I told her we could work it out once Dare made up

his mind, and there was no use worrying too much about it until then.

But Claire's phone call made all the feelings I had kept pushed down all day rise up to the surface. I felt tense and anxious and scared.

At five-fifteen the sun was beginning to go down, but I could still see Dare out the kitchen window, sitting there on the carriage house steps, his shoulders hunched over. Waiting.

I cut a piece of chocolate cake, wrapped it in a piece of paper towel, and brought it out to him with a large glass of milk.

"I don't want it," he said.

"I'll just leave it here, and you can eat it later. Bring the glass back up to the kitchen in a while."

"Dad said he was going to leave last night and go part of the way, so he could get here by two," said Dare suddenly. "He said if he didn't do that, he'd leave at eight in the morning so he could be here by four. He said he'd take me out to dinner anywhere I wanted tonight." He paused. "But he doesn't like to get up early. If he didn't leave last night, he probably wouldn't've left till, like, late in the morning. I mean, he might not be here till tonight sometime."

But Dare sat out there waiting until nine-thirty, when I left the kitchen. His father didn't come at all. And he didn't call to tell Dare that he wasn't coming.

It was awful. But Dare had to learn. If he couldn't, then, as Lissa had said, he had to deal with that. I couldn't protect him any longer. It was destroying both of us. But why did it have to happen then on his birthday, after his dad had let him down?

"Dare," I said at last, softly, "come on in, let me fix you some dinner. And we've *got* to talk now."

Dare dragged in and sat slumped at the table. I had seen Dare angry, I had seen him elated, but he was now totally down and defeated. He looked even worse than the night I had found him downtown, when I had offered to start feeding him on leftovers at the hotel.

"I don't want to eat," he said.

"Are you sure? I could—"

"I *said* I don't want to eat!"

"All right, all right," I said. "But we've got to talk. NOW."

"Just let it wait, Chrysta."

"It's already waited too long. You've had nearly a week to think about it, but it's been hanging over us for at least a month. This is a bad time, but—"

"Next week, Chrysta."

"No," I said, and it was about the hardest thing I've ever done. "*Now.*"

He looked at me, and slowly walked to the stairs. I heard him sigh. I followed him up to his bedroom.

I watched him find the old pillowcases, the Snoopy and the plain white one, which were now washed and folded in one of his dresser drawers. And he started stuffing his junk into them. He stuffed faster and faster.

I didn't want him to leave. Not on his thirteenth birthday, when his father hadn't showed. But what could I do?

Unless he *chose* to stay, it would get worse. I still think I was right, too, in spite of what happened.

"Do you want *this* back?" he asked, holding the clock radio out. His voice was shaking, low—through his teeth. The tension in the room was stifling.

"No," I said, "it's yours. Oh, Dare—"

He looked at me and I've never seen anyone stare with such hate. He walked over to the top of the stairs, lifted the radio over his head, and threw it down with all his might. There was a crash, as the radio hit a lamp that shattered on the hall floor. He grabbed his pillowcases and ran downstairs, with me after him. I wanted to stop him—to—I don't know, to grab him and shake him and tell him—tell him something, but what? Everything that was twisted inside of him—love and disappointment and pain—was exploding.

He dropped one of his pillowcases and I beat him to the door. "Look, Dare, goddamnit, listen! You can walk out that door now if you want, but you remember, *you're* the one *choosing* to leave, I'm not throwing you out! And it's not me you're trying to run away from, it's yourself! And sooner or later, you've got to face that! You've *got* to!"

He gave me a look of pure, unspeakable fury. Throwing down his pillowcases he strode to the fireplace, picking up the angel-wing begonia I had raised from Nettie's start. He raised it over his head and crashed it down onto the hearth, then quickly did the same to the Wandering Jew. I stood still, shocked, only my eyes moving back and forth from his twisted-up crazed face, like that of a little animal, to the mess on the floor. Standing against the door, I felt glued, unable to move.

Then he found the fireplace matches.

He dragged a handful of them against the hearth, and they ignited. He hurled them into the air, and most of them went out, but some stayed lit until they burned into the carpet, leaving small, smoldering circles. We stared at each other, neither of us moving.

Then Dare, his eyes still on mine, reached into his pocket and took out his new pocketknife. He clicked it open and walked toward me slowly. Then he stopped.

"Dare," I said, "you're *choosing*. Even now, you're choosing."

Dare's eyes narrowed further. "I'm not *choosing*

anything, Chrysta. I never chose anything in my life."
And then he moved quickly, knife up, toward me—I
shut my eyes. Felt the rush of air and movement
hurtling by my face. Heard the knife sink into the wood
of the door just to the right of my temple. Heard him
pull the knife out, heard his footsteps on the porch.

I opened my eyes. All I could see of him was his back
as he trudged up the path, the pillowcases slung over
his shoulders. I looked around the room. The shattered
lamp, the broken radio, the pieces of pottery and
spilled dirt and crushed leaves, the dark spots where
the matches Dare had thrown had burned into the
carpet before going out. There was a singed smell.

Finally I stepped away from the door. I examined the
gash in the wooden door frame and I closed my eyes.

And what I saw was myself, shaking out that blood-
red catsup onto that white dress.

I sat down in the middle of the carpet in the desolat-
ed living room then, and I wept.

I never saw Dare again.

34

It's now February, almost three months since Dare left.
I live in Fayetteville, with Luke. I've been here since
the hotel closed for the winter, the day after Thanksgiving.
I go to Vo-Tech, where I'm studying restaurant management. Mr. Dewling is paying for it, in return for my
agreeing to come back to the hotel next summer. Lissa

and Peter live in Excelsior now, and I only owe about $300 to the Excelsior Hospital and $200 to Dr. Besum. Luke is still going to the university.

Luke, as I said when I started, urged me to write this. I didn't want to go through it again, writing it all down. But on January first I started, and every day now, after school, I come home and write for a couple of hours. Now I'm almost done.

Luke and I love each other more and more. He's asked me to marry him. I want to. But not yet. I'm still working it out in my mind. Lissa's right, I *am* straighter by the day: If I get married I want it to be till death do us part, the whole forever bit. Luke feels the same, but you'd expect it of him. But me, me, the sixteen-year-old runaway C-cup punk-queen misfit? I've come a long way, but I need to come a little further. I need to believe in myself 100 percent before I say yes to Luke, to believe that good things can happen, that I can make them happen, that I can make my own happy endings. Unlike Dare. Unlike my parents.

"Luke, are you sure you want to marry someone who can't have kids?"

"Not someone. *You*."

"But—"

"Chrysta, we can adopt kids when we're ready, you know we can. Kids like you and like Dare, kids whose parents didn't want them. We can give them something really good."

"I know . . . but . . ."

"But what, darlin'? Don't cry, Chrysta. Or cry if you want to, that's all right too."

"Oh, Luke, it's just that . . . when we make love sometimes and it's so . . . When I don't know where I end and you begin, I think about if we *could* . . ."

"Oh, sweetheart..." Luke holds me. He strokes my hair. He hugs me. He kisses my wet cheeks and wipes my eyes. When the handkerchief gets soaked he gets up and gets a tissue and wipes my eyes with that.

"Sweetheart, yes, in a perfect world someday if we could have children, our own children made of us, it would be... Oh! I'd love it, and I know you would too."

I cry even more.

"But, darlin'... that's just a tiny, tiny piece of the whole thing. The minute they're born, kids start being their own people, not their parents. Look at us. Look at Dare, or Nettie, or anyone."

"Oh, Luke, I know, but..."

"Chrysta, I want you. *You*. You're my friend and my sweet, sweet lover, and you're the woman I want to be with for the rest of my life. There's no little voice in the back of my head saying go look for someone else who *can* have kids. *I love you*. Believe it, Chrysta."

I sigh, a long sigh, and slowly I stop crying. I get up, go to the bathroom, and splash cold water on my face. And there a new idea occurs to me. I come back into the bedroom. "Luke," I say slowly. "Luke? Do you think part of the reason I took in Dare was because I had just found out that I couldn't have any kids of my own?"

Dare, the crazy little mixed-up kid even crazier than I was. I was only sixteen. Even a real together sixteen-year-old isn't ready to take on being a mother, right? Someone who is sixteen hasn't finished growing up herself. Especially someone like me with all my stuff about my parents, me with that long scar on my belly.

When I think about it, I guess I must be made out of pretty strong stuff. Stronger than I knew.

And not just strong. GOOD.

Sure, there might have been some sicko motivations in

my taking in Dare. Like that I had just learned that I couldn't ever get pregnant and so I had to "have" a child immediately. But also, let's face it, Dare needed help himself, badly. And screwed up as I was, I tried to give it to him. I tried my damnedest. I did.

Because I do try. I'm a hard worker. I work hard, and I try hard, and I love hard, and I'm good. I'll make a damn good kitchen manager and a damn good wife to Luke, and someday, I'll make a hell of a good mother to the kids we're gonna adopt. I know it!

"Luke," I said, after I'd finished writing this. He looked up. "Luke, I've got to call my parents now."

He looked at me. There was so much in that look: love and respect and admiration— How did I get so lucky? "Want me to come with you?"

"Nope, I've got to do this alone."

"I understand."

Looking at his shining eyes, I knew he did.

Walking over to Collier's, the big drugstore that stays open to ten and has a nice quiet phone booth, I look up. I see the stars, small and far away, glittering in the winter sky. The air is cold against my cheeks. I feel very small and very large at the same time. Everything's changed. Everything is sharp and vivid and extraordinarily clear. Why didn't I ever see it before? Surely this clarity has always been here. And surely it will never leave. Cars on Dickson Street, stopping at the red light, going at the green, the snow crunching under my feet, the warm furry lining of the parka around my cold face—it's all in such perfect harmony. All in order.

I dial direct. The operator comes on and tells me to deposit $2.90. I do. I thank her.

The phone is ringing. I can see it, squat and black,

crouched on the hall table downstairs, on its plastic doily, in Benton, Illinois. And even that phone, and even my parents, they're somehow part of the order. And it doesn't even matter very much if they know it or not. Because *I* know it. Somehow, I'm here. Through Hugh Dewling and Nettie and Lissa, through Steve Darwin and Joanie and Harold Jenkins, through dearest Luke, but most of all, mysteriously, through taking in Dare (who could have been me, but wasn't), through taking him in *and* letting him go—I'm here. Safe. Home. No more running.

Which means I forgive them. Screwy as my parents were, if they had done anything differently, I might not have wound up here, filled with joy and wonder and this certainty that everything's just exactly right, here in—of all places—the Collier's phone booth in Fayetteville, Arkansas! It's so funny, it's so perfect, I'm breathless, I'm laughing, I'm free!

"Hello, Mom? Yeah! It's me! Yeah, your daughter! Me! Chrysta! Chrysta Perretti, that's who I am now."

ABOUT THE AUTHORS

CRESCENT DRAGONWAGON was born in New York in 1952, but since 1972 has lived in a small town in the Arkansas Ozarks, where besides writing, she gardens vegetables and flowers and reads a lot. She is married to historic preservationist Ned Shank and has a cat named Beanblossom. With their friend Bill Haymes, the Dragonwagon-Shanks own a small bed-and-breakfast inn, Dairy Hollow House. Dragonwagon, a vegetarian, is an excellent cook. She likes to visit New York occasionally, see as many plays and movies as she can in as short a time as possible, and return home. She has always wanted to write. *To Take a Dare* is her first novel, though she has previously published picture books, cookbooks, poetry, and magazine articles. She is currently at work on her second novel, *Just Like in the Movies*.

PAUL ZINDEL is no stranger to young readers, having written some nine novels, including his most recent book, *The Girl Who Wanted a Boy; I Love My Mother*, a picture book; and several plays, including *The Effect of Gamma Rays on Man-in-the-Moon Marigolds*, for which he was awarded the 1971 Pulitzer Prize for Drama. Zindel is married to Bonnie Zindel, also a writer, and they make their home with their two children in Beverly Hills, California.

TEENAGERS FACE LIFE AND LOVE

Choose books filled with fun and adventure, discovery and disenchantment, failure and conquest, triumph and tragedy, life and love.

☐	22605	**NOTES FROM ANOTHER LIFE** Sue Ellen Bridgers	$2.25
☐	24529	**LOVE'S DETECTIVE** J. D. Landis	$2.50
☐	23321	**THE KEEPER OF THE ISIS LIGHT** Monica Hughes	$2.25
☐	23556	**I WILL MAKE YOU DISAPPEAR** Carol Beach York	$2.25
☐	23916	**BELLES ON THEIR TOES** Frank Gilbreth Jr. and Ernestine Gilbreth Carey	$2.50
☐	13921	**WITH A FACE LIKE MINE . . .** Sharon L. Berman	$2.25
☐	23796	**CHRISTOPHER** Richard Koff	$2.25
☐	23370	**EMILY OF NEW MOON** Lucy Maud Montgomery	$3.50
☐	22540	**THE GIRL WHO WANTED A BOY** Paul Zindel	$2.25
☐	25233	**DADDY LONG LEGS** Jean Webster	$2.50
☐	20910	**IN OUR HOUSE SCOTT IS MY BROTHER** C. S. Adler	$1.95
☐	23618	**HIGH AND OUTSIDE** Linnea A. Due	$2.25
☐	24392	**HAUNTED** Judith St. George	$2.25
☐	25029	**THE LATE GREAT ME** Sandra Scoppettone	$2.50
☐	23004	**GENTLEHANDS** M. E. Kerr	$2.25
☐	24781	**WHERE THE RED FERN GROWS** Wilson Rawls	$2.75
☐	20170	**CONFESSIONS OF A TEENAGE BABOON** Paul Zindel	$2.25
☐	25901	**SUMMER OF MY GERMAN SOLDIER** Bette Greene	$2.75

Prices and availability subject to change without notice.

Buy them at your local bookstore or use this handy coupon for ordering:

Bantam Books, Inc., Dept. EDN, 414 East Golf Road, Des Plaines, Ill. 60016

Please send me the books I have checked above. I am enclosing $_____ (please add $1.50 to cover postage and handling). Send check or money order —no cash or C.O.D.'s please.

Mr/Mrs/Miss _____

Address_____

City_____ State/Zip_____

EDN—2/86

Please allow four to six weeks for delivery. This offer expires 8/86.

BANTAM
SHOP·AT·HOME
C·A·T·A·L·O·G

Special Offer
Buy a Bantam Book
for only 50¢.

Now you can order the exciting books you've been wanting to read straight from Bantam's latest listing of hundreds of titles. *And* this special offer gives you the opportunity to purchase a Bantam book for only 50¢. Here's how:

By ordering any five books at the regular price per order, you can also choose any other single book listed (up to $4.95 value) for only 50¢. Some restrictions do apply, so for further details send for Bantam's listing of titles today.

Just send us your name and address and we'll send you Bantam Book's SHOP AT HOME CATALOG!

BANTAM BOOKS, INC.
P.O. Box 1006, South Holland, ILL. 60473

Mr./Mrs./Miss/Ms. _____
(please print)

Address _____

City_____ State _____ Zip _____
FC(B)—11/85